BLOODRAGE

BOOK THREE OF THE BLOOD DESTINY SERIES

HELEN HARPER

CHAPTER ONE

I WAS ON MY HANDS AND KNEES YET AGAIN, PALMS SCRATCHED BY gravel, face no doubt an attractive shade of green, whilst I retched my guts up onto the ground.

"Are you quite alright, Miss Mackenzie?"

I couldn't help but note the lack of solicitude in the inquiry. I dragged myself to my feet. "Yes," I muttered, embarrassed. "I'm fine."

"Then we should go in. The Dean is waiting for us." Without pausing any further, the mage beside me swept through the door of the large sandstone building in front of us.

I glanced around, taking in my surroundings. We were at the end of a long driveway; in front of the training academy were large manicured grounds, covered with a layer of icy frost. A few crows cawed overhead, sweeping their way across the sky in search of some scarce winter food; to my left, the portal through which we had entered shimmered briefly in the air. I sighed deeply, turned, and followed inside.

My escort was waiting, a look of exasperated irritation on his weathered face. He didn't say anything further, however, merely moved deeper inside through the main vestibule area before turning right down a scuffed corridor. A young teenage girl

1

bustled out of a door just up ahead, carrying a few china plates with the remnants of some half-eaten food on them. Whatever the recipients of the plates had eaten, it didn't look particularly appetising, especially to my still-nauseous stomach. It was probably just as well that the meals weren't fresh though, because when the girl looked up and saw me, her eyes widened and her mouth dropped open with a comic half 'oh' of surprise and dismay, and the plates went crashing to the ground. I paused, kneeling down to help her pick up the shards, but she backed away like a frightened rabbit.

The mage tutted to himself. "Really, Miss Mackenzie. We do not have time for this."

He cast a stern look towards the poor girl, who seemed to be getting whiter and whiter by the second and was evidently praying that I'd just leave her and the smashed contents alone. I gave up and straightened. The mage made a *moue* of distaste and then continued forward.

At the end of the corridor a wooden door lay slightly ajar. He knocked on it briefly. A deep voice from within muttered something I didn't quite catch, and then my ever-so-friendly guide motioned me inside. I gave him a dazzling smile, ignoring the flickers of heat in my belly caused by a mixture of my nervousness and his rudeness, and went in.

Sitting behind a large desk that was strewn with all manner of books and oddities was an older man wearing a pair of half-moon spectacles perched on the bridge of his nose. He stood up as I entered, clasping his hands behind him, and I realised that he was wearing an antiquated black academic gown in the ilk of someone who felt the need to proclaim his importance to the world. He gestured at me to sit down on a small chair in front of the desk and then seated himself again. The chair I was on was cushioned and fairly comfortable, but it was also considerably lower than the chair of the man in front of me, making me feel somewhat like a small child. It was a very old intimidation ploy, although knowing that it was a trick still didn't stop me from actually feeling intimidated. I leaned back, trying to look relaxed.

For several moments, silence hung in the air. I bit my tongue to refrain from saying anything stupid. It was possible, well probable really, that I was going to be here for five years. The deal I'd made with the Arch-Mage in return for the mages freeing Mrs Alcoon, my old employer, from a particularly disagreeable stasis spell, meant that I had promised to submit to training here at the mages' academy. Apparently the average length of time before graduation was five years; I was determined, if not for my sake then for Mrs Alcoon's, to be much quicker than that. Pissing off the dean of the school probably wouldn't help my cause much, even if he was being pissy himself.

Finally, he looked up from whatever he was doing to appear busy and stared at me over his glasses with a look that would no doubt freeze the balls off many young schoolboy wizards. If he thought that looking at me was going to scare me though, then he hadn't read the full report from the Arch-Mage. I might have been feeling intimidated by my surroundings, and by what was going to be expected of me, but I'd faced down scarier things than teachers. I straightened my back and gazed at him straight in the eye.

"So, Mackenzie Smith."

I stayed silent and just continued to look at him. He raised his eyebrows slightly. "Your name is Mackenzie Smith, isn't it?"

"Oh, I'm sorry," I said innocently. "I hadn't realised that you were asking me a question." I smiled at him pleasantly. "Yes, my name is Mackenzie. But please call me Mack."

The Dean refrained from smiling back. "There is no need to get smart with me, young lady. We don't tolerate attitude from students."

Young lady? Attitude? Why that jumped-up little... I continued to smile. "There was no, uh, attitude, intended, Mr Michaels."

"Dean."

"Huh?"

"Dean Michaels. We expect you to display appropriate humility whilst you are here. You will address me as Dean Michaels. You will address everyone else with their full titles. The trainers you will address as Mage, followed by their surname. And that same humility goes for your attitude towards the other students who are here due to their lineage and ability – neither of which I believe you possess. You will address them as Initiate followed by their first name."

Well, I actually did have some ability. In fact, I had a pretty nifty trick with fire that I could happily show him. But I reminded myself that I was trying to be conciliatory and unthreatening, so I just gave a perfunctory nod and ignored the seething coils of fire inside me.

"I apologise, Dean Michaels."

He didn't appear particularly mollified, but he inclined his head slightly and continued, shuffling more paper around. "You will start at Level One with all our other initiates. You are expected to attend every lesson and every gathering unless told otherwise. There are certain events which are reserved for real mages only and we will not expect you to attend them."

Or want me to attend them anyway. That was okay. I was pretty sure my ego could survive not having to pitch up to some dull-as-dishwater magic parties.

"Breakfast is served at 5.30am. Lessons begin at 6.00am. You will have to master all five disciplines before you can move on to Level Two studies."

I cleared my throat.

He blinked at me and flicked a finger in my direction. "What?"

"What are the five disciplines?"

The Dean stared at me as if I had just sprouted purple horns with yellow polka dots. "You mean you don't even…" His voice trailed off, and he rolled his eyes. "Kinesis, Divination, Protection, Evocation and Illusion."

"Ah, I see." I nodded sagely.

"You have no idea what any of those actually are, do you?"

"Kinesis is moving things around, I guess. Protection will be warding, I imagine, and learning how to kick the shit out of nasty things."

The Dean winced. "Language, please."

"Oh, sorry. Learning how to utilise one's alchemical hocus-pocus in order to suppress and extirpate the existence of any objectionable entity that threatens either to subjugate or generally cause botheration." I crossed my legs and leaned back again.

He didn't look very amused. "Trying to be clever here, Miss Smith, will not help you. Neither will showing off, provocation or violence. I have been ordered by the Arch-Mage to train you, and train you is what I shall do." He stood up, towering over both me and the desk. "But that does not mean that you are to be anything other than tolerated. You are not a mage and you will never be a mage. You are a thug that we have had foisted upon us. I expect you to be seen and not heard, and not to bother me in this room again until it is time for you to leave. You will not bring shame and disrepute upon our institution. The oath-taking ceremony begins at dawn tomorrow, after which point you are bound by our laws. Break them and suffer the consequences."

He lowered himself slowly back to his seat and looked down at his desk, picking up a squat pen. "You may go now."

I stayed in my chair for one slightly stunned moment, before gritting my teeth and standing up. I opened my mouth to say something back to the stupid old fool, then thought better of it, and turned back to the door, curling my fingernails into the palms of my hands. I told myself that there was little else that I could really have expected. Absolutely the best thing that I could do would be to excel in every area that this jumped-up Hogwarts offered and get out with my dignity intact and Mrs Alcoon's consciousness restored. My bloodfire was screaming at me to do differently, but thankfully sanity prevailed.

My escort was waiting outside, smirking at me. Clearly he

had heard every single word. I gracefully resisted the impulse to slam my fist into his face and forced the edge of my mouth into a smile.

"Well, that was fun. The Dean is such an inspirational and motivational guy."

The mage ignored me. "I'm going to take you to your room now." He pushed himself off from the wall and motioned down the corridor. "It's this way."

I followed him again, back down the corridor and then up three flights of stairs. We passed several people, some of whom seemed to be students wearing different-coloured robes, and some who were older and were no doubt teachers, judging by their black academic gowns, which mirrored the Dean's. None of them appeared particularly thrilled to see me, in fact more than a few moved swiftly out of my path in case they might happen to brush past and actually, shock horror and heavens forbid, touch me. It didn't matter. I wasn't here to make friends, and after already being thrown unceremoniously out of Cornwall where all my real friends were, I was pretty sure that this bunch couldn't do much to hurt my feelings.

We passed a row of rooms that were filled with bunk beds, and a few terribly young-looking girls, again wearing robes of various colours, were milling around inside them. Great. Not only was I being put through all this ridiculous rigmarole, but I'd have to share a room with some giggling adolescents. I had a flicker of a memory of my old bed in the dorms at the keep in Cornwall and pushed it out of my mind. What was past was past.

Instead of entering any of the dorm rooms, however, we went past every single one and ended up at the end of the corridor, heading up a rickety spiral staircase. At the top there was a small door. The mage pushed it open and walked inside. There was a tiny, narrow bed and a small sink, and not much else. A sliver of a window let in a minuscule shaft of light.

"This will be your room," he announced, with no small hint of satisfaction in his voice.

I looked around. The Ritz this most certainly wasn't, but the single bed at least was reassuring. "I don't have to share with anyone?"

He snorted. "We didn't think it would be fair to impose your presence on any of our students."

"I think you'll find that I'm also one of your students."

His lip curled in derision. "Yeah, well, that remains to be seen."

I scowled at the mage. "Hey, I didn't choose to come here. But I will be here until such time as I graduate, because this is what it is going to take to free a harmless old lady that your lot have decided to keep in a coma so you can hold me to ransom. Don't blame me for being here."

"Don't presume to think that I give a shit what your situation is," he retorted. "Make yourself at home. I will be back in five minutes with a robe." He turned on his heel and walked out.

"Hey! Can you get me a toothbrush as well?"

Silence rebounded back at me. Out-fucking-standing.

I tugged at the tight hairband holding my hair in place and pulled it out, wishing I still had some silver needles concealed there so that I could have poked his eyes out with painful ease, then ran my fingers through my hair, unknotting the tangles, and lay down on the hard bed, closing my eyes. A moment later there was a knock at the door.

"Hello?" called out a tentative, yet surprisingly cheery-sounding voice.

Jeez. What now? I opened my eyes again and swung my legs to the side, sitting up. "Come in," I muttered.

A smiling face peered round the door. "Hey! You must be Mack."

A girl of about seventeen with short, dark hair and a purple robe came in, sticking out her hand. She looked vaguely familiar for some reason. I stared at her outstretched palm for a heartbeat and then shrugged and took it. She shook my hand enthusiastically.

"I'm Mary. Level Four. I can't believe you get your own room! Only the trainers normally get their own rooms." She wrinkled her nose for a moment. "It is a bit, er, stuffy though, isn't it? Maybe we can get you some air freshener or something."

I continued to stare at her. I seemed to have been set upon by the human teenage equivalent of an over-enthusiastic Labrador.

Without appearing to even stop for breath, she continued. "So, did you meet with the Dean? He normally greets everyone when they arrive for the start of the academic year, but of course you're a bit late for that. I'm sure you'll catch up really quickly – I've heard you're, like, amaaaazing at Protection."

I finally found my voice. "Um, yeah, I did meet with him. He wasn't very friendly."

"Ah, he'll get over it." She bounced down onto the bed. The mattress springs let out an alarming groan that she seemed not to notice. "Can you show me?"

"Show you what?" This girl was becoming more and more confusing by the second.

"The green fire thing that you do. I've never seen anyone with any colour other than blue. I'm not really much good at that myself. Illusion is, like, more my kind of thing, which is a bit boring really." Mary looked at me expectantly, with an eager glint in her eyes.

I tucked my hair behind my ears and regarded her steadily. "How do you know about that? And why are you being so friendly? Everyone else seems terrified of me."

She laughed out loud. "Gosh, I'm so sorry, I should have explained properly. I have an older sister – Martha?"

Dawning realisation hit me. Martha was the mage who had come to pick up my theoretically comatose body in Inverness. Except it had been Mrs Alcoon who was comatose, not me.

Mary carried on. "She says you met her and that you, like, saved her life. She's a pain in the arse, really. I mean, I love her and all but she's a bit full of herself sometimes, working for the gatekeepers and all. So it's kind of cool that you managed to beat her in a fight. And, don't tell her, but it's also kind of cool that you rescued her. She asked me to make sure that you're all right and don't get bothered that much. She thought things might get kind of messy."

I raised my eyebrows at her. "Do you ever pause to take a breath?"

"Hahaha! You're funny! Martha always says I talk too much." She beamed at me happily.

"You said Martha's a gatekeeper? What's that?"

"Oh, they're a bit like the police. They're mages who excel at Protection," she raised her eyebrows pointedly at me as she said this, "and who are recruited to keep the peace, watch out for rogue mages, deal with any incursions from other planes that we might be called upon to sort out. That kind of thing."

Hmm. Well, Martha, who had unexpectedly – and rather pleasantly – become my apparent benefactress, might be a gatekeeper but Alex, the surfer-dude mage who had helped me out in Cornwall, clearly hadn't been. He had been terrified of any kind of fighting. So that would mean that with his skill at tracking, he was probably into Divination. My 'attitude' had stopped the Dean from telling me more about the five disciplines, but this seemed like a good opportunity to find out more.

"So," I said slowly, making sure I was getting this right, "Divination is about tracking things, then. With that blue light?"

"Yup. As well as a bit of fortune telling, and thought sensing for some mages."

Right. So that would be what Mrs Alcoon had a small amount of skill in then. I definitely didn't particularly like the idea of coming across any more talented mages who might be able to 'sense' what I was thinking, and made a mental note to find out later if there was a way to block my thoughts and maintain my privacy.

Mary continued, "Illusion speaks for itself really – we can make things appear differently to what they are. You know, so if, like, a great lumbering giant appears out of a portal, we can make him appear normal to the humans so they don't freak out. Kinesis moves objects around. Some mages who are really good at it can send something from here to an address in Australia in almost the blink of an eye."

"You mean like email?" I asked drily.

She gave a surprised giggle. "Yeah, I suppose a bit like email. And Evocation is the hardest one. There aren't many mages who are skilled in that area. It's when you, like, summon spirits to do your bidding. You know, fight for you, or create things. That sort of stuff."

Interesting. None of this sounded like anything I could do. I wondered if they'd let me off if they realised that I was utterly unskilled at anything other than lighting a funny-looking fire? It was worth investigating.

I smiled my gratitude at Mary for her explanations. "That was really helpful."

She beamed back. "Why don't I show you around the school? That'll help you too. It's a bit of a maze until you get used to it, and you'll want to make sure you're on time tomorrow to take your oath. The Dean gets a bit angry when people are late, especially when it comes to the ceremonies and stuff."

"Thanks, Mary, I appreciate all the help I can get." And I really did. It was refreshing to have someone being nice to me. "I should probably stay here though. The 'not quite so helpful and forthcoming' guy who brought me here is bringing some robes. Hopefully some toothpaste and a toothbrush too."

"Oh, you mean Jeremy? He's an idiot, but he's okay when you get to know him. In fact…" Mary's voice trailed off when the door creaked open and the man himself stood on the threshold.

"Initiate Mary, you do realise that vespers are about to begin?"

She scrambled off the bed. "Sorry, Mage Thomas."

"You'd better run," he said pointedly.

She shot me an apologetic look, and a rueful grin, then escaped behind Jeremy – Mage Thomas – and out of the door.

Once she'd gone, he held out a bundle for me. "Here you go.

Inside you will find a blue robe, some soap, toothbrush, toothpaste, electric razor, scissors and," his lip curled distastefully for a moment, "clean underwear."

I almost laughed for a moment but then paused, thinking about what he had said. "Um, electric razor and scissors? Why?"

"You need to shave your head, of course."

I gaped at him, my stomach dropping. "What?"

"You heard me. All initiates are required to do so."

"But why?"

He shrugged. "Tradition. Who knows really? You need to have it done regardless before the oath-taking ceremony tomorrow. It starts at dawn so you'll need to be dressed and ready before 5.00am. I will come and pick you up here and take you directly there tomorrow morning. You will need to dispose of everything you are currently wearing." He nodded at my neck. "Including that." My hand flew to the necklace I'd worn every day since Mrs Alcoon's alleged friend had placed it around my neck and caused all these problems in the first place.

"I was told not to take it off."

"Well, now I'm telling you to take it off."

It was becoming hard to ignore the supercilious tone in his voice, but I focused on the orders themselves instead to avoid snapping unhelpfully back at him. I wasn't sure if I was going to be glad to get rid of the necklace, or sad that I'd miss its now familiar weight. I was damn certain, however, that I was going to miss my hair. Mage Thomas, for his part, seemed to know exactly what I was thinking because he placed the bundle down on the bed and smirked at me again as if he was suddenly amused. My eyes narrowed. Was he one of the telepathic mages?

He winked at me and made for the door. "Sweet dreams."

Tosser.

CHAPTER TWO

I woke early, well before my 5.00am pick-up time. It was probably something to do with having the lumpiest, most uncomfortable mattress this side of the equator, but at least it gave me enough time to sort myself out – although it didn't help that I'd had several disturbing dreams involving a lithe black panther stalking me through the empty cobbled streets of London. I did not have a crush on Corrigan, I told myself firmly. That had been a mere blip caused by feeling a bit lonely and needing someone to reach out to. Shaking off the vestiges of the dream, I pulled myself off the bed and splashed my face with water to wake up and get a grip on myself.

It took me several moments to find my way into the blue robe that I'd been given to wear. There was some kind of strange, complicated twist of fabric involved that had me cursing aloud. When I finally managed to fit myself into it properly, I sat down heavily on the edge of the bed. I lifted a strand of hair and gazed at it mournfully in the pre-dawn darkness. Maybe I'd take the necklace off first instead.

I reached round the back of my neck, searching for the clasp to undo it. My fingers couldn't seem to find it, however. I felt all the way along the length of the chain, but whatever mechanism had originally been in place now seemed to have disappeared. Okay-dokey. Feeling rather weirded out, I yanked at the chain instead, trying to snap it. Nothing happened. I pulled harder but the thing remained stubbornly round my neck. It occurred to me that maybe I could squeeze it over my head and try to wiggle myself out of it, but when I started to pull it upwards rather than outwards, it seemed to tighten itself infinitesimally, and I couldn't even scrape it past my chin. I was vaguely reminded for a moment of Frodo's one ring and wondered idly whether the mages would free Mrs Alcoon if I threw myself into the fires of Mount Doom. It probably wasn't an option. I shrugged to myself. If they wanted the necklace off that badly, then they'd have to help me with it. After all, I figured, it was a bloody mage who'd put it on me in the first place so it would just have to be another bloody mage to take it off.

Of course it did mean that I was already putting myself in the position of incurring even more wrath from the Dean. I really needed a good report card if I was going to progress here and get out. Damn it. I reached over and picked up the scissors that Mage Thomas had left the night before. My fingertips began to tingle with a drumming heat that snaked its way up my arms, pulsing through my entire body. My bloodfire was clearly mirroring my unhappiness. I walked over to the sink with a heavy heart and poised the blades over a hank of hair. Screwing my face up tight, I began to cut, using the scissors to take off most of the length, then I grabbed the electric razor and switched it on. Its buzz reverberated through me and I almost threw the fucking thing against the wall to smash it to pieces, then swallowed down my angst and vanity and began to run it over my scalp, inch by inch.

It was difficult to know whether I'd managed to get all the hair off without a mirror to look into. I ran my hands over my head and was pretty sure there weren't any odd tufts left. On the floor around me were all the forlorn remnants of the red hair that I was so proud of. It didn't feel like that long since I'd managed to get out the dye that I'd used to look nondescript in

Cornwall. And now I was completely bald. It would probably take months, even years, for it to grow back to a reasonable length.

I paused for a moment. Mary had short hair, but I was sure that I'd seen lots of students the day before with longer hair. I tried to remember what colour robes they were wearing, but before I could progress any further with my thoughts, there was a knock at the door.

I stepped over and opened it. Mage Thomas was there, waiting. When he caught sight of my newly shorn head, his eyes widened and something flashed through them for a quick moment before disappearing.

"Like what you see?" I grunted.

He pursed his lips and didn't reply, just waved at me to follow him.

I sighed and followed him yet again. This seemed to be becoming my life, trailing around after good old Mage Thomas and his winning ways.

I'd been expecting the oath-taking ceremony to be held in some grand ballroom-type arena, but surprisingly the mage led me outside towards the back of the school and down through a garden. The morning air was crisp and cold, and I was starting to shiver. You'd think that the mages would come up with some kind of garment for winter that would be more insulating. But, then again, perhaps I was so cold because I no longer had any hair to cover my head. Certainly, my ears were starting go numb around the edges and the slight breeze blowing around my naked skull felt extraordinarily peculiar.

When we finally came to a halt, I realised that there was a small gathering of people awaiting our arrival. A stone statue of some berobed man stood majestically over everyone, watching with sightless eyes. In front of the statue was a small altar and the Dean, holding a large worn-looking book in his hands. There was an element of surprise in his eyes as he looked at me, making me wonder if he'd thought that I would turn tail and run after our little chat the day before. He wasn't going to get rid of me that easily. Still, he beckoned me over to stand beside him.

"We meet here, next to our founding father, to welcome a new initiate into our midst," he intoned.

I wasn't convinced that 'welcome' was quite the right word for him to use, but I managed to keep my mouth shut.

"Initiate Smith, place your hand onto the book, and then repeat after me."

I began to place my palm onto the tome that he was holding and then immediately snatched it away. It felt as if I'd received an electric shock. The Dean's eyes narrowed at me, so I tried again, this time trying to ignore the painful buzz the book was giving off. I hoped that this was normal and wasn't something to do with the fact that I wasn't really a mage and shouldn't really be here.

"I, Mackenzie Smith," he began.

"I, Mackenzie Smith," I dutifully repeated.

"Do swear to uphold the rules and traditions of the Ministry of Mages."

"Do swear to uphold the rules and traditions of the Ministry of Mages."

"I shall not abuse my power but shall instead seek to fulfil the precepts of the mage covenant of altruism, benevolence and compassion."

I almost choked at those words – where was the altruism, benevolence or compassion as far as Mrs Alcoon was concerned? However, I managed to get them out of my mouth without drawing too much attention to myself. The Dean continued, laying out a range of rules and concepts that I was now bound to follow. The majority seemed to involve making sure that I followed orders. I sighed inwardly. I probably wasn't going to be particularly good at that part.

The sky was lightening, with just the merest tinge of red in the east, when he finally finished and lowered his head. "Congratulations, Initiate Mackenzie."

"Thank you," I replied automatically.

His lips curled almost imperceptibly for a moment, and then he brushed past me, heading back towards the school building. His entire entourage followed.

Mage Thomas stayed behind and raised his eyebrows at me. "Well, well, well."

"What?" I snapped. I think up until this point I'd been hoping that someone would jump out from behind a bush and tell me that they'd made mistake and they'd let me off. Now that I'd taken the oath, there was no turning back.

"I believe it's time for breakfast. I will show you to the dining room, and then you should prepare for your first lessons."

My soul lightened immediately. At least if I could get some coffee down me then I'd start to feel a bit more human. Human probably wasn't the right word, but I didn't dwell too long on that part, instead I just followed (again) quickly at the mage's heels.

* * *

THE DINING HALL was already busy when we arrived. Mage Thomas dumped me as soon as he could, without making any apologies or giving further explanations, so I headed straight for a large, welcoming-looking urn and poured myself a beautifully thick and gloopy mug of caffeine, then picked up a muffin and sat down.

I was just savouring the bitter coffee when someone shouted in my ear.

"Oh my fucking Founder! What the hell have you done to your hair?"

It was Mary.

"What do you mean?" I asked cautiously.

"You've shaved it all off! Jeez! Is it, like, some kind of protest? I mean, I know you didn't really want to be here that much but it was so beautiful!"

Several unpleasant slots clicked into place. "So I don't have to be bald to be an initiate, then?"

"What? No! Who the…?" Her voice trailed off suddenly, and her gaze fell on that bastard Thomas who was at the other side of the room in deep conversation with someone else. "Oh."

I carefully put the coffee down on the table in front of me. The flames inside were roaring, licking their way up through my intestines and seeping out through my skin. My vision was darkening, but I was still dimly aware of flickers of green flame sparking at my fingertips. I stood up, pushing the chair back.

"Uh, Mackenzie…" started Mary.

"It's Mack," I said calmly.

"Mack, I don't think this is a very good idea."

I ignored her. Several heads were starting to turn in my direction and the buzz of conversation was hushing. I ignored that also. I began to walk over to the mage with single-minded determination. When I was about halfway across the room, he realised what was going on. He turned and faced me, whilst his companion backed away. I shot out a stream of green fire towards him, which he blocked with one hand. It didn't matter. I just kept on walking.

"You've just taken an oath, Initiate Mackenzie," the prick called out. "It would be wise to re-consider your actions."

Only because he knew I was about to beat him. There had been nothing in the oath about not taking revenge once provoked. I flicked out another jet of green flame. Again he blocked it, this time answering back with his own blue fire. It hit me dead in the chest, making me gasp, but I swallowed down the pain and focused instead on the fire inside me. He let out some more attacks, his face impassive. A couple of the shots slowed me down, but they weren't really going to stop me.

When I was a few scant feet away from him, I eyeballed him and hissed, "Did you really think you could get away with this?"

"You're talking about your hair, right? It's not my fault if you're such a gullible bitch that you'd fall for something that stupid."

My bloodfire blazed. I leapt in the air, kicking out one leg and catching him on his chin so that his head snapped back, then sent one punch to his midsection, leaving him doubled over. Several other mages who were clearly trainers rather than students hastily got to their feet to stand beside him, each one with their attack fire gleaming on their palms.

"My fight is not with you," I growled. "But if you get in my way, then I will take you down."

They didn't answer, but instead looked at each other as if in silent communication and then, all at once, sent out a stream of blue flames towards me. Their fire combined into one deadly shot, but I somersaulted in the air and to the side, letting it miss me completely. By the sound of things, it did some rather catastrophic damage to the tables behind me, but I stayed focused on the real action.

I kicked over some of the tables in front of me so that they formed a barrier between myself and the gang of bully mages. I sensed, rather than saw, a flicker of fire coming at me from the left so I sprang backwards to avoid it, then sent out my own green answer. The yelp of pain assured me that my flank was covered, so I turned the spray of flame onto the tables, setting each one alight and creating a wall of hot light that Thomas' friends couldn't get through.

Three of them began to concentrate on my barricade, attempting to douse the flames with their own, whilst the others began to send out a steady stream towards me. A section caught my shoulder, knocking me backwards, but my hand found a plate on the floor and, as I scrambled back up, I sent it flying towards the trapped mages, hitting one smack bang on the middle of his forehead. There was no thought now; it was pure adrenaline and fire. I reached out for more plates and sent them out towards the others, one after another. Every time one connected, I was rewarded with a gasp, shout or scream of angered pain. Good.

I focused back on Thomas, who was still doubled over on the floor. I took a running jump and leapt over my own flames, then twisted my body so I was behind him, and pulled the crook of my arm around his neck, beginning to squeeze. He choked and gurgled but I yanked harder.

"You're going to pay, Thomas," I snarled. He answered with a gasp. I tightened my grip even further. There was a pounding in my ears. The heat in my veins and arteries was almost overwhelming. I looked out across the room. It seemed that everyone had left, abandoning the scene as soon as they realised what was going on. I could vaguely make out shouts from outside as no doubt reinforcements were being mobilised. My eyes looked across to Mary, who was still standing where I'd left her, a lone, silent figure surrounded by the carnage and debris of overturned tables and smashed china. Her eyes were filled with horror, and what gallingly appeared to be pity. A tiny tendril of sanity made its way through my brain. Fuck. I released the mage and he fell forward onto the floor, clutching at his neck and gasping for breath. Then I sat down on the floor next to the prone and groaning bodies and covered my face with my hands.

CHAPTER THREE

I ASSUMED THAT THE DOOR TO MY LITTLE BEDROOM, TO WHERE I'D been frogmarched by a posse of grim-faced mages, was locked. Regardless, I didn't bother trying it. How could I have lost control so utterly and completely? I moved my hand up to my hair to run my fingers through it in an almost unconscious movement, then remembered I had no hair left and my hand fell back down to my side. The narrow bed I was sitting on felt just as uncomfortable as it had the night before. I tripped through everything in my mind again. I had indeed been an idiot to fall for Thomas' trick. All the signs had been there that he'd been fooling me; I just hadn't paid enough attention. To attack him though…that was beyond the pale. They say that revenge is a dish best served cold. I supposed that only worked when you weren't blazing hot inside.

I curled my fingers into a fist and punched the mattress. All I'd had to do was to keep my mouth shut and my head down. Now the mages were probably going to fling me out or put me in prison or something and I'd never manage to get Mrs Alcoon freed. I couldn't see any way out, and I couldn't envision any way in which I could talk myself out of this. Perhaps if I told them what I really was they'd be more understanding. But I doubted it.

They'd probably then be even more keen to make sure that I never saw the light of day ever again. There wasn't anyone I could call on for help this time; I was truly on my own and it was completely my own fault.

I pushed off the bed and began to pace up and down like a caged cat. The room was so small that I could barely take four paces; every time I reached a wall I lashed out and slammed my fist into it before turning on my heel and doing the same thing again. Before too long my knuckles were bleeding. For a moment I wondered if Solus, the Fae who had tracked me through my blood back in Inverness, could sense what was happening through the mages' wards. It didn't really matter if he could, however. He'd refused to come within half a mile of the Ministry building so it was unlikely he'd try to get anywhere near here either. I'd lost count of the number of times that I went backwards and forwards by the time there was finally a knock on the door. I immediately stilled and pulled my shoulders back. It was time to face the music. Taking a deep breath, I went to the door and opened it. It was the Arch-Mage.

He stared at me silently for several moments. I tried to return his gaze, but ended up dropping my eyes to the floor. He'd given me a chance and I'd blown it.

After what seemed to be an eternity, he finally spoke. "So, it seems that you've gotten yourself into quite a lot of bother. I have to admit, I'd rather hoped that you'd manage to hold out longer than a day." He stepped inside the tiny room. "So what do you have to say for yourself? The Dean is really rather keen that you never darken his door ever again."

My cheeks warmed involuntarily. "I'm sorry. I just have a bad temper. I flipped out and I know I shouldn't have. I'll accept whatever punishment you choose, but you can't take this out on Mrs Alcoon. It's not her fault. I'll do anything and go anywhere, just please let her go."

"We've been through this. The deal was that you'd go through training so that we know you can control your impulses and your magic, and then we'd take the spell off. There doesn't seem to be very much control in the slightest on your part. By the Founder, you only took the oath less than thirty minutes before you attacked a mage without any provocation!"

I lifted my head. "That's not fair! I was provoked! He tricked me into shaving off my hair. I was just trying to do what I was told so that I could be a good initiate. When I found out it was all just a joke on his part, I got angry. That's all."

The Arch-Mage stared at me. "Do you mean to tell me that I had to interrupt a Council meeting to come all the way here because of a little hazing? I thought you were tougher than that."

"I'm sorry. It won't happen again, I promise."

He sighed heavily and sat down on the bed and then, apparently appreciating how uncomfortable it was, changed his mind and stood back up. "The thing is that I'm sure you mean that right now. But if you can't even control your temper, then all this is for naught. What happens next time you feel provoked? The point of you being here is to learn control so that you don't misuse your power. It appears that all you are really learning, Miss Smith, is how to be as violent as possible."

"Please," I said in a very small voice. "She's depending on me. I really will be good."

He stared at me for a long moment while I held my breath. I knew that the Arch-Mage was a decent sort; our previous encounter in London when I'd broken into the Ministry had proved that. But I also knew that I hadn't given him all that many options after almost killing one of his mages. I could well imagine that the Ministry, ninety-nine per cent of whom were already baying for my blood as it was, were putting extraordinary pressure on him to deal with me once and for all.

"You have one final chance," he said finally.

My heart leapt in my chest, but he held up a single digit in warning.

"However, there is a caveat. Once a week you will attend anger-management counselling in London. And if you so much as send a dirty look in the direction of anyone else at this facility, then there will be nothing else I can do."

I was nodding vigorously. I'd take any olive branch, even if it meant talking to some shrink about my feelings.

The Arch-Mage stared at me, hard. "I mean it, Miss Smith. One more fuck-up and you're done."

"I won't let you down. I promise."

He didn't look as if he entirely believed me, but I would just have to prove otherwise to him. And maybe the counselling would help a bit. God knew that I needed to do something to start controlling my temper. It seemed to be getting worse and worse as each day went by.

"It's for the best if you stay in your room for the remainder of the day. I will have some food sent up to you. You can begin your studies tomorrow, with Friday afternoons off for the counselling. I will smooth things over with Dean Michaels for now." Something flickered across his eyes as he said that. For a moment, I thought it might be a gleam of self-satisfaction, but it was gone before I could really analyse it.

I blinked my acknowledgement, and the Arch-Mage left without another word. Sinking down onto the floor, I exhaled loudly. I was pretty sure that I'd had a very lucky escape.

* * *

THE NEXT MORNING it was Mary who came to escort me to the dining hall. I guessed that she had volunteered for the duty; it was more than likely that after the display yesterday, no-one else was keen to be my escort. I hoped that Thomas was alright. I didn't like him, but that didn't mean I wished pain and suffering on him. Mary at least smiled at me tentatively.

"You know, it'll probably grow back really quickly."

"Yeah," I said quietly, "it probably will."

She stuck close to me all the way to the dining hall, but didn't say anything else. When we entered the large room, the conversation died instantly and I could feel a hundred pairs of eyes on me, both teenage and adult. I took a quick glance around, noting with some relief that the room had been put back into order and looked exactly as it had the day before, prior to my tantrum. I strove hard to ignore the stares, and helped myself to the coffee, drinking it quickly and scalding my tongue so that I could get out of there as quickly as possible. Once I was done, Mary nodded and jerked her head to the door.

When we were back outside, she spoke again. "You have Kinesis first. The mages have decided that you will have private lessons, seeing as how you are, like, so new and, well, you know."

Unfortunately, I did know. I trailed after her along various narrow cobbled pathways, from either side of which loomed different buildings of all manner of shapes and sizes. I hadn't fully appreciated just how large the academy's complex was until this point. We eventually ended up in a smallish room at the far end of a squat structure that seemed to be some considerable distance away from the main building that housed the cafeteria and dorms. Waiting inside was a rather nervous-looking mage of about thirty years old. I didn't envy him this task, I had to admit. Who would want to teach the psycho bitch to move things around with her mind? Mary stated that she would be back in two hours' time to take me to my next lesson. I tried to give her a warm smile of gratitude, but she was already turning back to the door to leave.

The nervous-looking mage stuck out his hand, and then thought better of it, suddenly withdrawing his palm even before I could begin to reach for it. My soul sank an inch inside as he hastily introduced himself as Mage Slocombe, and then immediately positioned his slumped body at the opposite end of the room, as far away from me as he could possibly get. I tried hard not to let it affect me, and straightened my posture and lifted my chin.

In the centre of the room, inside a small chalk circle, lay a tiny little pebble. Mage Slocombe instructed me in a small, reedy voice to sit down and watch the stone. I did as he bade, hunkering down cross-legged on the floor, and awaited my next instructions. No more were forthcoming, however. I stared at that damn pebble for the whole two hours, all the while wondering if I was supposed to be doing something to make it move. My eyes smarted and my legs were so numb when Mary returned to pick me up that it took me several moments to be able to stand properly and move. I thanked the mage quietly for his teaching, trying so very hard not to acknowledge the shaft of pain that ran through me at the look of sheer relief on his face that the session was over, and then we left.

"A bit of good old stone staring, huh?" Mary was clearly feeling a bit more talkative now.

Relieved that her naturally bubbly personality was re-asserting itself, I nodded vigorously. "Yeah, what on earth is that all about? Is something supposed to happen?"

She grinned, cute dimples appearing in her cheeks as she did so. "Perhaps. You'll just have to wait and see. Some initiates spend months with the staring thing, and others pick it up in, like, just a few hours."

"You know I'm not actually a mage though, right?"

"I guess you'll be doing a lot of staring, then." She giggled a bit, leaving me feeling no better whatsoever, and deposited my unhappy self outside a shiny, aluminium-looking door that appeared completely out of place in this old building. Apparently this was for Evocation.

Once inside, the mage, who seemed even more nervous – if that were possible – than Slocombe had been, warned me very carefully that I could only perform Evocation magic inside one of the specially proofed rooms. Should I choose to attempt it anywhere else, then there was the danger that I would summon some kind of spirit that would wreak all kinds of havoc before it could be contained. It quickly became clear, however, that I was a long way off summoning anything at all. I was given a quick demonstration with some kind of water sprite, but even though I followed the mage's instructions to the letter, when I tried it for myself, absolutely nothing happened. By the end of the lesson, sweat was dripping off my face and seeping through my robe, and I had accomplished nothing whatsoever. The mage shrugged and then almost pushed me back out of the door.

Mary was waiting outside with a grin on her face. "How did it go?"

"This magic stuff is as hard as it looks," I commented, wiping my brow with my sleeve.

"Ah, you'll get the hang of it in no time. You've got a bit of time now to grab a bite to eat, and then you need to hit the library."

"Library? Thank God – maybe this is something I can do."

Mary grimaced. "Yeah, perhaps. You'll need to start with all the Level One reading to match your practical skill sets in the different disciplines. Everyone starts at One. There are five levels to get through and, believe me, it gets harder as you go along. At your level right now, most of it is pretty dry. It's a lot of background knowledge, history, that kind of thing."

I felt relieved. At least I knew that I could read. "Sounds right up my alley. When do I start the other disciplines?"

"You'll begin Illusion and Divination this afternoon."

"And Protection?" I tried – and failed – to keep the hope out of my voice.

Mary's expression, however, was rueful. "Sorry. The trainers have decided that you've already passed Level One in Protection, even though you can't throw a basic ward yet. I guess they want you to focus on the other disciplines rather than the stuff that might, you know, kill people."

Fuck. That had been the only discipline that I felt I really needed to study to help me control myself a bit. Not only that, but it was definitely the only discipline that appeared I'd have any hope of mastering.

"So," I began, not entirely sure I wanted to hear the answer, "I need to pass Level One in all disciplines before I can move up to Level Two?"

"Yeah. And then you need to achieve Level Two in all disciplines also, although after that you can specialise in just the one or two that you're particularly talented in."

Great. Forget this taking five years, it was more likely to take me five hundred. That is, if I didn't get thrown out beforehand. I wasn't a quitter, however. I wouldn't let myself become defeated after just one morning.

"Forget the food for now," I said decisively. "Show me where the library is."

Mary looked surprised, but shrugged and nodded acquiescence, and we headed off.

I hadn't quite been prepared for the grandeur that the exterior of the training academy's library suggested was on offer. Up until now, the rooms had looked much like those of any other institution, strange metal surrounding the Evocation room aside, of course. However, even on approach, the doors of the library proclaimed both style and substance. They were vast masterpieces of construction: heavy oak panels with carved designs of different flora and fauna expertly inlaid into them. I couldn't help but trace my fingers over them in awe, coming to rest at the edge of a dragon's tail that curved its way across one of the panels.

"Wouldn't it be cool if, like, dragons really did still exist?" commented Mary wistfully.

I looked at her sharply but she didn't really seem to notice. "Well, they do exist," I said, trying to aim for a matter-of-fact air.

Her brow furrowed for a moment, then cleared. "Oh, you mean the wyverns, right? But they're not really dragons, are they? They're more like dragon-lite."

"They're apparently distant cousins," I said absently, still running the tip of my finger over the dragon's body.

"Of creatures that don't exist any more though."

I made a non-committal noise. This probably really wasn't the time to be getting into chats about dragons.

"Have you ever seen one?" Mary asked suddenly.

"What? A dragon?" Only every time I look in the mirror, I thought. "Um…" God, I was a useless liar.

"No, silly – a wyvern."

"Oh, yeah, sure. I had to take lots down when I lived in Cornwall." Funny how those memories were now so precious. I smiled to myself. "There was this one wyvern that was such a bright blue colour and had such a loud shriek that we were sure that the villagers nearby were going to either hear or see it and come and investigate. You know us shifters don't have skills like you do. We can't just wave our hands in the air and make things appear to be different to what they are. It's a lot more complicated for us to hide the Otherworld from humans than it is for you."

Mary was staring at me. "What?" I asked.

"You said 'us shifters'."

I squirmed, suddenly embarrassed. "Oh. I didn't mean that. I'm not a shifter, I just…I just spent a lot of time around them, that's all. I grew up with them."

"Aren't they a bit scary? I mean, we hear stories that they, like, eat their young and that kind of thing."

I gazed at Mary in astonishment. Surely she had to be pulling my leg. The sincerity in her eyes suggested differently, however. "Fuck, no. Where on earth did you hear that? All mages can't think that, can they?" I thought of Alex. He hadn't ever seemed to think that the shifters were cannibalistic. Why on earth would any mage agree to work with them if they believed that tripe?

"Well, I don't know. The trainers say it's not true, but you kind of hear some stories now and then, you know?"

"No, Mary, I don't know. Shifters are the most trustworthy, loyal and friendly people you could ever meet. They would never do anything as awful as that." A little voice poked inside me, suggesting that I'd thought some pretty terrible things about the

Brethren, who were technically the Shifters, with a capital 'S', of the shapeshifter world.

"Okay, I'm sorry. I've never met one, so it's difficult to know these things."

"Yeah, but mages work with shifters all the time," I protested.

"Only when the Arch-Mage makes them and so that there can be some kind of peace between us. Not because we like them."

I was absolutely horrified. "Is that what you really think?" I had no idea what Corrigan and the Brethren's opinion of mages was, but I was certain that the local shifters, such as my old pack in Cornwall, had never held any animosity towards the mages. Some wariness, sure – who wouldn't be wary of someone who has a range of magical powers at their disposal? But to be so hostile as to suggest that they ate their young and that we didn't like them? I shook my head. The world was a much more complicated place than I'd ever realised when I lived in my quiet little pocket of Cornwall.

Mary shrugged. "I'd never really thought about it much." She peered at me anxiously. "You're not, like, angry, are you?"

I guessed I deserved that little note of worry. "No, Mary, I'm not angry. Just a bit sad is all, I think."

She was clearly relieved. "Oh, okay, cool. Listen, I think we can smooth things over with the others if we can show that you can be a good sport. You know, let bygones be bygones, that kind of thing?"

I didn't really think I cared that much about what a bunch of adolescent pre-mages thought of me, but I thought it'd probably be best to play along. "Sure, how do we do that?"

"We come up with a nickname for you, you know, now that you're bald. We could call you, um, baldy? Or maybe egghead? That would fit with you being so keen to go to the library and all."

I kept my face carefully expressionless. "A nickname. Yeah. What a great idea. Or we could, you know, just not do that."

Mary missed my lack of enthusiasm. "Awesome! I'll start

thinking of some names and then you can pick the one you'd like the best." She beamed at me. "This is really going to help you, like, fit in more." She glanced down at her watch and her faced paled suddenly. "Oh, I've got to go. Are you okay from here? Can you make it back to your own room and to the dining hall without any problems?"

"Sure," I reassured her.

"Okay. Lunch is at 1.00pm and then you've got Illusion, Divination and then dinner at 7.00pm. The librarian inside who's called Slim will tell you what to do." She gave me a big wave and then ran off.

I watched her go and then reached out to touch the wooden dragon just one more time. "Hey little guy," I whispered to it.

Then I pulled my hand away and opened the door.

CHAPTER FOUR

An inadvertent gasp left me. I hadn't expected anything on this scale, even after seeing the ornate library doors.

The entire room was massive. Vast stained-glass windows surrounded two sides, letting in bolts of coloured light that danced over the towering teak bookshelves housing stacks and stacks of books. I took a step forward and looked up in awe. There must have been at least three storeys housed inside that one cavernous space, and every inch was filled with space, light and knowledge. There was a curving wrought-iron staircase to the left of the room, leading up to a mezzanine level that contained even more stacks. The glorious scent of old ink and vellum wafted towards my nostrils and I inhaled deeply, briefly closing my eyes. Here, more than anywhere else that I'd visited in the academy, I felt at home.

I moved forward to the first row of bookshelves and slowly walked down it, trailing my index finger across the titles, feeling the different textures and embossed letters engraved on the covers. Some of the books appeared old, perhaps by even hundreds of years, whilst others could have been published yesterday. Every so often a title caught my interest, and I hooked it off the shelf to peer at the cover before sliding it back into its place. There were the inevitable tomes relating to the five disciplines, but also histories, treatises on different denizens of the Otherworld, spell guides and instructions... I took in the range incredulously. My thoughts inevitably flickered back to the smouldering remains of the Clava book shop. Mrs Alcoon would love it here. I loved it here.

Thinking of my old friend reminded me of my purpose so, taking in Mary's words, I reluctantly left the books alone and went in search of Slim, the librarian. I wandered in and out of the aisles, occasionally glancing upwards to admire the windows and the way they distributed the light around the entire floor. It took quite some time to cover the ground floor, by which time I'd determined that it was empty. Finding it hard to believe that there weren't more students here making use of such a marvellous space and range of books, I headed for the staircase and climbed upwards. I could feel the beginnings of a headache forming behind my eyes, but my surroundings allowed me to regard it as little more than a nuisance. Instead I let myself soak up the view of thousands upon thousands of books that were laid out on the floor that was now below me.

As I'd surmised from my stunned view around as I'd entered, the next floor showcased more shelves and more books. Behind me were a range of several closed doors, no doubt small carrels for private and quiet study. Ahead of me, the mezzanine seemed to stretch backwards for miles so I headed in that direction, moving deeper in.

"Hello?" I attempted calling out. "Miss Slim?" My voice echoed back towards me, hinting at the absence of any other being. I thought for a moment, then called out again, "Mr Slim?"

Nothing. I shrugged and kept moving forward. Gender distinctions notwithstanding, Mary had been sure that the librarian would be here, so I probably just had to look a little further. The area I was moving into was considerably less well lit than everywhere else, probably because the stacks of shelves on this level were so tall that they were starting to block out the sunlight streaming in from the windows. The hackles on my skin were starting to rise for no apparent reason, and I suddenly shivered. Telling myself that it was just the slight drop in temperature now that I was no longer bathed in the warm sun, I continued on to a small door that I noticed at the back of the room. Set into the wall on its own as it was, I reckoned that this was not just another study carrel, but either a cupboard or a doorway to another part of the vast library. I reached out to twist the doorknob to check when a sharp voice with an oddly Irish-sounding lilt interrupted me from behind.

"What the feck do you think you're doing?"

I blinked and began to turn around. Finally. "I'm looking for…" My voice died away as I took in the owner of the voice.

In front of me, hovering in the air at about eye level, was what I could only describe as a chubby, purple gargoyle. But this creature was most definitely not made of stone or affixed to some ancient building. Small wings attached to its back were fluttering in the air. It seemed impossible that they would be capable of supporting the creature's weight in flight, and yet that's exactly what was happening. A pair of dark flashing eyes were narrowed at me from under a set of bushy white eyebrows that curled out further than should really be allowed. The creature placed its hands on its hips, creating such a comical image that it was suddenly impossible not to smirk.

"What the feck is so funny?"

I wiped the grin off my face with a struggle. "Er…nothing. Sorry." I licked my lips and composed myself. "Are you…" I glanced downwards from the creature's face for a moment, feeling my cheeks warm ever so slightly. Definitely not a Miss Slim, then. "…Mr Slim?"

The small creature growled at me. "Of fecking course, I am. You'll be that fecking hairless trouble-maker then, I suppose? This area is completely out of bounds to you. You are only allowed on the ground floor." He fixed me with a beady-eyed glare as if daring me to argue. "Dean's orders."

"I was looking for you," I hastily protested, most definitely not wanting to create yet another enemy for myself. I may have been somewhat tardy with that wish, however, because Slim wheeled round in the air with a large snort and flapped off back down towards the staircase, clearly expecting me to follow him.

I sighed and followed the little creature as he continued to snort and mutter to himself. I only caught a few snatches of words, but the gist appeared to be along the lines of 'why the feck had he been lumbered with educating a great oaf like me'. I supposed that at least I'd finally met someone today, apart from Mary, who wasn't terrified of getting on my bad side.

When we got back down to the ground floor, he led me to a desk area in one of the corners. There was a pile of about ten books lying next to a pad and a pencil. Slim jerked his head towards them.

"There are your fecking books. Read them. Here. Then there's a test." He brushed some imaginary dust off his shoulder with a clawed hand. "Don't touch anything else. You are not permitted to take any books out of this room. And don't fecking bother me." He sniffed and then fluttered off until I lost sight of him among some of the stacks.

I turned and looked down at the books, feeling a twist of regret that I apparently wasn't to be given more freedom to explore the library in more depth. Still, reading a few books had to be easier than staring at a stone for two hours or trying to summon a sprite. I pulled out the chair and sat down heavily on it, picking up the pencil and running my hand over my naked skull. No problem.

* * *

SEVERAL HOURS LATER, my brain was swimming. The language in the books was virtually archaic. Facts and figures merged together into dizzying nonsense, and my head was pounding. At different points, I'd been vaguely aware of other people entering and leaving the library, but they'd all given me a wide berth. I supposed that I should be thankful for being able to have uninterrupted peace and quiet in order to study. I pushed the chair back and was about to stand up when Slim appeared, hovering at my shoulder.

"Are you ready for the fecking test?"

The pain in my head protested and intensified at the idea of having to continue to think and focus, but I nodded dumbly and reached behind my neck to massage it. The little creature remained expressionless, and instead placed a sheet of paper in front of me that he'd seemingly magicked from nowhere. He also picked up the pile of books, raising a single bushy eyebrow at me as he did so. I was vaguely impressed that he managed to balance the pile of books in one hand, and vaguely insulted that he thought that I'd cheat and so had to whisk them away from me. I had to try hard not to bite out an annoyed comment and instead tucked the chair back in, curling my ankles around the legs. I rubbed my forehead and began.

All the books had been incredibly dry documents detailing long histories and laws relating to the ridiculously complicated mage society. I now knew more about the state of legal affairs within the wizard system than I'd ever wanted to. Fortunately for me, I'd had the shifter Way Directives hammered into me from the moment I'd arrived in Cornwall at a young age, so I was pretty confident that I could absorb ridiculous rules and regulations without too much bother. The best thing was that there were remarkable similarities between the mages' system and that of the shifters. Other than some different terminology relating to specific magic details, the rules could virtually have been written by the same person. Once I started answering the questions, I realised that I was able to block out the pain in my head and fly through the answers.

When I'd finally finished, I put down my pencil and stood up. Looking around, I could see no sign of the little gargoyle. I was tempted for a moment just to leave my answer sheet where it was and let him pick it up when he deigned to reappear from behind whichever pile of books he happened to be hovering at this point in time, but I was cognisant of the possibility that if some other mage like Thomas, who was keen for me to fail, came across it, then it would mysteriously disappear into the ether. There was no other choice but to find Slim and put it into his purple paws in person.

The light in the library had a different hue now than when I'd arrived, casting softer dapples across the floor and shelves. The growl in my stomach attested equally to the fact that I'd been here for some time, and I started to wonder what time it was and whether I was too late for lunch. There were a few mage-like figures hovering in between some of the stacks, but I didn't bother asking them for help in locating Slim. I had a pretty good idea by now of how helpful I could expect them to be. Instead I continued to wander up the vast corridor, peeking left and right as I went and breathing in the familiar and comforting smell of old books. My headache had returned with a vengeance now and seemed to be getting worse, throbbing more and more the further into the annals of the library I went.

I was starting to feel the familiar heat of irritation uncoil itself in my veins when a title crammed tightly onto one of the shelves to the left of me caught my eye. My eyebrows raised in surprise, and I reached over to pull it out. I'd been right. This edition was older than the one I'd used in John's office all those months ago but it was definitely the same Fae–Human dictionary that I'd used to break the password and hack into his computer. Almost unconsciously, my fingers turned through the pages until I found the entry for Herensuge – the Basque definition for dragon. My chest tightened when I found it, and again I couldn't help wondering just how much John had really known about my heritage and why he'd never told me. I sighed, pinching the bridge of my nose. I'd never know the truth so it was pointless wondering. Snapping the dictionary closed, I leaned back to the shelf to attempt to slide it back. It was a tight fit and I was struggling to squeeze it in when someone rudely pushed past me, jolting my body against the rows of books. I inadvertently lost my balance and half tumbled to my knees, cursing. Fucking mages. At least shifters had some semblance of manners. Even Anton wouldn't have been so crude as to get a kick out of a move like that.

I would have gone after the offending mage, promises to the Arch-Mage be damned, but the throbbing in my skull had transformed itself into a searing pain that was making it hard to think straight. The idea that maybe I'd incurred some kind of serious injury at some point, and now had a blood clot or brain tumour invading my body, flitted through my mind with the unerring whisper of every hypochondriac's worst nightmare. Squeezing my eyes tightly shut, I tried to will away the pain then, when that didn't work, I pushed my palms against the uneven surfaces of the books to try and bring myself back up to my feet. And that was when I felt it.

It was a soft tingle against my fingertips, as if one of the books was almost vibrating. I'd felt that half-buzz before. I half opened one eye and squinted towards where the sensation was coming from. My jaw tightened when I realised that I wasn't mistaken. Without thinking further, I reached over and pulled out a dusty-looking book, the now forgotten Human–Fae dictionary dangling half off the shelf above me where I'd been trying to push it back in. I focused instead on the new tome in my hands that was continuing to hum against my skin, and moved down and sat on the floor, carefully turning to the first page. The familiarity of the opening image floored me: a stunningly beautiful landscape with undulating emerald-green hills in the background, a shining blue river and what appeared to be a pomegranate tree. I turned the next page, but I knew what I would see before I got there. It was a Fae rune, singly screaming itself at me from the pristine white page. This was exactly the same book that I'd come across in the Clava book shop, the one that had freaked me out so much and made me really doubt what the old woman had been up to.

I tried to rationalise it to myself. I'd been in a book shop. What else would you find in a book shop other than books? Now I was in a library. Hello! And it was a vast library stocked with hundreds of thousands of titles, no less. Of course there would be copies of the same book. But in such a large library, was it really credible that I'd come across such an unusual and rare book without even looking? I moved my hand up to my scalp to twist my fingers thoughtfully through the hair that I no longer had, and then stopped abruptly in mid air and brought my fingers to my nose instead, sniffing. Oh God. There was a definite whiff of stale bonfire clinging to them. I raised the book itself up to my face and sniffed again, even more cautiously this time. The smell was even stronger. As if the book had been in a fire and the pages had been burnt. I flicked quickly through the rest of it, not looking to see what was inscribed within but instead hunting for any signs of damage. There were none.

I rocked back. Okay, so it could be a coincidence that I'd come across the same book. Coincidences happen all the time; in fact, it would be a coincidence if there were no coincidences (I struggled mentally with that one, although I think I got it). But could it really be a coincidence that a copy of the book that I last saw burning in the debris of Mrs Alcoon's shop now turned up here with the definite and distinctive odour of burnt paper? I wasn't completely stupid. Something was going on here. I glanced down at my blue robes and realised that they would actually have some use after all. Taking a quick glance around to make sure that no-one was within eyeshot, I hiked up the robes and shoved the book under one of my arms. The robes would drape over my body well enough to conceal its shape and I'd be able to sneak it out of the library and examine it in more detail later. Assuming I didn't have to move my arms very much, that was. Another thought struck me, and I reached up and scooped out the dictionary that was still half hanging off the shelf above me and did the same, only this time shoving it under my other armpit. Hopefully I wouldn't sweat too much into the books.

I stood up and smoothed the blue material down, trying to crane my neck around my body to see if the corners of the books were suspiciously poking out. They seemed to be hidden well enough from what I could judge. Carefully squatting down so as not to disturb their positions, I grabbed my test answer sheet from the floor where it had fallen when I had initially been shoved against the shelves. I tried not to think about whether that was a coincidence or not as well, and instead stiffly got myself back to standing position and walked back out into the main area of the library, keeping my arms firmly at my sides to hold the books in place. I realised that the headache that had been bothering me so very much had now completely vanished. It must have been psychosomatic, I told myself. If not, then it had been a tension headache from the stress of having to take the stupid test in the first place. It wasn't that the book itself had given me the pain to alert me to its presence. No. That would be impossible because it was an inert object. Not alive. Nor could it have been reincarnated from a fire on the other side of the country. Definitely not.

"Now what the feck are you doing?" came a familiarly gruff voice from behind me.

I turned slowly, attempting to look natural. "I was looking for you. Here," I said, uncomfortably bending my elbow at the joint in order to pass over my answer sheet to the librarian without the books dropping from their precarious position under my robes, "these are my answers. I think you'll find they're all in order."

Slim snatched them from me and scanned down the sheet, huffing as he did so. He pursed his lips. "Very well. I suppose you've passed." He looked up from the sheet and stared at me, the wings at his back continuing to flap. "Can't say I think much of your fecking penmanship though."

I inclined my head slightly and muttered that I would work on it. The floating gargoyle stared at me for a moment, and I could feel myself starting to sweat uncomfortably. Then he blinked with what seemed to be some kind of dismissal and turned, flapping off in the other direction.

I exhaled slowly. I might just have made it. Making an odd shuffling turn that would have looked bizarre to anyone who was watching, I manoeuvred myself towards the library doors and stiffly walked out.

CHAPTER FIVE

I FELT CONSIDERABLY MORE CONFIDENT ONCE I'D LEFT THE LIBRARY and began the hike back to my little attic garret. Both books were tight under my arms and, although I had to take care to grip them tightly, I passed several mages who didn't seem to notice anything peculiar. Of course, they all veered considerably far out of my way when they saw me coming and averted their eyes to avoid meeting my gaze, and I knew that once I'd passed them they were all staring at me in wide-eyed fascination, safe in the knowledge that I wouldn't then be able to catch their eyes. So far, however, no-one was shouting anything about the crazy bitch who wasn't really a mage trying to steal things and hide them about her person.

I was particularly glad that the thumping headache was showing no signs of returning, despite my muffled alarm that it really had been caused by the Fae book alerting me to its presence. I kept whispering in my head that I was being ridiculous, but I didn't really manage to fully convince myself. However, I did feel a sense of churning nausea that resembled an odd sensation of oily seasickness at the thought that my thievery would be discovered. I was pretty sure that I'd pushed the

Ministry of Mages to the limits of its patience with me. I didn't have much of an idea about what they would do if all this training stuff didn't work out, and truthfully I didn't really care all that much about what happened to me. Other than Mrs Alcoon, there was no-one any more who depended on my existence or who would probably even miss me that much if I was gone. Imagining a tiny violin playing in my ear, I scowled. I wasn't feeling sorry for myself, I really wasn't. I was just facing reality. Solus was a Fae, therefore notoriously fickle, and would forget me in a heartbeat. Alex would probably be thrilled that he'd no longer be held accountable for my actions. Betsy and Tom had each other and would do fine, while Julia was far too capable on her own, even crippled as she was, to need me underfoot causing the problems that I repeatedly seemed to involve myself in. And Corrigan...? Well, I didn't really know what he'd think. Regardless of all of them, though, if I didn't make it through this training, then Mrs Alcoon was finished. That was completely unacceptable. Therefore it was imperative that I kept my nose clean and didn't do anything else that was stupid. Like getting caught sneaking books out of the library.

I considered whether I should just have left the books where they were. The fact that both of them had materialised under my nose – and that fate had conspired to force me to trip over right next to them – suggested to me that it hadn't been an option. Certainly not if the headache had been going to continue, anyway. No, I had done the only thing I could do. And the overwhelming curiosity to discover exactly what lay inside the Fae book was searing its way through me.

I swung round past the dining hall and took a quick peek inside as I went past. The entire room was empty and it seemed pretty clear that I'd missed lunch by at least an hour. I knew I had Illusion and Divination classes to get to, but I reckoned that I could easily make it back to my room first to drop off the books and hide them somewhere safe before I found out where I was really supposed to be.

As I reached the staircase up to the dormitory level, I noticed with a sinking feeling that Thomas was standing there, arms folded, watching my approach. His back was ramrod straight, exactly as if the metaphorical poker up his arse reached through his spine and into his skull. That probably accounted for the lack of brain cells, I figured sardonically.

I made it just past him and was on the step beyond, when he decided to speak.

"So, I hear that your classes didn't go so well?"

Smug bastard. I resisted the impulse to turn and just carried on walking, ignoring him completely. Unfortunately, he decided to join my ascent up the stairs and continued to talk.

"That's a real shame, you know," he said, without a trace of apparent emotion in his voice. "It'll be interesting to see how you do this afternoon, though."

I ignored him and continued walking up the stairs, keeping my arms closely clenched to my sides. It was probably fortunate for both of us that when he grabbed my shoulder, I was sentient enough not to react physically.

"What?" I snapped.

"Look, Mackenzie, I'm sorry."

I paused, entirely befuddled. Thomas continued, "I shouldn't have done that. With the whole, you know, shave your hair thing. It was immature."

Well, score one for the idiot in a frock. I stared hard at the mage, trying to work out what he was up to now. "Yeah, it was, Thomas."

He flicked at an invisible strand of hair. "I feel like we got off on the wrong foot. Perhaps we can start over." He took his hand off my shoulder and thrust it out, palm extended upwards.

I fixed my gaze on his hand. I had no idea whether this was some kind of trick or not, but I was pretty sure that if I reached out to shake his hand in a gesture of peace, I would lose my grip on the filched books. I didn't think that he'd be so friendly if they fell to the floor and exposed my sneaky theft. I prayed to myself that he couldn't actually read my mind while my bloodfire swirled nervously around, flickering through my veins with dulled heat. I cleared my throat, "Well then, I apologise if I hurt you."

His hand remained outstretched. "Fortunately we have some dedicated healers whose talent is virtually unsurpassed."

I thought of Julia and had my doubts at that, but I shrugged anyway and hoped he'd go away. No such luck, however.

Thomas had apparently worked out that I wasn't going to shake his hand in return. He shrugged and withdrew his arm, but there was a flash of something indefinable in his eyes. "Still, it did have one positive outcome," he said, his voice somewhat flatter now.

I turned to face him, exasperation getting the better of me. "What? What positive outcome did it have?"

His eyes gleamed. "You will start Protection lessons tomorrow after all. And they will be with me."

Oh fucking hell. "Great," I muttered. "Except I think I've proved that I'm better at Protection than you."

"At attacking, perhaps. But being truly gifted at Protection involves learning how to hold back and use control." He bared his teeth in what I suppose could be called a smile. "So that's what we'll be doing. I will be making you learn how to control yourself. I've realised that it's not fair for me to judge you so harshly. Of course it's not your fault that you act like an untrained creature. After all, you did spend all that time with the shifters. It's no wonder you have base feral instincts."

Bloodfire roared in my ears with the unfiltered rage of a thousand angry devils. The only thing that brought me back from the brink and saved Thomas – and me – this time was that at that particular point one of the books tucked under my armpit chose that moment to suddenly begin to slide down. I clenched my arm tighter to my side and willed it to stay put, biting my tongue until I tasted the hot, iron-rich blood.

"I hope that we can put all this unpleasant business behind us and become, if not friends, then collegiate colleagues instead." He reached out to squeeze my shoulder again, but this time seemed to think better of it and let his hand drop back down to his side.

It took every fibre of my being not to flinch, and instead to grit my teeth and smile back at him. The book slipped an inch further down and I could feel the trickle of sweat at the nape of my neck.

I cast my eyes down so I didn't have to look at him. "I thank you for your gracious tutelage, Mage Thomas."

He was silent for a moment, clearly wondering whether I was taking the piss or not. Then he shrugged nonchalantly and nodded to himself. "You'd best be on your way then, Initiate."

I didn't want to move until he did. I was sure that if I started walking back up the stairs, there was no way that my now sweat-damp skin would be able to keep the book gripped in place. Perhaps I could mimic conformity and make it appear that I was waiting for him to go first to show respect. He stayed motionless for a heartbeat longer, but my fake tractability must have worked, because he eventually moved off and back down the staircase, calling out behind him, "Looking forward to tomorrow, Initiate!"

The bloodfire flared inside me for a moment, leaping up to my throat, then I tensed my body to attempt to keep the book in place for just a few minutes more, slowly turned and walked up the stairs and away from Thomas.

Fate was finally smiling down on me as the entire dormitory corridor was empty of people. Everyone had to be out studying or in lessons. With the risk of discovery lessening by the minute, I picked up speed and eventually made it back to my small room. Of course, by the time that I did so, the second book had also started to slide its way down my side, whilst the first was virtually at my hip. As soon as the door closed behind me, I let my muscles release their grip and both copies fell to the floor from under my robes with staggered thumps.

Then I reached out towards the bed and yanked it from its place, flipped it on its side and screamed.

* * *

ONCE THE TENSION and potential bloodfire eruption had both been released, I calmly straightened the frame of the bed back to its original position and scooped both of the books up from the floor. I thought through what Thomas had said and struggled to make sense of it. Out and out aggression I could deal with. I knew how to react to that; for goodness' sake, my blood knew how to react to that. Let's face it, I'd had more than enough practice over the last year or two. But coping with someone who was passive–aggressive was new to me. What was I supposed to do? On the surface he was apologising and handing out an olive branch. Which, I conceded, I'd probably ruined somewhat by refusing to shake his hand. The barbed comment about my 'feral instincts' however? If it hadn't been for the books clutched under my sweaty armpits, I wasn't sure what I'd have done. There was a good chance that the Arch-Mage would have been scraping what was left of Thomas from the polished staircase and I'd have condemned Mrs Alcoon to spending the rest of eternity in stasis. I frowned to myself, vowing to do better next time. What was it Shakespeare had written in Macbeth? 'Look like the innocent flower but be the serpent under't'. Well, if Thomas wanted to play that game, then I would rise the challenge.

I forced him out of my mind and focused instead on the matter in hand, thoughtfully turning the books over. The Fae tome continued to hum against my skin, although not unpleasantly. I scanned my small room. There were absolutely no hiding places anywhere within its confines, other than perhaps under the pillow, which just seemed both ridiculous and pointless. Musing it over, I decided that the smartest thing to do would be to hide them in plain sight. There was nowhere I could put them where they wouldn't be found, so if I pretended ignorance and just left them lying around as if I hadn't just sneakily spirited them away, then perhaps no-one who entered my room would think of them as anything other than a little extra study material. Maybe I could feign ignorance and pretend I hadn't heard Slim tell me in no uncertain terms not to remove any books from within the library's walls. I nodded to myself, then left them both casually on the bed sheet. Each one felt rather unpleasantly moist from the contact with my body. I'd just have to hope that there wasn't any lasting damage to either.

From outside I heard the distant tolling of a bell, and then a clustered buzz of chattering voices as the next lesson changeover took place. That meant I had just enough time to get myself to my Illusion class. I wasn't entirely sure where it was, but maybe I would bump into Mary along the way so I wouldn't be too late. I'd have to hope I didn't see Thomas again too. Casting a quick glance back at the books to reassure myself that they were both there, and sending them a quick promise that I'd be back to look at them properly later, I left the room and headed off in what I presumed was vaguely the right direction.

I still felt unpleasantly damp under my robes. As I walked through an arched courtyard area towards the building where my lessons had been earlier, I attempted to take a surreptitious sniff of my armpits to see if they really were as bad as I was imagining. My actions didn't go unnoticed, however, as a group of green-robed initiates, whose acne explosions advertised their youth, started snickering loudly. I glared at them and they abruptly stopped. I tipped my chin up and increased my stride, trying to make it look as if I knew exactly where I was going. I'd be damned if I'd ask any of these pimply teenagers where I was supposed to be.

Several minutes later, I was regretting my stubborn stance. Any initiates who had been milling around had since disappeared, and I had absolutely no idea where I was. I ducked into one door that looked vaguely familiar and found myself inside the strangest interior that I think I'd ever seen. Every surface was blood red: the floors, the ceilings, the doors. Even the sodding doorknobs gleamed scarlet. Swallowing hard, and hoping that I hadn't suddenly discovered that the Ministry was actually some kind of bizarre sacrificial cult instead of the upright and upstanding organisation it proclaimed itself to be, I darted right back out again. I most definitely had no need to investigate the dark depths of the academy. Ignorance is bliss, I told myself firmly.

I tried re-tracing my steps, but just seemed to be going round in circles as a few minutes later I ended up back at the scary red room. Cursing aloud at my lack of spatial awareness, I briefly wished that I'd already had a Divination lesson. Maybe then I could conjure up some blue snaky light to show me where to go. But then, given the lack of magical prowess I'd so far displayed, it was barely credible that I'd be able to manage even that. I ground my teeth together. I'd travelled through other planes, for fuck's sake! How could I not manage to navigate my way through one sodding school? This was getting ridiculous. I tried to imagine the layout in my mind's eye. I positioned the main building, with the dormitories at the front. The weird garden where I'd taken the oath was behind there. The red room was here, where I was. This morning, I'd been...nope, I was drawing an absolute blank.

Abruptly, up ahead I spied a group of students emerge from another door, walking away from me. I felt a brief surge of hope. Maybe if I followed them, I'd end up somewhere useful. I realised that such rationalisation was probably fatal, but I appeared to have little other choice at the time. I was tempted to jog up to them to ask them where to go, but for some reason I couldn't quite make my legs move fast enough to gain on them.

"Coward," I whispered to myself. They were just kids. What did I think they were going to do? Clique me into submission?

Someone pointedly cleared their throat. My head snapped to the right but there was no-one there. I turned round, feeling like an idiot, but again there was no-one else even vaguely near me, and the students up ahead had rounded the corner and disappeared. Then something whizzed past and hit me smack bang on the middle of my shaven head. Okay, this wasn't funny any longer. Frowning, I lifted my gaze upwards and saw that, looking down upon me, was an old, wizened-looking face.

"Well?" it said irritably. "You're late. Get up here."

I threw out my hands in a gesture of utter exasperation, trying to convey that I didn't have the faintest idea how to get up there. The owner of the face sighed dramatically and flicked a hand in the air. And just like that, a door appeared in front of me. For fuck's sake.

"What did you expect?" called what I now presumed to be my teacher, with what could only be described as a cackle, face disappearing back inside. "This is Illusion."

I stood there for a moment, clenching and unclenching my fists. Oh, hysterical. I glanced down at my fingers and saw little flickers of green flame appearing and disappearing. Goddamnit. I was absolutely not going to let my temper get the better of me. No way Jose. I straightened my shoulders and entered the now clearly delineated doorway. The whole red rooms thing had probably been another 'funny' trick. I wondered if this happened to all the initiates or if I was getting extra-special treatment just to point out how little of a mage I was now or was ever going to be. Muttering the whole way, I stomped up the stairs and entered the room from which I was pretty sure the face had called to me.

Inside was a tiny, hunched-over figure wearing the now familiar black robes of the fully confirmed mages. It was difficult to judge whether the figure was even male or female to start off with, until the cackling started up again. Okay, female then. I ran my tongue around my mouth, trying to stay calm and not let the continual grating laughter get to me. It was far from easy.

Finally, the figure waved me over to a wooden chair. "Sit there," she said with an imperious tone that belied her somewhat frail exterior.

I could feel some inner part of me rebel at even this one small order. Did she think I was a child like the other students? The old woman looked at me. It occurred to me that there was something very odd about her face that I couldn't quite put my finger on. Her eyes were a sharp blue, even if the skin around them was wrinkled and pale. I bet not much got past this witch. I battened down the overwhelming urge to spin on my heel and walk right out of the room and instead did as she bade, chewing on my tongue to prevent myself from saying anything I might later regret.

The woman cackled again, briefly, then gave me a small bow, withdrew a round stone from within her robes and placed it on the floor about a metre in front of me. I felt my insides droop with resignation. Another bloody stone.

"The key to Illusion," she intoned solemnly, "is belief. Believe that you can transform the stone…" she flicked a finger and the thing began to grow before my eyes, "and then you shall achieve. Have faith…" she flicked another finger, and the stone bizarrely elongated itself, twisting one way then another, "and who knows what can occur."

I leaned forward. What once had been just a lump of rock was now a tiny bonsai tree, its limbs misshapen into a typically elegant Japanese contortion. She snapped her fingers and it returned to its original shape. I tried to look blasé, but I was pretty sure that I completely failed.

"Hold out your hands," she instructed.

I did as she bade, and she dropped the rock into them. It felt cool and heavy.

"Now close your eyes, and believe. This is not stone. It isn't hard or cold to touch. Consider the surface. It's soft and warm, like a blanket."

I rubbed my fingers over the edge, feeling the minute porous bubbles against my fingertips. It still felt like a rock.

"You do not believe!" she stated sharply.

"Give me a break," I huffed, eyes still closed, "I'm trying."

"There is no try," came the old woman's voice.

"Let me guess," I said drily, "there is only do."

"You mock me."

I opened my eyes. "No, no, I'm sorry. I'm not trying to make fun of you. I've just heard that saying before. I'll try – I'll do harder."

She pursed her lips. In that instant I realised what it was that was ever so slightly odd and off-putting about her face: she had absolutely no eyebrows or eyelashes whatsoever. For some odd reason, I found this really rather terrifying.

"It is of no matter. Your time is up."

"What?" I spluttered. "I only just got here."

She whipped the stone from my hands and secreted it away in her robes again. "You were late."

"Only because you hid the fucking door!"

The woman gave me a baleful glare.

"I'm sorry," I apologised. "I didn't mean to swear. But I would like another shot. Please." If nothing else, at least this mage was prepared to talk to me, unlike the others I'd met so far. I had to start learning something if I was ever going to get out of here.

She just looked at me. I looked back. Clearly she wasn't going to change her mind. I eventually nodded in resignation and left.

Once I got back outside, I kicked the wall of the building in frustration, then cursed at myself as my foot answered back with a smarting shot of pain. I took a moment to attempt to compose myself but the burn of my bloodfire remained, lingering like heartburn in the centre of my body. Running my hands over my bare skull, I tried to pull myself together. I had to get to Divination now, and I was damned if I was going to be late again.

Fortunately this time things seemed a little easier. I followed the cobbled pathway, heading back towards where I presumed the main building was. Almost immediately I noticed a large, red-brick building to my right with a sign hanging over the doorway that proclaimed itself to be for Divination. It seemed somewhat ironic that the one mage discipline that taught you how to find things was the one place that actually managed to signpost itself properly so that you could find it.

Standing outside was a diminutive-looking mage, rubbing his palms together. As I got nearer, he smiled slightly and bowed.

"Mackenzie Smith?"

I nodded and tried to smile back, although I was aware that it was probably more of a grimace at this point than a full-on grin.

He gestured towards the door, encouraging me to enter. Instead, I gestured back at him, playing the polite game of insisting that he go first. Not that I was trying particularly hard to be polite, of course, I just didn't enjoy the sensation of having people behind me where I couldn't see them. Especially when those people had inexplicable and dangerous magical powers. After several almost comedic moments where we silently told the other to 'please go ahead', the mage gave up and went in first.

Once inside, he bowed again and introduced himself as Mage Higgins. He had a friendly face, with laughter lines at the corners of his eyes and a mouth that seemed to be permanently smiling. His demeanour was somewhat standoffish, but I could forgive him for that given my academic record so far. At the very least, he was the most approachable teacher I'd had so far and, despite the lingering traces of fire inside me, I felt considerably more relaxed.

"What do you know about Divination?"

I thought for a moment, casting my mind back to what I'd seen Alex do and what had happened when I'd been trying to escape through the Clava Cairns up in Inverness. I shrugged. "It tracks things. Or people. If you want to find someone, then you wave your hands, a blue light comes out and leads you to where you want to go. Oh," I added, remembering what Mary had told me, "it also means that you can see into the future and read minds."

I felt ridiculously pleased with myself. There! I knew something and I was not the class dunce for once. Mage Higgins, however, frowned at me in displeasure. "Divination is an art form. It enables the user to ascertain the potential truth, whether that is in the foretelling of the potential days to come, an understanding of and empathy with a situation, person, place or thing, or the discovery of elements unfound. It is not as crude as fortune telling or mind reading."

I barely managed to avoid rolling my eyes. That was what I'd said, just in not so many words. I swallowed down my thoughts, focusing on the relief that what was inside my mind was my own after all, and waved my hands in the air with a flourish. "Of course, Mage Higgins. An art form. That is what I meant."

He stared at me for a moment, brow slightly furrowed, as if he couldn't work out whether I was being serious or not. I gazed back innocently. Eventually he gave up. "Very well, then. In order to begin with Divination, the most complex and sophisticated of all disciplines, one must start at the beginning."

He lifted his hands up into the air and connected his middle finger with the thumb on each hand, forming a sort of circle. All at once, a beam of floating blue light appeared from each hand, rising dramatically into the air and circling around the mage's head.

"The atmosphere is made up of rivers of silent consciousness. Tap into that consciousness and you can twist it to your purpose."

As I watched, the swirls of blue light joined together to form the shape of a perfect circle, then dissipated into mist and re-formed into a square.

"So the atmosphere is alive?" I asked cautiously.

"Not in the sense that it is a mere creature like you or I," answered Higgins. "It is far more complicated than that. Rather think of it as particles of being instead of a being. Each one is interlinked and each one can be put to use." The blue square became a helix, connecting lines together almost ad infinitum. "Look behind you," he commanded.

I turned, and realised that there was a painting on the wall. I took a step closer to examine it.

"It's a wonderful piece, isn't it?" Higgins sighed in happy ecstasy. "Escher created it as a lithograph around the same time as his Waterfall piece. He gifted it to us before his career took off."

"Escher was a mage?"

"You'd be surprised at how many artists have formed part of our community at one time or another. That, Initiate, is what comes from appreciating the true aesthetic of the world."

I gazed at the painting. It depicted a natural scene, unlike other examples of Escher's work that I'd previously come across, although this one maintained the same intricacies that had catapulted him to fame. Water cascaded down, across and up a fast-flowing river, with rocks and trees penetrating out at unusual and unfeasible angles. I found it virtually impossible to take in the whole image at once, and instead had to focus on small, individual parts at a time.

"Once you appreciate the connections within and without our world, then you can begin to manipulate and control them. Why do you think there are so many planes and dimensions?"

I started. I'd not really thought about it before. They just existed, much in the same way that France did, or Alaska. The 'why' of their existence seemed like a pointless question. I turned back to face the mage, who was smiling at me benignly.

"Okay," I said slowly. "Everything's connected and interwoven. Like an eternal tapestry."

"Yes! You get it!"

I really didn't. But he seemed pleased and I figured I could fake it. I nodded, trying to appear thoughtful and wise. "This is a revelation to me, Mage Higgins."

He clapped his hands together. "Most excellent. Now we can begin." The mage half turned and pointed towards the window. "Between here and the outside world there are the brooks, streams, rivers and currents of being. If I do this," he flicked a finger and sent out a trickle of blue light, "then you will see that it travels along the currents. The inveniora finds the currents in order to travel and reach its destination."

I could see that the bolt of blue did indeed seem to waver and shimmer along the air as if it were floating steadily down a river of air. The light reached the window and dissipated slowly. "So the blue snaky light is called inveniora?"

"If you must use such basic terms to describe it, then yes. The blue snaky light is inveniora." When he pronounced the term, Higgins' voice took on a tone of hushed reverence. This was indeed someone who loved his day job.

"Okay," I nodded vigorously. "I get it."

"Then discover it for yourself, Initiate. Send out your energy and find the current."

Sighing inwardly, I really wished that he would stop calling me 'Initiate'. Still, this lesson was already going considerably better than the last one, so I managed to keep my irritation level to a tiny simmer. "Uh, how do I do that?"

"Reach inside yourself," said the mage. "Pull out the part of yourself that is connected to your integral energy and send it out to join the world. It remains as part of you, but it also enters the currents of consciousness."

Okay. Integral energy and currents of consciousness were equally baffling, but I thought I had a vague idea about what he meant. I concentrated on my stomach, where I instinctively felt that my 'energy' resided. In my mind's eye, I saw myself pulling out an invisible thread that made its way up through me, past my heart and through my shoulders and down my arm and...I flicked my fingers and shot it out.

Nothing happened. Higgins raised his eyebrows and folded his arms. I took a deep breath. This really didn't sound that hard. Out of everything I'd experienced so far at the academy, Divination seemed about the only discipline aside from Protection that I had any hope of understanding, so I had to try harder.

I did the same again, visualising the same thread, just more slowly this time, giving it the opportunity to take shape and become real. Yet again, there was nothing. A flame curled inside me, the residue of my earlier annoyance from Illusion. I tried to ignore it, this time pulling my magical inveniora thread from the soles of my feet, allowing it to gather impetus as it travelled up and up and up and through and…fuck it.

"If you get frustrated," stated Higgins calmly, "then you cannot tap into the currents."

"I'm not frustrated." I yanked violently from inside myself this time, picturing not a skinny thread of blue light but instead a fiery ball of bloody flame. And this time I really could feel it. The sphere of bloodfire travelled through my system, singeing my gut and searing my lungs until I had to hold my breath. Then I forced it out at maximum velocity down through the veins in my arm.

A sparking red light appeared in the air. I beamed, proud of my efforts and turned to Higgins to seek his approval. Instead of pleased satisfaction on his face, however, there was a look of growing alarm. I turned back to see my own inveniora growing. It wasn't just a snaky light of red, it was a blossoming and overpowering cloud. Tendrils reached out across the entire room, hitting the pockmarked walls and bouncing back, then multiplying further and further. They danced their way through the air in every possible direction.

"Stop it!" yelled Higgins.

"What? How?" I shouted back, now almost unable to see him through the veins of red. The acrid smell of burning reached my nostrils and dread filled me. Oh God, not again. I flailed my arms around, panicking, trying to gather back in the inveniora.

"I can't breathe," choked the mage.

Fuck, fuck, fuck. I reached out desperately to try and get hold of the trails of light, but it was to no avail. They just seemed to be growing and growing. Taking a deep breath, I ran over to roughly where I thought the window was and felt my way along until I was sure I had it. Then I drew back my fist and punched through, smashing a hole through the glass, which in turn ripped through my skin. Blood ran from my hand, splattering onto the floor, but I didn't have time to worry about that now. Instead I focused on trying to use my mind and arms and every part of me to push the inveniora out into the open air and away from Higgins.

Bit by bit it seemed to start working. The clouds of red light shoved their way out through the small hole. I tensed my body and leapt up, kicking through the rest of the glass, shattering the rest of it until there were only a few shards left clinging to the edges of the window frame. The remainder of the scarlet haze escaped, rising up into the sky as it did so in a ball of hazy mist. For a second I watched it, checking that it wasn't going to continue to enlarge or re-form or do anything remotely dangerous. Mercifully, instead the edges started to show signs of evaporation as it mixed with the rest of the atmosphere. Thank fuck.

I turned back to Higgins who was curled up, foetal-like, on the floor, muttering to himself. I pulled him up to his knees and looked into his eyes, searching for any signs of damage or pain. He coughed painfully and stared at a point somewhere behind me.

"No," he moaned. "No, no, no, no."

"Ssshhh," I soothed. "It's okay, it's gone. You're okay now. We're okay." From outside in the corridor I could hear some shouts and calls of concern.

"No," he groaned again.

I looked back and saw with a sinking heart what it was he was actually complaining about. The Escher lithogram, even protected as it had been behind a plate of glass and frame, appeared irrevocably damaged. Its finely etched lines were dulled and the paper had taken on a red hue, almost like a rash. The rocks and trees were virtually obscured now and the confusing twists and turns of the water no longer appeared to distort reality and perspective. Instead they were smothered by taints of crimson smudges.

The door banged open and two black-robed mages who I didn't recognise came bursting in. They took in the scene with one glance and glared at me with seething hatred. I held up my hands, palms upwards. "I didn't do anything! I didn't! I was just doing what he said."

Higgins continued to moan. They scooped him up between them and pulled him out of the room. Then Thomas entered, mouth twisting as he looked around.

"Mage Thomas!" I babbled. "This isn't my fault. I tried to stop it – I broke the window. I'm sorry but I didn't mean for this to happen." All I could think of were the Arch-Mage's last words to me about just having one final chance left.

He strode over to me and looked down. "You're telling the truth," he stated grimly.

"Of course I'm fucking telling the truth! Why would I do otherwise?"

"Why would a simple Divination lesson cause such havoc?" He shook his head at me.

"I'm sorry," I gasped again.

He sighed deeply and put his hands on his hips. "Come on. I'm going to escort you back to your room. It's probably best if you stay there for the rest of this evening. We'll need to get that blood cleaned up as well."

I glanced down at my hand and the blood now covering half of my arm that was continuing to drip remorselessly onto the floor. Shit. Panic seeped through my consciousness at the thought of the repercussions that spilling that amount of my stupid Draco Wyr blood might have. Thomas offered me his arm to help me up, but I had no other choice but to ignore it and clamber to my feet myself.

A spasm of irritation crossed his face, but there was nothing I could do about it now. Past experience had taught me that whenever others came into contact with whatever weird shit was within my system, then strange stuff started to happen. The last thing I needed was an untrustworthy mage knowing more about me than I needed him to.

"It's fine," I muttered. "I'll make my own way back."

"Suit yourself." He turned on his heel and stalked out of the room. Loudly exhaling the angst and anxiety of the afternoon, I followed him out.

CHAPTER SIX

I ENDED UP FOLLOWING THOMAS ALL THE WAY BACK TO MY LITTLE room. Whilst I'd been glad to have him along thanks to all the stares and hushed whispers from the collection of initiates and mages as we passed, I felt more and more nervous as we approached the dorms that he would come in and immediately spot the books I'd nabbed from the library. I cursed myself and my stupid actions. I should have put them under the pillow after all, then at least I'd have had a chance of concealing them. Now, between what had already happened between Thomas and myself, and the fact that I'd completely freaked out an experienced mage and destroyed what was probably a priceless painting, the discovery of the books would completely signal my downfall.

Fortunately for me, he just left me at my door, silently leaving to return to whatever he'd been doing before I'd interrupted with my spooky red inveniora catastrophe. I'd wanted to ask him whether everything was okay – that my Divination creation had all vanished into the ether and wasn't now making its way to smother some nearby human inhabitants with its noxious redness – but I was kind of afraid of the answer. I also naturally wondered how much trouble I was in now. Deep down inside, I had to admit that maybe it would be better for everyone if I put a stop to all this foolishness now. Mrs Alcoon might be permanently trapped in her state of enforced inhibitory gnosis, but at least she was alive. At the rate I was going, if I became much more successful at any of these disciplines, I was liable to kill everyone within a ten-mile radius.

I moved over to the small sink with a heavy heart, then twisted on the cold tap and thrust my hand underneath the stream of water, watching as my blood mixed with the cold water and swirled its way down the pipes. I'd need to see if I could get hold of some tweezers or something to pull out all the tiny shards of glass.

I was still standing there, staring down at the white ceramic bowl and the splashes of blood continuing to drip inexorably down into it, when there was a knock at the door. Startled into action, I jumped and managed to call out, "Just a minute!" in time to hastily flip over the corner of the bed sheet to mask the books that still lay there. Then I turned off the tap and creaked open the door an inch, peering through the gap to see whether it was the Dean coming to take me away.

"Hey, Mack! Look what I've brought!"

Relief flooded through me. It was Mary, holding up a first-aid kit. I opened the door all the way and ushered her in.

"Hi Mary," I said weakly. "How are things?"

"Awesome! Although, I mean, like, wow. You've really been tearing things up, huh?"

"I guess." I took the kit from her and unzipped it with my teeth, then searched through until I found tweezers. "Is Higgins okay?"

"Mage Higgins? Yeah, so I hear. I think he's just a bit shaken up. What on earth happened?"

"Honestly, Mary, I have no idea." I headed over to the sink and turned on the tap again, then bent my head and began digging into the wounds to get out the glass that remained embedded in my flesh. "Have you heard anything about what the Dean is going to do?"

Silence answered me, so I craned my neck backwards. Mary was staring at my hand with a faintly sick-looking expression on her face. "Does that not hurt?"

I blinked in surprise and then looked back down at my bloody hand. "Um, yeah, I suppose. A bit." I hadn't really thought about it much. "Have you heard about the Dean?" I prodded her again.

She shook herself. "Uh, no. I don't think he could do anything even if he wanted to. Mage Thomas checked and says you were telling the truth that you were just doing as you were told. His Divination skill is good for that." She shrugged. "That makes it the fault of the teacher for not taking appropriate precautions."

I yelped slightly. Higgins? "Fuck!" I swore. "It wasn't his fault."

"Was it your fault?"

"No, but, he didn't know that would happen. I mean, I didn't know that would happen either, but that doesn't mean he's to blame."

"He kind of is," said Mary gently. "That's why he's there, to make sure that nothing goes wrong."

Yeah, but he didn't know that he had a fucking Draco Wyr who had no idea what she was capable of doing in front of him, did he? Now I had the guilt of making him look bad to add to everything else. I turned off the tap again. "I need to see Thomas."

Mary ignored me and rummaged inside the kit, pulling out a small bottle. "Here's some disinfectant."

"I mean it, Mary."

"He won't see you. He said that he's busy or something, and that I should make sure you're all cleaned up and that you get some food, and then some rest."

I bristled at Thomas' seeming solicitude. Yeah, he was a wanker. One minute he was forcing me to shave all my hair off and the next he was pretending to look after my well-being. I trusted him more when he was just being nasty. I grabbed the disinfectant from Mary's hand and rubbed it on, hissing slightly at the sting, then took a pristine white bandage and wrapped it tightly round my hand and wrist.

"When was the last time you ate?" Mary enquired.

My stomach growled in answer.

"Yeah, that's what I thought," she said. "You didn't even have lunch, did you?"

I could feel myself getting annoyed. The last thing I needed right now was to be mothered by a teenager. She beamed at me. "Let's head down to the cafeteria. It'll just have opened so the food'll be fresh."

I pasted a smile onto my face, forcing the corners of my mouth to curve upwards. "Fine."

I took a surreptitious look at the lump on my bed where the books were as we left. If Mary had noticed it, then she hadn't thought to mention it. I mentally crossed my fingers and prayed it was going to be alright, along with poor Higgins. As we walked down to the cafeteria, Mary gushed away about her day, and the success she'd had in conjuration with "like, making a dryad appear in the middle of the room." I briefly wondered whether I should tell her just how painful it was for a dryad to be even a short distance away from the trees they called home, then decided it would serve little purpose now. Clearly responsibility towards the rest of the Otherworld wasn't something that was high on the mages' agenda.

I was getting quite sick of the wave of silence that seemed to precede our journey to the canteen with every room we passed. It was even worse when we entered the dining area itself, as at least forty pairs of eyes immediately swivelled in my direction and then quickly looked away as if to pretend that they hadn't seen me. One swaggering teenager stood up and walked towards us as if he was going to say something to me, then brushed past, his elbow barely catching the edge of my robes. The group sitting at the table that he'd risen from sniggered nervously.

"Ignore them," said Mary confidently at my side. "It's just truth or dare. All the initiates play it at some point."

"Let me guess – I'm the dare?"

She flicked a rueful glance at me. When the teenager twisted back for a return shot, I couldn't help myself from snapping right and snarling animalistically in a manner that would have made any of my old shifter buddies proud. He was so startled that he half fell backwards, skidding on the polished floor. I tried not to laugh, but it was a struggle. Then I reminded myself soberly that I had to start giving off a better impression of myself.

We joined the back of the queue for some food. The smells wafting up were delicious: homemade bread, something pungent with garlic and tomatoes and, if my senses hadn't completely deserted me, coffee. Realising how hungry I was, and how much better some food would make me feel, I began to relax. That's when Mary tapped the shoulder of the initiate in front of us, who turned stiffly and awkwardly.

"Hi Mary," he said nervously.

"Hey Brock! Have you met Baldilocks?"

The guy muttered something inaudible then limply stuck out his hand. I had only just worked out that Mary had been referring to me, so I was momentarily frozen until I got hold of myself and managed to reach out and shake his hand back. He muttered something again and then turned back to face the queue.

"Baldilocks?" I hissed at Mary.

"Yeah! D'you like it? I think it suggests a sense of humour, but reminds people that you're just a girl and not, like, this big, scary ogre or anything."

I curled my nails into the palms of my hands. "It's great," I said through gritted teeth, "but I think Mack actually suits me better."

"No way, like I said, a nickname will do wonders for your reputation! Everyone will realise that you're actually kind of fun."

"I'm actually not kind of fun," I growled back at her, but she missed it as she leaned over to give her order to the serving lady.

Once we both had piles of steaming food on our plates, we headed to sit down. I veered right, making straight for a nearby empty table, but Mary tugged at my sleeve and irritatingly took me to a table filled with initiates who looked to be about the same age as her instead.

She introduced me to them all, yet again as 'Baldilocks', to which I was barely able to suppress a shudder. Mary then proceeded to keep up a stream of chatter the entire time. I watched her for a few moments, mouth half agape at the bubbly enthusiasm that never seemed to quite abate, then my stomach growled loudly again, almost making the kid to the right of me jump half out of his seat. So instead I smiled pleasantly, and began to dig in.

It was virtually impossible for the table to remain silent and stony under the onslaught of Mary's chatter. By the time we were done, I knew all the initiates' names and backgrounds. I knew that Brock, the poor boy who'd been forced into an introduction with me at the dinner queue, was particularly gifted at Evocation, but that he really, really wanted to do well in Kinesis instead as that was his family's business. I also knew that Deborah, whose family bloodline ran all the way back to the Pendle witches in the seventeenth century, had a huge crush on Thomas (I found that particularly difficult to fathom but managed to refrain from commenting further) and that Aqmar had travelled all the way from Indonesia to chilly England to train here because this academy was meant to be one of the most prestigious in the world. I managed to deflect many awkward questions about my own background, well aware of what Mary had said earlier in the day about shifters, and instead gave the teenagers the chance to talk about themselves. Inevitably, however, by the time we were all finishing up, the conversation drifted to Protection.

"I hate it," groaned Aqmar. "All we ever do is work on protecting ourselves and defence spells instead of how to actually fight back."

"Mmmph," agreed Deborah through a mouthful of food. "I've got Mage Atterton for Protection and he's a complete waste of space. Now if I had Mage Thomas," she said with an arch look in my direction, "things might be different."

Mary bounced up and down in her seat. "But that's perfect!" she exclaimed. "Baldilocks, you can teach us Protection."

My eyes widened in alarm. "Um, I'm not sure that's a very good–"

"That's a great idea! You've been out into the real world, you know what it's really like," cried Aqmar.

Deborah joined in. "And you can show us what Mage Thomas shows you."

"I don't really think–" I began again.

"We can do it on Saturdays when we've got, like, time off," Mary suggested. "Out in the old field. You know, the one that never gets used any more."

"Let's do it!" Aqmar's eyes were shining.

I looked from one face to the other and sighed inwardly. "You'll need to get permission first," I finally conceded. "I'm not sure that I'm really allowed to do this."

"Brock can go to the Dean – he's like the pet initiate."

"I am not," he spluttered. "I just know him from outside the academy 'cos I've met him a few times at family things, that's all."

"Yeah, but you'll ask him, won't you?"

He looked uncomfortable but Deborah put a perfectly manicured hand on his arm and purred up at him. "Come on, Brocky."

He shot me a quick look from under his eyelashes and then gave in. "Okay, I'll go talk to him. I'm not promising anything, though."

"Yes," I agreed hastily, "I'm not convinced that the Dean would be happy with me contaminating your young minds with thoughts of violence."

"Tosh! Don't you worry, Baldilocks, he'll agree."

I winced yet again at the ridiculous moniker. I figured rationally, however, that having some of the academy's best and brightest on my side couldn't do any harm. I was fairly certain that I could put them through their paces without getting them to do anything dangerous, and I supposed that at least it would keep me busy. With that, I made my excuses and left them to it, all of them jabbering away at poor Brock to sort out exactly what he'd say to the Dean to make him acquiesce to their request.

* * *

WHEN I GOT BACK to my little room, I flipped over the sheet and stood staring down at the books for a moment. The night was already drawing in, so I flipped on the light switch, allowing the bare bulb that was hanging from the ceiling to flicker on with a faint buzz, then I propped up the pillows at the edge of the wall and sat down, pulling the Fae text towards me. If anything, the tingling sensation when I picked it up seemed to have intensified, as if the book itself knew that I was finally going to have the chance to read it properly.

Shifting uncomfortably on the narrow, lumpy bed, I carefully turned to the first page, glancing yet again at the illustration. There was no telling where it was from, whether it was even of this plane or not. Carefully, I turned the page again to the first Fae rune that loudly proclaimed the title. I hadn't realised that I'd been holding my breath until my lungs started to ache. I slowly exhaled. Tracing the rune with my finger, I reached over for the dictionary to begin the laborious process of looking it up.

It was a simple rune, as far as runes go, with merely two strokes inked in next to a teardrop-shaped etching, so after several moments of flicking through the dictionary, I found what I was looking for. When I read the definition, I sank back slightly into the pillows, considering. It translated directly as 'fire'. And yet the picture on the preceding page clearly was not one that suggested death or violence or fiery hell, but rather tranquillity and mother nature. I'd certainly have to hope that was the case. I didn't need any more death or destruction in my life.

Turning the page again, I was confronted by a considerable

amount of closely written text. Heart sinking, I realised that working out what all this meant was going to take more than just one evening with a Fae dictionary. I pondered my alternatives. I could see if I could sneak the book out when I went to anger-management counselling tomorrow. Then, I might be able to find a way to contact Solus and pass him the book for translation. But I might not be able to get hold of him; I might not get any time alone even if I could contact him; in fact, I might even get caught with the book itself, and I was pretty sure that it would be harder to explain away how it ended up in my possession outside of the academy's walls than inside. No, I would just have to do it the hard way. Feeling a wave of exhaustion flood through me, I closed my eyes briefly, thinking that I'd just grab a quick catnap and then make a proper start on translating it. Even if I only managed the first page tonight, it would be a start, and I reckoned I'd probably get more adept at it as I went along.

It was probably the ache in my neck that woke me several hours later, still fully clothed in the blue robes and with a trail of drool leading to my shoulder. The Fae book remained open on my lap, at exactly the same page that I'd left it. Angry with myself for letting my physical weaknesses get in the way of what I needed to do, I pushed the book off to the side and stood up, stretching, then padded over to the window and looked out.

The night sky was a deep, midnight blue, with a considerable amount of cloud cover preventing any stars from shining through, and although I could just hear the night calls of some distant animals, everything else was quiet and still. I sucked the air deep into my lungs, appreciating the moment of peace, and gazed upwards. The wind must have picked up at that point, as the clouds suddenly cleared in one corner, revealing the bright luminescence of the moon above. I could feel my bloodfire leap into my heart for just one brief moment as it registered deep within me that it was a full moon. That meant that every shifter, all over the country, was right now outside enjoying the night. I could picture it in my mind's eye almost as clearly as if I was there with them. Even though I'd obviously never been able to shift myself, I had still always appreciated the freedom and abandoned joy that the full moon had provided. I'd go out with the pack and, while they shifted into their weres, I'd run and play-fight and feel.

Fuck it. I shoved my feet into my shoes and quickly covered the books with my sheet again, then opened my room door slowly, trying to be quiet. The spiral staircase and then the corridor that ran along the other dorm rooms were both as silent and still as the world outside my window had been. Nonetheless, I tiptoed along, wary of any creaks that the old floorboards might yield up as my weight landed on them. However, I managed to sneak my way down and onto the ground floor with the minimum of sound. Trying the handle, it became clear that the front door was locked and that I'd need to find another way out, so after thinking for a moment, I slipped along to the cafeteria.

The tables and chairs, which had been so full just scant hours before, lay dark and empty. The moonlight, now fully bared, drifted in, creating eerie, twisting shadows amongst the utilitarian furniture. I picked my way across the room until I was standing in front of the large windows that looked out over the driveway. Pulling up one chair, I stood on it and reached up for the clasp, just managing to grab it enough with the tips of my fingers to flip it over. Then I hopped up, hands curling over the frame, and head-butted it open as I dragged my body over to follow. The wounds in my hand throbbed as the window banged against them, but I paid them little heed and focused instead on squeezing myself out.

Eventually making it out into the cool night air, I took another deep breath and filled my lungs. The damp, earthy scent of dew and soil and just sheer goodness rose to my nostrils, and I closed my eyes briefly, savouring the moment. Then I took a quick glance around, registering the absolute stillness of the night and the fact that I was, indeed, truly alone. Moving forward ever so slightly, my foot caught the edge of the crumpled initiate robes that I was still wearing. I barely hesitated before pulling them over my head and leaving them in a pile beside my feet. I still had my underwear on, if the unlikely happened and I ran into someone while I was out here. Personally, I doubted whether anyone would be all that keen to view my unattractive and somewhat utilitarian smalls anyway. Besides, just for now, for this moment, I needed the sense of freedom and the connection, however tiny, to my old life.

And then I took off. The academy-issue shoes weren't really designed for running, but it didn't matter. I was out and in the open. Life was good. I jogged at an even pace round to the back of the house, occasionally jumping over the odd bush. Once in the garden where I'd taken the oaths, that somehow seemed almost a lifetime away now even though it had actually only been a couple of days, I skirted round the statue and sped up, sprinting now. I passed perfectly planted rose bushes, devoid of flowers now it was the dead of winter but with thorns still gleaming in the moonlight, pruned hedges and carefully raked soil just waiting for the first sneaking sign of spring before being sown and tended. There was no wind, but the cool night air still brushed arrogantly past my naked skin as I continued to pound my way around.

After a while I veered off left and ended up on the cobbled pathways, which twisted through the buildings that housed the different disciplines. I reached out and scraped my fingertips along the rough walls as I ran, almost as if I was double checking that they were real. When I reached the door that led through to Illusion, I slowed for a moment. The gateway remained firmly in place this time. Then I dismissed it and continued.

By the time I got back to the windows of the cafeteria, I was breathing hard. My skin and muscles felt pleasantly tingly all over as the enjoyment of exertion rippled through me. I felt better than I had done in a long time. Picking up the robes from where I'd left them, I decided not to bother trying to strain myself to clamber back inside them. Instead I jumped up and clung onto the edge of the window frame and shoved them through, pushing myself after them. The sleeve of the robes caught against something so I tugged hard without thinking, realising too late that had been a dumb move as the fabric ripped violently. Oops.

I yanked them off whatever had snagged them and peered down in the darkness, trying to ascertain what damage had been done. The moon took that opportunity, however, to sneak its way back behind the clouds. Shrugging to myself, I balled them up in front of me and headed back to my room to sleep.

CHAPTER SEVEN

WHEN I WOKE AGAIN A FEW HOURS LATER, I STRETCHED OUT LAZILY like a cat, enjoying the slight tautness in my muscles. Then, humming to myself, I sprang up and padded over to the sink, splashing my face with water. My night-time jaunt had clearly done wonders for my mood, and I felt lighter and more carefree than I had done in a long time.

Craving several cups of dark chewy coffee, I picked up my robes from where I'd left them in a haphazard heap on the floor and shook them out. The only other replacement robes I'd been given had already been sent to the academy's laundry room the previous morning, and I knew from what Mary had said that I could expect them back by Saturday, but, even in this era of attempting to conserve energy and water by not continually washing, I felt that I – and everyone else, in fact – deserved at least one other outfit. All these magic lessons involved expending a lot of energy, often surprisingly physical, and being surrounded by adolescents going through sweaty puberty did not exactly offer much opportunity to enjoy an odourless society. I gave the robes a sniff, but fortunately my foray into the front gardens had somehow imbued them with the soft but not unpleasant smell of damp grass. Less happily, they had the appearance of having been crumpled into a ball and left for several hours – which, of course, they had. Sighing, I smoothed them out as best I could and began the daily routine of contorting my body so I could put them on. At the very point of achieving success and completing the final manoeuvre of yanking my head and neck through, I distinctly heard the sound of another fabric rupture.

Looking down, I realised that there was a tear running from the bottom hem of the robes to halfway up my thigh. Shit. Perhaps I could get a safety pin from someone later on, I thought hopefully. I moved around a bit trying to see just how obvious the damage was, but it seemed that fortunately the robes were billowy enough for my modesty to be more than adequately covered. I shrugged and figured they'd just have to do. I quickly changed the dressing on my hand, noting with satisfaction that the lacerations caused by punching through the window yesterday were healing nicely, then ran my hands over my skull, feeling the beginnings of stubbly re-growth. I supposed part of me should thank Thomas for the fact that I didn't have to worry about bad hair days any more. Then I snorted. The day I'd thank him for anything would be the day that dragons flew through the sky again.

Once back in the cafeteria, where I was oddly starting to feel rather at home, I ignored the fruit plates and baskets of bread and croissants and instead made straight for the coffee urn. The cups on offer were rather on the small side, so I poured myself three and then balanced them precariously over to an empty table.

I was savouring the dregs of the second cup when someone plonked themselves down beside me. Startled, I flicked my eyes up.

"Hey," said Brock, placing down a tray covered with a mass of fried food that only a teenager could eat and not feel guilty about.

"Uh, hey," I replied, somewhat nonplussed.

He lifted up his plate and gestured at me to try some kind of doughy, sugary ball thing. I shook my head and lifted up cup number three instead. Brock grunted and began to wolf down his food at an alarming rate, finishing before I'd even drunk down to the end of my coffee.

Then he pushed his chair back and grunted, "See you."

I genuinely smiled. "Bye, Brock." Wonders would never cease. It would appear that I may have made another, if perhaps rather taciturn, new friend.

"Initiate Smith?" called an unpleasantly familiar voice from the other side of the room.

Fucking Thomas. I'd been hoping that I'd have time to sneak another cup of coffee. I sighed and stood up whilst he crooked his little finger at me, beckoning me over. A flash of heat travelled down to my toes as I walked over to join him. Jeez, wasn't I just becoming the well-trained little sham initiate?

Once I reached him, he smiled down at me, although it didn't somehow quite reach his eyes.

"I hope you're ready to begin your Protection lesson," he said, looking over my wrinkled attire with a disapproving frown.

"I can't wait, Mage Thomas," I replied, injecting as much fake enthusiasm as I could possibly muster.

A grimace crossed his flat features. "You're going to have to, of course, get over your aversion to me touching you if you are going to have any chance of succeeding."

I started guiltily at his words. I didn't have a problem with him touching me: he just tried to do it at the most inopportune moments. With no appropriate answer, I just shrugged innocently and followed him out of the cafeteria.

When we were outside in the fresh air and heading towards what I presumed was the Protection building, Thomas chose to speak again. "So, I hear that you are starting to win over some new friends."

I couldn't help myself from grinning and nodding. "It's all Mary really. That girl is like some kind of unstoppable force of nature. Once she puts her mind to something, I don't imagine much gets in her way."

Thomas gave a short bark of laughter. "I can think of someone else not too far away who is much the same as that."

I blinked. I rarely got my own way with anything. If I did, I'd hardly be trailing after Thomas wearing a stupid powder-blue nightgown in the middle of the Ministry of Mages' national training academy. "That's hardly true," I protested.

"Really?" projected Thomas with a heavy hint of sarcasm. He began ticking off his fingers. "The Arch-Mage is prepared to free a potential hazard – your friend – from stasis simply because you asked him to. You are getting mage training at the best," he put considerable emphasis on those last two words, "training academy in the world, even though you are not a mage. You attack me and, instead of being thrown out as you should be, you are offered counselling. You destroy a priceless painting and send a well-respected teacher into therapy and nothing happens. And," his voice rose half an octave higher, "you have now been given special dispensation to offer Protection lessons to a group of Level Four initiates at the weekends that focus on attack instead of defence as the rest of us actual teachers are forced to give."

Wow, bitter – much? I had to admit that I was surprised that the Protection lessons for Mary and her friends were going to be allowed to go ahead, and I still felt guilty about Higgins, but I didn't think that Thomas was seeing the whole picture.

"Do you think I want to be here?" I snapped. "There are a million places in the world that I would rather be than this sodding place. The Arch-Mage will free Mrs Alcoon – that's her name, by the way, she's actually a person, a human being – because she's not done anything wrong and is no threat to you whatsoever. Of course your amazing Magnificence will only do so after he's forced me to spend fucking years at this stupid school! Damaging that Escher lithograph was an accident and, anyway, I was just doing what I was told. I'm sorry about your friend Higgins and I hope he recovers soon, but those Level Four initiates asked me to teach them, not the other way around, so get off your fucking high horse and chill out."

Thomas was silent. You'd think that spurting off my diatribe of woe and getting it finally all off my chest would make me feel better, but instead I just felt angry. Sparks of heat shot along my veins and arteries. I scowled and went to thrust my hands in my pockets, then remembered that the robes I was wearing didn't have any and cursed aloud, kicking a stone at my foot instead. It went clattering off across the cobbles, bouncing for several feet.

"And here we get to lesson number one," Thomas finally said softly.

"Oh right," I drawled sarcastically, "of course, pissing me off is just so you can raise some kind of salient teaching point and show off with just how wise and knowing you are."

"Look at your hands."

I glanced down. Flickers of green flame ran along my fingertips. I clenched my fists, hiding them from sight. "So fucking what?"

"If you can't begin to control yourself, then you can't begin to control an attack."

"Oh yeah? Because if you look at one of the reasons why I'm here, you'll see that I'm actually pretty damn good at controlling attacks. Better than your bloody mages, anyway."

"And naturally you'll only ever have to fight mages," Thomas muttered. "Not earthquake-inducing terrameti, or one-eyed monsters or demi-goddesses, that are stronger, faster and better than you."

I spluttered. "How the hell do you know...?" Goddamnit, if that had been Alex blabbing then I'd bloody well kill him.

"The Lord Alpha was most forthcoming about your exploits. He thought that it might help your progress here if we knew more about you. There's actually a rather thick file with all sorts of information in the Dean's office."

Hot, fiery blood pounded in my ears. Corrigan. I might have fucking known it.

Thomas drew a deep breath. "Baldilocks? Is that what you want to be called?"

I swore at him violently.

"Okay, okay," he said, palms held upwards. "Initiate Smith, then."

"It's fucking Mack."

"Alright, fucking Mack," he said in a placatory tone.

I rolled my eyes at him and clenched my teeth.

"Sorry, I couldn't resist. Mack, you need to understand that the fury you get yourself worked up into is your downfall. If you can control yourself better, then you will be more successful at whatever it is you want to do."

I muttered at him.

"Pardon?"

"I killed the terrametus. I might not have managed to get rid of Iabartu on my own, but I killed the fucking terrametus."

"Okay," Thomas said. "Well done. But now let's get to work so next time you can kill the goddess too."

* * *

I STILL DIDN'T LIKE him. And I was seething with rage at Corrigan and the way he'd given me up to the mages at the earliest opportunity. But I was starting to concede to myself that maybe there was more to Thomas than I'd initially been led to believe. If he thought that I was going to play the willing little student, then he was sadly mistaken, but perhaps I'd listen to what he had to say. Some of it at least. I'd not entirely forgotten his comment about me having feral instincts because of living with shifters.

He led me into a battered-looking building that was considerably more worse for wear than any of the previous ones I'd been into. Thomas noted my reaction and mistook it for judgement.

"You've spent too much time with the pack," he commented wryly.

"What on earth do you mean?"

"Just because they have unlimited wealth, that doesn't mean that we do also."

"You're kidding me, right?" I scoffed. "You charge up and down the country getting payment for services rendered everywhere you go. You forget that I've been to your headquarters in London. It's hardly falling down due to lack of money or disrepair." In fact, from what I could remember, it was positively gleaming with wealth. Marble floors, expensive portraits, that thick, fluffy carpet that your feet sank into…

Thomas grimaced. "We have to keep up appearances. You have no idea how much money it takes to maintain all of these buildings."

I gaped at him. "And you think that the shifters don't have lots of buildings to maintain as well? They are dotted all over the country! You guys get to stay in one place and then materialise by magic through whichever portal you decide to create. You don't need to keep a presence in every corner of the country." I couldn't believe that I was sticking up for the shifters now after Thomas' revelation about Corrigan's deceit, but this at least was the truth.

"And you don't have to spend years training and buying materials to maintain your art. You just attack whichever Otherworld creature happens to be nearest and then collect your payment. We actually pay attention to what's going on and do what we can to keep the equilibrium between all facets of the Otherworld."

I blew out air in exasperation. Keep the equilibrium? What a load of bollocks.

"I suppose you don't eat your young either," I said sarcastically.

Thomas laughed. "Oh, you've heard that little nugget, have you?"

"Yeah, I mean, seriously? Who believes that shit?"

"It doesn't hurt to keep the ranks suitably wary of the pack."

I couldn't keep the disgusted disbelief out of my voice. "So you make up stories about the monster in the closet?"

"No," he answered calmly, "we just don't do much to dispel them, that's all."

"The pack is nothing like that as far as you're concerned. We have always treated the Ministry with respect."

"That's bullshit and you know it. When you need some magic, you call us in and then treat us like the hired help. Don't think we're not aware that you all think that what we do is mumbo-jumbo claptrap."

"That's not fair! We don't think that!" I paused and then back-tracked slightly. "Okay, not everyone thinks that, anyway."

"See?" Thomas pointed out. "You're not any worse than we are."

"You shouldn't say that, really, you know."

"Say what?"

" 'You'. I'm not actually one of them, remember?"

"I'll stop saying 'you' when you stop saying 'we'. And anyway, if you're not a shifter and you're not a mage, what are you?"

I swallowed, then replied as evenly as I could, "I'm human, of course, you numbskull."

Thomas laughed again, humourlessly this time. "I'll believe that when fish start climbing trees."

Slightly offended, I backed away from him. Straying into dangerous territory as we were, I wasn't stupid enough to let this conversation carry on further, however, so I stayed silent as we moved into a large gymnasium-type space and hoped that the mage wouldn't pursue it. Green paint was peeling off the walls in a depressing manner, and an old gymnastics horse stood forlornly in one corner. Thomas motioned me towards a mark on the scuffed floor, thankfully getting down to the actual business of teaching rather than poking around to glean what he could about my background. He then stood in front, facing me.

"Do what I do," he instructed, and inhaled deeply, cupping his hands in front of him as if he were holding a ball.

I copied his movements, feeling like an idiot. He tutted and shifted over to me, gently tipping up my head but pressing down slightly on my shoulders until I relaxed. Then he nudged my feet further apart until they were pointing slightly outwards. He moved back to where he had been before and returned his hands to the cupped position, remaining there for several moments before lifting up his arms and pushing them slowly out in front of him. I mirrored his movements. When Thomas picked up one leg and placed it diagonally in front of him, shifting his weight onto it, then I did the same. When he took his left wrist and curved it downwards, joining each of his fingers to his thumb, and then scooping it out into the empty air, so did I. After thirty minutes of this, I was panting as if I'd been sprinting down a racetrack, despite the fact that every movement was slow and deliberate. Every single thing that Thomas had done had impressed me with its sheer fluidity and grace. Next to him I felt like an awkward heffalump.

When he eventually stopped, drawing his feet together and bowing towards me, and I did the same, I stared at him suspiciously.

"That was just t'ai chi, wasn't it?"

Thomas arched an eyebrow. "It's called t'ai chi ch'uan," he corrected.

"Whatever," I dismissed airily. "It's got nothing to do with protecting myself against Otherworld nasties. That demi-goddess you spoke of before would have laughed in my face if I'd tried that."

He sighed heavily. "Mack, you have a very long way to go."

I rolled my eyes, looking away for a moment, then flicked a glance back at the mage. I guessed it was time for the unthinkable after all.

"Thank you," I said quietly.

He seemed surprised. "For what?"

"Calling me Mack. Not many people do."

Thomas grinned, suddenly appearing terribly boyish. Then he

glanced down at his watch and abruptly changed demeanour. "Come on, it's time to go."

"Go where?"

"Anger management, of course. Not that I see it doing much good, though."

My contented mood evaporated in an instant. He just couldn't help himself. I nodded, trying to hang on to my former feelings of tranquillity, but the irritation was starting to take over again. Stupid mage. I ignored his look of bedevilled amusement and stalked out of the gym.

CHAPTER EIGHT

The portal was already set up and waiting by the time I arrived back at the main building. It shimmered green and purple in the morning sun. If I didn't know better, I thought ruefully, I'd think it was pretty. Instead my stomach was already churning at the idea of having to travel through one yet again. God knew how the mages managed to do this all the time and not end up with some permanently dodgy stomach condition. I tried to steel myself, imagining a wall of iron surrounding my intestines. It'll be fine, I whispered to myself.

A black robe who I'd not yet met stood towards the edge of it, but I barely registered him, instead focusing on the swirling shapes and flickers of light. I took a step towards it, suddenly wishing that I'd not agreed to the counselling. Why in the hell couldn't it just be held at the academy? I was pretty sure I could conjure up a few other names of mages who would benefit from spending an hour or two with a shrink.

I sneaked a peek at the mage who continued to stand stoically at the side, pointedly not looking at me. It didn't appear as if I'd get any quarter from that area, so I took a deep breath and walked forward, pushing through to the other side.

Inevitably, as soon as I came through, the bile was rising in my throat. I did my best to fight it, swallowing it down and trying to focus on breathing deeply. It didn't work. I managed to run a few steps away from the portal itself and then immediately began regurgitating the remnants of the coffee. It occurred to me that if anyone ever wanted to take me down, then it would be pretty damn easy for them just to wait for me to materialise through a portal. My temporary, nausea-induced incapacitation would then quickly become permanent and there'd be fuck all I could do about it.

I rubbed my hands over the top of my head. At least I didn't have to worry about ending up with bits of vomited carrot in my hair, I figured. I shrugged thoughtfully. Maybe I wouldn't bother re-growing my hair. Then I reminded myself of the charming nickname Mary had designated for me, and thought otherwise.

Looking around, it was clear that I was on the roof of a building somewhere. I walked over to the edge and peered down, but didn't see anything I recognised. Not that it was such a huge surprise that I didn't know where I was. After all, I was hardly an expert on London. I had kind of thought that maybe it would be near the Ministry, but it didn't seem to be. Shrugging, I turned back, making for a small door that could only lead down to the counsellor's offices.

The staircase heading downwards was considerably more plush than I'd been expecting. The walls were dotted with photos of what I could only presume were successful clients. I stopped at one that looked vaguely familiar. Damnit, I knew I'd seen him somewhere before, I just couldn't work out where. I felt slightly comforted at least that there were others who were brave enough to attest to the fact that they'd been here before. I wouldn't be letting anyone even think of putting my photo up here, though. Absolutely not.

I emerged from the stairs into a small waiting area. Creamy leather couches stood against a lightly coloured mauve wall. There was a chrome coffee table, upon which sat the obligatory range of magazines to cater to different tastes, and a blonde receptionist behind a desk, smiling professionally at me.

I cleared my throat. "Er, I'm here for an appointment. My name's Mackenzie Smith."

The receptionist's eyes widened slightly. I didn't like that reaction very much and frowned to myself. She beckoned me to sit down on one of the sofas and then practically ran out of the room to get 'refreshments'.

My eyes narrowed. Something was going on here that I definitely did not like. Out of habit, I reached behind my head for the silver needles that I used to keep secreted away there, then I remembered that they had been taken away from me far too long ago. Instead of sitting down, I leaned over the desk to look for something I could use in case this was an ambush. I had no idea who or what might be after me now, but experience taught me that you could never be too prepared. My eyes fell on a silver-coloured fountain pen and I smiled grimly. That would do.

Unscrewing the top, I palmed the pen, concealing it within the sleeves of my robes. It might not be a throwing dagger but it was better than nothing. Down the corridor from where the receptionist had disappeared, I heard a door open. My body tensed, and I moved to the opposite wall where I'd have optimum access if this really turned out to be something that required more than my usual attention.

Adrenaline began mixing with bloodfire and I could feel trickles of anticipatory heat filtering through. I realised that there was a part of me hoping that this actually was some kind of nasty out to get me. It might even help me get rid of some pent-up aggression before the real anger management. I frowned. As long as it wasn't actually the counsellor himself who was hoping for a bit of action, of course. The sound of heavy, measured footsteps approaching down the corridor filled the small space. That definitely wasn't the receptionist returning. I clutched the pen tighter and prepared myself for whatever it might be. The footsteps got louder and louder, and then abruptly stopped just around the corner from where I was. I knew that their owner would be able to see that the couches were empty. That was unfortunate as it meant that I might just have lost the element of surprise. It was of little matter, however; I was confident enough that I could take on whatever was coming.

And then I inhaled.

"Fuck!" I slammed my hand against the wall and pushed myself off, rounding the corner to greet the unwelcome owner of that ever-so-familiar citrus spice aftershave.

"Hello, kitten," purred Corrigan.

I shoved a hand into his chest as if to push him away, but he remained immobile, smiling down at me with the predatory gleam of his were. His green eyes danced with amusement.

"What the fuck are you doing here?" I snarled.

He painted on a look of melodramatic hurt. "Why are you being so aggressive? I thought we were friends now."

"We were never friends," I enunciated carefully. "Now tell me just what exactly you're doing here."

Corrigan took a step towards me and, before I could twist away, grabbed hold of my wrist. The pen clattered to the floor. He raised an eyebrow. "Are you going to ink me to death?"

"Get your hands off me!" I shrieked with a wail akin to a banshee.

His grip, in answer, merely tightened. I sucked in the scent of him, aware of how close we were. He'd clearly completely recovered from the effects of the red fever, and was looking far too good in a crisp white shirt that dazzled against the tan of his skin and his inky black hair. I swallowed and yanked my hand away harder, this time succeeding in pulling loose.

He gazed at me, a faint line of puzzlement etching its away onto his brow. "What's going on? I thought we parted on good terms."

I looked away, unable to deal with those emerald eyes searing their way into me. "You told the mages all about me! About what happened in Cornwall and the fact that I wasn't strong enough to beat Iabartu."

He reeled back momentarily, then recovered. "No," he said slowly, "I told the mages that you were stronger than virtually any shifter I'd ever come across, and that you did well by almost besting a demi-goddess. I wanted them to appreciate your strength. By knowing more about you, I figured they could help train you to be even stronger than you already are."

"Do you have any idea how patronising that sounds?" I spat, raging at the idea that he thought I needed his protection. "And besides, I know it's bullshit. You're just pissed off that I decided to go with them instead of staying with you. Well, guess what, buster? I'm having a great time! It turns out I am pretty good at all this mage stuff. I don't need you sticking your nose in."

"Is that right? Because the way I hear things, you're not doing so hot. In fact there was something about you almost getting kicked out for losing your temper. Isn't that why you're here?"

I turned back to look him in the eye. "You're getting reports on me? You have no right, Corrigan. I'm not part of the pack so you can fuck right off."

"You saved my life," he said softly. In fact so softly that I barely heard him. "In some cultures that means that you're now responsible for me for life."

"Well it's just fortunate that's not my culture then, isn't it?"

A muscle throbbed in his jaw. "This is not going quite how I'd planned it."

"My heart bleeds for you." I spun around and went over to the sofa, plonking myself down and crossing both my arms and legs. "Now please leave. I have a very important appointment to keep."

He ignored me and moved over to the opposite couch, carefully sitting down himself. "Your new haircut, it, um, suits you. It's quite dramatic."

I eyeballed him angrily. 'Oh, you're going to have to do so much better than that, Corrigan."

He leaned over, forcing me to uncross my arms so he could

take both my hands in his. An involuntary shiver ran up my spine. "So give me the chance then."

"Fuck off."

Corrigan sighed irritably and then frowned and looked down. His body tensed in anger. "What the hell happened to your hand?"

I was rather taken aback by the vehemence in his voice. "Nothing. I just needed some air so I punched a hole in a window, alright?"

"Did someone hurt you?"

"No." I pulled my hands back and crossed them against my chest again.

"Mack, I mean it." The look in his eyes was frightening. "Did one of the mages do this to you?"

"No, Corrigan," I said tiredly. "I did this to myself."

He stared at me for a moment, as if trying to ascertain the truth. "Fine, then. But, know this, I'm on your side, whether you believe it or not."

I snorted, then wished I hadn't as the noise that came out was quite ridiculously unladylike.

"And anyway, Mack," he continued, "if you really want to avoid my attentions quite this much, then you should perhaps not flash me quite so much skin."

My head jerked up at him, confused. He smirked broadly and gestured downwards. With horror, I realised that the rip in my robes had somehow increased even more since I'd put them on in the morning and they were now gaping open all the way up to the edge of my hip. I stood up hastily, more annoyed by the flush of embarrassment now flooding my face than anything else. Corrigan leaned over and chucked me on the chin.

I'll be seeing you, kitten.

I growled at him again, but he pulled open the door and left, laughter rebounding back across the room. For my part, I kicked the coffee table, overturning it and sending the magazines flying. Out-fucking-standing.

* * *

I WAS PICKING the magazines back up when the receptionist came back into the room. She flicked me a nervous glance.

"Whatever happened to patient confidentiality?"

"Um, excuse me?"

"Patient confidentiality," I repeated, annoyed, then gestured at the door through which Corrigan had just left.

"That was the Lord Alpha," she explained patiently.

"I know it was the Lord freaking Alpha!" I yelled. "How did he know I was going to be here?"

"Ohhhh, I see." She nodded sagely. "I have no idea. He just showed up and told us he was going to wait for you. Certainly no-one from this office told him you were going to be here. Why on earth would we?"

The look she sent me left no doubt as to the fact that she patently had no idea why the leader of all shifters would have any kind of interest in a bald girl wearing a crumpled blue robe that had a huge rip up the side and who spent her free time going to anger-management classes. Actually, maybe she had a point there. But that didn't change the fact that not only couldn't I trust Corrigan, it also meant I couldn't trust the mages either. One of them must have blabbed to the shifters about me being here. Probably the same person who thought it would be fun to let him know I was flunking out of magic school.

I scowled to myself.

The receptionist cleared her throat nervously. "Uh, Miss Smith? You're, uh, burning."

I glanced down at my hands. Both were aflame with deep-green light that danced over my skin. I sniffed and realised that not only had the bandage round my hand caught alight and burnt away almost to nothing, but now the sleeves of my robes were on fire too. Jesus. Couldn't the bloody mages have been smart enough to pick some flame-retardant cloth for their stupid uniform?

"The bathroom's down that way," the receptionist said helpfully.

"Great, thanks," I muttered, before heading down the corridor to douse myself with water. This was not one of my better days.

When I emerged from the small bathroom, a man wearing a well-tailored suit was standing outside waiting for me.

"Miss Smith? It's a pleasure to have you here. I'm Jacoby Bryant. Please, if you're now quite ready, perhaps you can follow me?"

I glanced down at myself. The sleeves of my robes were hanging down in ragged wet strips, slapping the edges of my bare skin, while the rip in the fabric up my leg was high enough now not to look out of place in any good stripper bar. One of the wounds on my hand had decided to open up and was oozing bright-red blood, so I quickly moved it up to my mouth to suck it away. Judging by what had happened so far, this was definitely an Otherworld venue so I'd have to be careful with where I spilt my blood. I smiled through my hand and curtsied with as much graciousness as I could muster and as if I looked like this every day of my life.

"Of course, Mr Bryant. It's a pleasure to meet you."

For his part, at least, his gaze didn't flicker. He just gestured me further along the corridor to a small room. Once inside, he pulled out a chair for me and then sat opposite.

"So Miss Smith, why don't you tell me where you feel the problems are?"

I looked at the man, and felt a deep inward pain. I couldn't even begin to tell him where my problems lay. How would the fact I'm secretly some kind of strange, dragon–human hybrid go down, I wondered? That I could barely control the hot, angry blood inside of me? I was tempted, oh so very tempted, to spill every little secret I had right there and then. But I knew deep down that no good would come of it. So, instead I rocked back in the chair and forced my body to relax. Then I looked him in the eye and just flat out lied.

* * *

By the time I returned, retching, to the academy, I had a whole host of calming techniques at my disposal. Bryant had recommended that I count to ten and practise some deep breathing and relaxation exercises whenever I felt the need to 'lash out', as he put it. They seemed like the sorts of things you'd tell an errant child having a temper tantrum, but he assured me that they really would work. I'd spun him vast and varied tales about what pissed me off and how I reacted to such situations. Not once did I mention that there was fire inside me that took over, so I kind of had my doubts as to how effective such techniques were really going to be. And as much as I wanted not to fly off the handle at every slightest thing, and to be in more control of myself, I also knew that my bloodfire was what kept me strong. It was what kept me alive. I felt as if I was being torn in two separate directions: on the one hand, I couldn't trust myself not to hurt others whenever the bloodfire flared, and on the other, I couldn't trust myself not to personally get hurt if I didn't let it happen. I eventually decided that context was everything. If I felt in danger – or if someone else was being threatened and I was there – then I'd let all hell break loose. If not, then I'd try counting and breathing, and if that worked, then great. Otherwise, watch out.

Needing to focus on something to keep Corrigan out of my head, I headed straight up to my little room and the mysterious book that kept tugging at me. I was bitterly aware of just how long it was going to take me to translate the sodding thing – but the one thing I had ample amounts of now that I was stuck at the academy was time. So I positioned myself cross-legged on my lumpy bed, opened both the book and the dictionary, and pulled out a pencil and notepad that I'd managed to snaffle earlier on.

Unfortunately I was more than prophetically right at how slow-going my weak translation efforts were. Not only that, but looking up individual words on their own wasn't aiding me particularly in making total sense out of what was on the page. After an hour of trying, I'd ended up with, 'In times past, tends steel dragon breathing fire was in the possession of the sky and the earth.' Ummm. Steel dragon? What the fuck was that? I supposed that I should probably be grateful that the book wasn't actually some ancient romance or pulpy thriller, and actually seemed like it might be something to do with me. But that just added to my overall frustration with the thing. If this sodding book kept trying to find me, and was indestructible enough to avoid being burnt to a cinder when the Clava Cairns book shop burnt down, then why on earth couldn't it help me work out what it actually said?

I kept Bryant's techniques in mind, and took a few minutes out to breathe deeply. Somehow or other it did indeed have a calming effect, and I eventually relaxed, and tried the next sentence. Chewing hard on the end of the pencil, and furiously flicking through the dictionary from one end to the other, the end result was, 'These majestic creatures ruled with no small scarcity of mercy and grace, their innate strength of mind and body power allowing the poise and compassion through every dimension.'

Okay, that seemed to make virtually no sense whatsoever. The dragon or dragons (made of steel?) were in charge but still full of grace and mercy? For some ridiculous reason, I had sudden visions of a benign dragon-shaped version of Ming the Merciless wearing armour and pirouetting down a street. Not helpful. That translation was then followed by, 'Is written and said and passed down through generations, that one such creature breathing fire and fell under the spell of the witch who were so impressed this charming dragon force they needed to harness their capabilities. Thus, worked her magic and true woman was able to convert the beast to the human form.'

I paused for a while, biting my lip. Dodgy pronouns and bizarre grammar aside, I thought I might just understand what was going on. Some female mage (of course it was a mage – who else would be stupid enough to stick their nose in where it didn't belong?) had weaved some kind of spell to turn a dragon into a man because she liked the look of him. This was all becoming just a little too Greek myth-esque for my liking. I sighed and gave up for the time being, and headed down to get some food from the cafeteria instead. At least the weekend had virtually arrived so, other than my promised session teaching Mary and the few other Level Fours who weren't too scared to talk to me some 'real' Protection, I was confident I'd have more time to attack the next few pages of the book with renewed gusto and verve.

CHAPTER NINE

I HAD BEEN TEMPTED TO SNEAK OUT AGAIN DURING THE NIGHT TO go for a run, as I'd done previously, however I'd had to admit to myself that my muscles were feeling more than a little tense and sore – surprisingly so – after the t'ai chi bout with Thomas. By the time I woke up on Saturday morning, with screechingly bright sunlight saturating my little room, I felt even more stiff. Cursing Thomas under my breath, I stood up painfully and did my best to stretch out the kinks and knots. I forced my fingertips upwards, aiming to reach high enough to brush the ceiling, then held that position for a few moments before curving first to my left side and then my right. My spine in particular felt sore, so I sank down to all fours onto the floor and worked on arching my back like a cat. Unfortunately doing this just put me in mind of Corrigan's muscular yet lithe and feline-like body, so I cursed again and instead got up to force myself into the daily torture of fighting my way into my blue robes. At least I now had some clean ones that weren't ripped to shreds.

I'd arranged to meet Mary, Brock and the others out towards the end of the back garden, far behind what I now thought of as the 'oath-taking' statue. My previous midnight jog at least meant that I was more confident at finding my way there and more able to get my bearings around the whole campus. I swung by the cafeteria, picked up one quick cup of steaming-hot, syrupy coffee and downed it, before re-filling it so I could take it with me on my way to meet them.

Overcome as I was with the simple yet heady joy of caffeine, I didn't immediately notice that the Dean himself was blocking my path outside. I'd not seen him since the oath, and I was pretty sure that I didn't really want to see him again, so if I'd registered his presence in time I'd probably have found some way to manoeuvre round and travel via an alternative route. No such luck, however. When he saw me approaching, he raised his eyebrows and folded his arms, clearly waiting for me to get close enough. Giving myself up to the inevitable, I walked up to him.

"Initiate Smith," he stated drily.

I inclined my head. "Dean Michaels." I made to move past him but he blocked my way.

"So, you think that you can train our initiates better than our own teachers, do you?"

One, two ,three, four, five. "Uh, no, I don't. They asked me to give them some extra help, and I said I would. You know, in the interests of the academy and all. In order to make them the best possible graduates you can ask for, so that when they enter the real world they are fully prepared." Six, seven, eight.

"I hardly think that you are best qualified to do so. Your track record in the real world, as you call it, is hardly exemplary."

Nine, ten. It wasn't working. Fucking Corrigan and his big mouth. "Well, if you think it's a bad idea, then I will happily tell them so."

"And have you turn my own students against me?" he hissed. "Don't think I can't see your petty machinations for what they are."

Wow, did this guy have a God complex or what? "I have no machinations, Dean. Nor do I have any designs or plans or ulterior motives." I looked at him directly in the eye. "All I want to do is to get through your training so that the Arch-Mage will release my friend. That's it."

He glared at me. "And what do you hope to achieve by meeting clandestinely with the Lord Alpha?"

I must have looked surprised at this because he laughed without humour and continued. "Oh, did you think I wouldn't hear about your little assignation? Do not suppose for one moment, Initiate Smith, that you can get away with telling the pack all about us. I will not permit it."

Assignation? I blinked furiously, feeling the inevitable surge of heat. "It wasn't me who told him that I'd be there. It was one of you lot. So if you don't want me to talk to him, then you'll have to do a better job of keeping your mages in line. Besides, if I want to talk to the Lord Alpha, then I'll talk to the Lord sodding Alpha." I didn't, of course, have the slightest desire to have further tête-à-têtes with Corrigan, but the Dean didn't have to know that.

"Oh, 'my mages', as you so eloquently call them, are more than loyal. But don't worry, I've already put in a report to the Arch-Mage. I don't expect it will be long before you hear more from him."

Oooh, scary, I thought sarcastically. I visualised a calm sea of tranquillity inside myself, one of the techniques that Bryant had encouraged me to utilise. "Then so be it, Dean Michaels. I shall look forward to his orders."

The Dean's face twisted momentarily, then he managed somehow to smooth over his features and dissemble. Without saying another word, he sidestepped from the doorway, unblocking my way, and gestured outside with a flourish as if to highlight that it was only through his whim that I was being allowed to venture outside. For my part, I didn't even bother trying to smile at him; I just kept my expression blank and slid past him and into the sunny freedom of the outdoors.

As soon as I'd gone a few steps from the building, I began to stomp, kicking up a spray of gravel as I went. Bloody guy. He seemed to be under some bizarre delusion that I was a threat to his stupid academy, or that I was meeting Corrigan voluntarily in order to undermine the entire Ministry. Idiot. Then I took several deep breaths and instead congratulated myself on not going nuts and attacking him. Perhaps I was making some progress after all.

By the time I made it out towards the back of the garden, I was feeling considerably calmer. Mary, Brock, Aqmar and Deborah were already there and waiting. I could feel a buzz of excited tension about the entire group of them. I felt a surprising twinge of trepidation. Sure, I'd coached Tom a few times on his technique back in Cornwall, but this was entirely different. I thought about what had been said about my failure to take down Iabartu on my own and wondered if it was just because I wasn't good enough. Maybe I'd just end up disappointing this group of over-eager teenagers too. Trying not to let my doubts show on my face, I strode up to them with purpose, and smiled.

In order to gauge what their skill set really was, I began by pitting them against each other, Deborah against Mary and Brock against Aqmar. They spent a lot of time circling each other aimlessly, occasionally jabbing out with a fist here and there. At one point, Aqmar lunged out with probably more force than he'd planned, and he caught Brock's cheekbone with his out-flung hand. Hissing in pain, Brock reacted without thinking, jetting out a shot of blue flame not dissimilar to that which I'd seen from the mages up in Inverness. However, Aqmar blocked it easily.

I watched them, thinking carefully. They just knew each other too well and were simply too cautious. Not only that but they had all been trained in the same way and probably by the same mages, so they knew exactly what the other was going to do before they did it. As all their training up till now seemed to have been focused on the defence element of Protection, I decided to test my theory. I had the boys and Deborah line up, with Mary facing them. Then I instructed Mary to attack them and for them to block whatever came their way. As I'd expected, every time Mary tried any kind of assault, the three of them easily managed to dodge, ward or even duck her attempts. I did the same with the others, rotating them round. The results didn't change.

Nodding to myself, I told all four of them to line up to block my own attacks. I decided to keep things simple for now, and avoid potentially hurting any of them with my personal experimentation, so I kept my green fire carefully extinguished within. Then I feinted left but twisted right and managed to knock over both Aqmar and Deborah with one shot. I danced back, trying not to smile at them both sprawled in an ungainly fashion on the wet grass. My robes were proving rather cumbersome and, whilst the handicap against me would probably not be a bad thing, it was just too annoying to deal with in reality. Figuring that mages were definitely not as used to nudity as shifters were, I resisted the urge to extricate myself entirely from the blue material and fight in my underwear, and instead bunched the folds up next to my hip and tied them into a knot, all the while keeping Brock and Mary clearly within my sights in case they tried anything. I think, however, they were a little too stunned at the speed with which I'd managed to dispatch their peers to consider trying any kind of counterattack.

Feeling a bit freer, but no doubt looking rather ridiculous, I judged the distance between myself and the remaining two. It seemed doable, and there was a large tree right behind the pair of them that would suit my needs perfectly. I ran towards the pair of them. Brock started to cower automatically whilst Mary, bless her, at least managed to form a weak ward with her magic in front of her body. But I wasn't attacking them from the front. Rather I leapt over them, using Brock's shoulder as a step to aid my ascent, then pivoted off the tree behind them, spinning in the air, and hitting both on the back of the neck. I didn't hit them hard, but they both went down, groaning. I dusted off my hands and strolled back in front of them. I didn't want to acknowledge how glad I was that I hadn't entirely lost all my fighting skills, even if my opponents were green students who would probably lose against a nymph, let alone someone trained by shifters.

Eventually they gathered themselves to their feet. There was a note of awe on all their faces that made me feel rather uncomfortable, so before they could say anything, I spoke up loudly.

"You're too complacent and too used to fighting, or rather defending, in the patterns you've been taught. If you do the expected, then you will always lose. The best fighters, the ones who win, are those who take the element of surprise and make it their own. You need to get yourselves out of the box that you've been trained into and play more dirty than that."

The four of them nodded vigorously, as if they were hanging off my every word. Again I felt a wave of discomfort, so I quickly assigned each of them their own tree, telling them that they had five minutes to 'fight' the tree, each time hitting it in a different way or in a different place. It took them a minute or two to get into the swing of things, but once they did, there was no denying their energy and enthusiasm. They all jumped around the poor trees like maniacs, hitting them first one way then another. I was pleased to note that they all attempted ducking and leaping, as well as lashing out. By the time they were done, the four initiates were panting hard.

Mary collapsed onto the ground. "By the Founder! Who would have thought that attacking a piece of wood would be so tiring?"

I laughed and pulled her to her feet, then set about showing them all how they could use their feet as well as their hands to develop and implement attacks. That was less successful, and both Aqmar and Deborah lost their balance twice, falling backwards and leaving themselves open to potential side attacks, but I was satisfied for now. I set them all homework: to come out and practise at least three times over the next week, and then left them to it, the four of them lying on the ground and giggling like school children. Which I supposed they actually were.

Heading back to the main building, I undid the corner of my robes and let them fall softly down to my feet, noting that once again I seemed to have managed to crumple and wrinkle the material. I shrugged to myself, for a moment idly wondering how on earth the other mages always managed to look so pristine and well turned out. At least the mages weren't obliged to always wear the robes once they were out of the academy, I figured. I still had a vivid image seared into my brain of the bizarre clothes that Martha, Mary's sister, and her Star Trek buddy had been wearing when I'd kicked the shit out of them up in Inverness, and I knew I'd definitely never seen Alex wearing any robes when he'd been in either Cornwall or London. Maybe their, um, individual attire was a direct result of being made to dress like idiots when they were training.

I rounded the corner of the main building, wandering back on a different route, this time swinging left rather than right so that I was closer to the training blocks than to the gardens. Humming away to myself with the success of the morning, I didn't notice the figure leaning against one of the walls until I'd virtually passed him.

"Well, someone's having a truly bodacious day," drawled a familiar voice.

I spun round, heart suddenly leaping in my chest. "Alex?" I bear-hugged him then pulled back to look him over. "I was just thinking about you! How the bloody hell are you? What are you doing here? Are you staying long?"

"It's good to see you too, Mack Attack. And I'm good, here to see you and staying for as long as you need me."

This was almost too good to be true. The last time I'd seen my magic surfer buddy had been after I'd broken into the Ministry's headquarters. I'd kind of had the idea that I'd perhaps gotten him into trouble by mere association. That, and the fact that he'd been a true friend to me by refusing to give up my real identity as a Draco Wyr to the Arch-Mage. I hugged him again.

"Really? You're really staying?"

"A little bird told me that you might be in need of a bit of help and support. So as long as there aren't any Otherworld nasties around that I have to fight on your behalf, then I am here, natch. The Arch-Mage dude has released me from my other duties. I will be the surf to your swell, the flat to your gnarly, the bomb to your point break."

"You realise I have no idea what you're talking about, right?"

"Mack Attack," he shook his head sadly, "nobody ever does."

I beamed my happiness at him, ignoring for once the stupid nickname.

He leaned over and whispered in my ear, "Mack, I also really need your help. I'm in so much trouble and I've really screwed up."

This time, when he pulled away, his eyes were filled with worry and his brow was uncharacteristically creased. Prickles of answering heat pulsated through my veins.

There wasn't any time for Alex to even open his mouth to begin to explain what the matter was before the damn bell rang again, presumably for lunch as today was a Saturday, and the area suddenly filled with initiates wearing robes of every potential colour under the sun. Fractious flames rippled up and down my spine at the forced interruption.

"Where on earth do they all come from?" I muttered.

Alex smiled half-heartedly and began to pull me in the same direction as the others were heading. "I'm now your Divination teacher," he said in a voice that was considerably calmer than the one he'd used to broadcast his whispered plea.

"Huh," I replied, mirroring his attempt to appear completely normal. An utterly pointless act given that anyone watching our movement through the crowds would have picked us out as anything but ordinary. It was as if there were some kind of strange, invisible barrier about a metre around the pair of us that no-one else dared to cross, even though they were squashed between the exterior walls of the various surrounding buildings. I would have been tempted to start veering off in different directions, just to see what happened, if it hadn't been for the gravity of what Alex had just said and my desire to get somewhere fast where we could talk without being overheard.

"So how did you swing that one, then?" I said, with every semblance of appearing unconcerned that I could possibly muster.

"Turns out it wasn't that hard after all. I went to speak to Higgins, the normal Level One Divination dude and he seemed only too happy to let me take you off his hands. It was almost as if he was frightened of you." Alex raised his eyebrows slightly, floppy blond hair falling to the side over his suntanned face. "I can't imagine why anyone would be afraid of a skinhead ex-shifter who can shoot freaky green fire from her fingertips and who was prepared to break into the Ministry stronghold just to have a little chat."

I shrugged. "The skinhead thing is only temporary. And it wasn't just a little chat that I wanted. I was trying to save my friend – I'm still trying to save my friend. It turns out your 'Magnificence' is the commitment type."

He put his arm round my shoulder and glared at a fresh-faced-looking initiate who was staring at me in what could only be described as the same way an arachnophobe would inspect a giant, hairy tarantula. And I'd thought that between Mary and her friends, relations between myself and the other initiates were improving. More fool me.

"Yeah, where is your friend?" asked Alex. "Last you told me she was in Inverness with you. I know the place you were in burnt down to the ground, and I know that it can be virtually impossible to move someone with enforced inhibitory gnosis even if they are as strong as you."

I was surprised that the Arch-Mage hadn't already told him, and despite the throng of students around us, I couldn't see that it was supposed to be a secret. "She's in Tir-na-nog."

I could feel Alex's muscles stiffen even through the thick material of my robes. "No way, dude."

I nodded solemnly. "Yes way, dude."

"Is that where you left your hair?"

I winced. "No, that's another story."

"Well, now I'm here full time, you'll have plenty of opportunity to spill it to me."

I smiled, trying to focus on my happiness that my old friend was here with me, and not on the tug of fiery worry that churned inside me.

CHAPTER TEN

RATHER THAN FOLLOWING THE STREAMS OF HUNGRY STUDENTS IN the familiar direction of the cafeteria, Alex and I peeled off and wound our way through the other buildings until we reached the end. He led me to a small stone bench set into a snug, bricked-off alcove round the corner of the crumbling Protection block. We both sat down, facing outwards.

Alex wrung his hands and sighed deeply. Then he turned to face me. "Mack Attack, I've really fucked up. I don't know what else to do or who to talk to."

I stared across at him, empathy and concern filling me. "You can tell me, Alex. What has happened?"

A bird chirruped overhead and he almost jumped out of his skin, his eyes tracking it nervously until it flew off. "You never know who might be listening," he muttered.

Feeling nervous now, as well as worried, I reached out and put my hands over his. "You know you can trust me, Alex."

He nodded, then looked up to me with angst-filled eyes. "I had a job last week. A Divination job. That's where I have to–"

I interrupted him. "I know what Divination is."

He shook himself. "Of course you do. Anyway, the job was to track down some daft *objet d'art* for this vamp."

"You work for vampires?" I couldn't prevent myself from recoiling ever so slightly.

"Of course we do. Do you think that shifters are the only ones who need to use a bit of magic now and then? They're not all bad, Mack, they just have some unpleasant eating habits. Anyway, are you going to keep interrupting or can I tell my story?"

I shook my head in apology, now more worried than ever. The note of irritation in Alex's voice was not at all the friendly surfer dude that I knew. I squeezed his hands to continue.

"Anyway, I had to retrieve this thing, some kind of statue. A wooden sculpture of Athena called the Palladium. According to mythology, it was held within the walls of Troy and the legend went that as long as it remained there, Troy would remain undefeated. So, unsurprisingly, Odysseus and his mate Diomedes sneaked in and nicked it, Troy fell and blah de blah. Then the Palladium ended up in the hands of the Romans, but of course it didn't stay there for long. The vamps somehow got their hands on it and used it as a symbol of their omnipotence and undefeat. Naturally it was all bullshit though."

"Naturally," I murmured.

"The vamps' stronghold was broken into years ago by a wraith thief called Tryyl, and several artefacts were taken, the Palladium among them. Tryyl was caught and tortured horribly and the vamps recovered pretty much everything apart from the statue. Nobody really cared all that much. It was ceremonial and the vamps felt their honour had been restored through the mental and physical destruction of Tryyl, so although they looked for it, they didn't really search all that hard, you get me?"

I nodded.

"But this old vamp, powerful dude, someone who's been around for several hundreds of years, was reminiscing with a bunch of his bloodsucking buddies and decided last month that he'd like to see if he could get it back. I think it was some kind of dare or something, I dunno. So instead of getting his own hands dirty, he calls me in– or rather, he calls in the Ministry – and pays us a bunch of money to get the Palladium back for him. I track it, eventually find it buried in an old cellar in a cottage up in the Lake District and give it back."

I was puzzled. "So what's the big deal? It doesn't do anything, it's not going to hurt anyone and you did your job."

"See, that's just the thing," said Alex, pulling his hands away from mine to run them through his hair. "When I initially started tracking the Palladium, my inveniora, that's–"

I nodded, "Yeah, I know what that is."

"Okay, my inveniora did something really strange. It sort of split off into two. At first I thought maybe it was because the statue had been damaged somehow and was in different sections – we've had that kind of thing happen before. So I just chose one randomly and followed it. When I got to the end, the statue was there all whole and shipshape and not damaged in the slightest, so I picked it out from the rubble and gave it to the vamp."

"Right. But?"

"But then I got curious. I wanted to see what else had triggered the inveniora. So I went looking and found this." He dug into a satchel that was lying by his side and pulled out a small wooden statue.

"Uh, Alex, that looks like it might be–"

"The Palladium," he said miserably.

"So what did you give the vamp?"

"Well, I checked up on the Othernet, trying to see if maybe there had been two statues. There hadn't. But what I found was another wooden statue called the Ancile. It's meant to have appeared on earth much later than the Palladium, but it's much more powerful. It's made of the same stuff as the Palladium, and is meant to be indistinguishable from other similar wooden statues if it's stolen. Which is why my inveniora couldn't tell the difference between it and the Palladium. What the Othernet also said is that it belonged to Mars himself, and that if wielded in battle and touched by blood, it would cause fire and war and destruction."

"And you think that you gave the Ancile to the vamps?"

"Yeah."

"And that because blood is their *dejeuner du jour*, you think that they will set off the Ancile if they touch it."

"Yeah."

"Okay. Well, why don't you just tell the vamps that you made a mistake? Get them to give you the Ancile in return for the real Palladium."

Alex looked unhappily down at his feet.

"Oh, I see," I said slowly. "Because you think that once the vamps realise what they have in their possession, then they won't want to give it up."

"Got it in one. Yeah, vamps aren't always as bad as everyone makes out, but they're not going to give up a relic of that kind of power just because I ask them to."

"Get the Arch-Mage to ask them to. Surely they'll want to keep in his good books."

"Yeah, I could do that. The thing is…" His voice trailed off.

"What?" I prodded.

"Well, the thing is that the Arch-Mage isn't doing so well right now. A lot of other factions are unhappy with the way he's running things. They're just looking for an opportunity for him to screw up and they'll jump right in there with a vote of no confidence." Alex looked at me with panic in his eyes. "Mack, I can't let that happen. I can't let my fuck-up be the reason that he's ousted from power. The Ministry will disintegrate. There'll be in-fighting and power struggles, and people will die. And it will all be my fault! And that's even if the vamps decide to give the Ancile back. If they decide that they're going to ignore the Arch-Mage – which they might well do – then things will be even worse."

I chewed on the inside of my cheek. Yeah, I could see how this was bad. And I had to admit, the Arch-Mage, for all of his posturing and his forcing me to come to the academy in the first place, was a pretty decent mage. I had actually had a few inklings as well that things weren't looking too rosy for him. I shuddered to think what things would be like if someone like the Dean ended up taking the reins of the Ministry's power.

"So, is there a way out? Is there some way that you can get it back?"

"Mack Attack, you know what I'm like. I'd be awful at that kind of thing. If I got caught, I'd be a blubbering wreck. And you know I'd get caught. I'm just not that kind of person."

I felt a heavy, sinking feeling of inevitability in the pit of my stomach. "But you think I could do it." It wasn't a question.

Alex just looked at me. I looked back at him and sighed. "Okay, what do I have to do?"

"Oh, Mack, I knew you'd help me. I knew that you'd save the day and come through and make everything right. That's why you're the Mack Attack!" He grinned suddenly and, for a flash, was back to his former self.

"Hey, hold on," I said seriously. "I don't even know if I can do this yet. Let's not forget that I'm stuck here at the academy in the first place. How am I even going to get time off to sneak into a vamp's lair?"

Alex shifted in his seat, abruptly looking uncomfortable.

"Alex?"

He budged around again and wouldn't meet my eye.

"Alex? Why do I get the feeling that I'm really not going to like this?"

"Okay, look. There's an easy way for you to get a night off."

"And how's that?"

"Someone important asks you out, you know, like for a date or something."

I had a nasty inkling that I knew where this might be heading. "But then I'm out on a date with this important person, not anywhere near the vamp's place where the Ancile is," I pointed out.

"Well, you see," Alex demurred, "that's where serendipity plays into our hands."

"Oh yes?"

"There's a party. Next week. All the Otherworld bigwigs attend. It's an annual thing, designed to encourage inter-species co-operation. And guess what?"

"Let me think," I said drily, "it's being held at this vamp's house."

"Got it in one! It's not his house so much as the vamps' actual stronghold, though."

"Is that supposed to make me feel better?"

Alex laughed slightly. "In order to keep things fair, the party's location is rotated through the places belonging to the leaders of the main different Otherworld groups. And this year we've struck lucky!"

I definitely didn't feel very lucky.

Alex continued, "So all you need to do is to wangle an invitation and the hard part of getting into the building where the Ancile is kept is already covered. And if you get an invitation, it's with someone important so that also makes it okay for you to leave the academy for an evening. The Dean won't be able to say no."

"It's like you planned the whole thing out."

"Yeah, dude!" Life leapt back into Alex's eyes as his personality started to re-assert itself. "You just get in touch with little old Lord Shifty – because, of course, he's going – and then you're in. And you can retrieve the Ancile and put the real Palladium in its place and then there's no fire or war or destruction and the Arch-Mage is safe and everybody's happy." He beamed at me, full wattage.

"Yes, I see," I said carefully, "except there's just one small flaw in your perfectly laid-out plan."

"What's that?" Alex looked confused and I was half tempted to bang his head against the stone wall.

"The part where I have to ask Corrigan if he'll take me to a party for all the VIPs of the Otherworld," I said, rolling my eyes.

Alex put his hands up. "Oh, but he thinks you're great, dude!

Everyone knows that you saved his life and saved the pack, and are the hero of the moment. You just need to whisper a few sweet nothings in his ear and hey presto!"

"Except for the teeny tiny little point where I just so happened to bump into him yesterday and we almost came to blows." Or at least I told him in no uncertain terms to fuck off, anyway.

"What? Oh, Mack Attack, no. Really?" The mage was visibly deflated.

"Do you have a back-up plan?" I asked gently.

He shook his head. "No. This is it. I've thought of everything else. This is the only chance there will be to get this done. And it needs to be done quickly or there'll just be more opportunity for the Ancile to be activated."

"The Dean really wasn't very happy about me talking to Corrigan yesterday. He'll be even less happy if I'm going out on an actual date with him. And that's even assuming I can get the Lord Alpha to invite me. You can bet he's already got some glamorous shifter lady signed up for that duty."

"Don't worry about the Dean," said Alex confidently. "If you can get our mate, Shifty dude, to invite you, I'll take care of the rest."

Somehow I thought that would be the hardest part of the whole operation. Alex's plan, to me, appeared to be balanced on the shuffle of far too many cards. I didn't have a problem with stealing back the Ancile thing for him, but fluttering my eyelashes at Corrigan was not going to be easy. If anything, I didn't feel quite right about lying to him. I might not be part of the pack any more but old habits die hard. I'd just have to look upon it as a challenge, I figured. Though a challenge that could well see my head ripped from my shoulders, of course.

CHAPTER ELEVEN

I GNAWED OVER MY CONVERSATION WITH ALEX ALL THE WAY BACK to the main building. I had absolutely no idea how on earth I was going to achieve any success with my magic training, plus translate the Fae book in the hope that it would give some clue as to my real heritage, as well as pull the wool over the eyes of the leader of the Brethren, and pilfer an ancient artefact from under the noses of all the vampires in the United Kingdom at the same time. Fucking hell. Alex, for his part, had muttered something about having to go and retrieve lesson plans and updates from Higgins in order to begin his (he hoped) short-lived career as a teacher, so I'd left him to it.

I decided that the best thing I could do would be to hit the library. There was bound to be something somewhere in there about the vampires' lair, surely? I could perhaps pretend I was reading up about Evocation for my next lesson. Although, come to think of it, that wouldn't be such a bad idea. I would just have to put the Fae book on hold for a while and hope that its disappearance from the library remained unnoticed. It was even possible that no-one knew it was in the library, of course. It definitely seemed, to all intents and purposes, to be exactly the same book that I'd come across in the Clava book shop.

That meant that perhaps it wasn't even catalogued in the academy library. I also wouldn't be able to contact Corrigan until much later that night, so there was no point worrying about that for now. I'd just have to figure out later what I'd say to him.

I swung by the cafeteria and managed to pick up a sandwich from the remnants of the lunchtime session, then munched it on my way to Slim's cavernous residence. I had absolutely no idea what the rest of the initiates were doing with their weekend; I'd just have to hope that very few of them were hitting the books themselves.

I'd swallowed down the last of the bread by the time I reached the library's vast doors. Repeating my actions from my last visit, I reached out with a single finger and traced over the elegant shape of the inlaid dragon, wondering this time if it was meant to be the one that had been transformed into a man by the female mage in the Fae book. She was certainly a brave woman to have taken it on, I mused, lightly touching the lethal-looking talons that had been carved there. Then I opened the library doors quietly and walked inside.

The space was as light, airy and impressive as it had been on my last visit. I looked around for Slim and, for a moment, thought that the little librarian had disappeared off into some nook or cranny yet again, until I heard an agitated fluttering coming towards me. I half turned, registered the purple figure and then smiled my awkward greetings.

"You again!" shouted Slim. "What the feck do you want?"

"Uh, hi. I would like to look at some books to help me with Evocation," I said as pleasantly as I could, keeping the smile firmly in place. "It might help me with my lessons. I'm, uh, not doing too well," I added in a conspiratorial tone.

The gargoyle snorted. "Well, blow me down with a fecking feather! At last a student in this place who has realised that they might actually learn something if they opened a book. Honestly, the number of fecking initiates I get in here demanding to be shown to the nearest Othernet station. As if we dabble in that rubbish here!"

I nodded my head wisely, glad that I'd not made that my first question. Instead I realised that I could kill two birds with one stone.

"Uh, Mr Slim, do you happen to have a cataloguing system that I could look through?"

"A cataloguing system? A fecking cataloguing system, she asks! Of course we have a feckin' cataloguing system. Come right this way."

He dipped slightly in the air then, wings beating harder, picked up again and flew stutteringly over to the middle of the ground floor where, next to the window, I realised were several large cabinets.

"Everything you'll need is here," Slim said proudly. Then a little furrow creased his violet forehead and he pointed over at the far-end cabinet. "But you can't fecking touch that one, mind?"

Curiosity arching through me, I nodded vigorously, promising not to go near the forbidden cabinet. Giving me a slightly suspicious look, the librarian turned back around and fluttered over to one of the desks. I could feel his beady eyes still on me, however, so I made good on my promise and stuck to the permitted areas, opening the first cabinet to get an understanding of the system.

I had to admit that I was really rather impressed. Everything was neatly labelled in meticulous handwriting. It seemed like a lot of work, and that the gargoyle's aversion to computers was doing him considerably more harm than good, but I figured that it wasn't really my problem. I skimmed through the first sections, skipping over the histories and treaties and sections on Illusion, then opened the next cabinet. Grinning slightly to myself, I noted that the cards here were all for Evocation and the unromantically titled 'Creatures'. This was perfect. I could ostensibly find the location of a book on Evocation, information on the vampires' stronghold and whether my Fae book was even listed all at the same time.

Aware that Slim's eyes were still on me, I began flicking through the entries for Evocation. I was kind of hoping that I would come across one helpfully entitled *Evocation for Dummies*, but I had no such luck. Still, I managed to find several titles that might just be vaguely comprehensible, so I made a quick note of them, then quickly moved on to the Creatures section. I wasn't entirely sure what to look for in terms of how the Fae book would be catalogued. There was an entire section on the Fae and I was sorely tempted to spend more time going through it to see if there was anything that might give me more information about Solus and who he really was. I had no time for idle curiosities, however, and there was nothing entitled Fire, neither in runic script nor in English, so I reluctantly left the Fae books behind and checked for information texts on dragons instead.

There were several books on wyverns: different breeds, ways of dealing with them, how to summon them and so on, and a few interesting-sounding books about the history of the species. None of it really seemed to be what I was looking for so, as a last resort and with my heart in my mouth, I searched for Draco Wyr. There was nothing. Not a goddamn thing. My gaze flicked over to the cabinet that was off-limits. I knew I couldn't entirely discount the fact that this huge library didn't include details of the mysterious Fae text or any others that might shed light on the Draco Wyr until I checked through all the catalogues. There was no way I was going to manage that today though, not with Slim hovering so closely. It was probably a good thing. I had all the time in the world to discover more about myself and my blood, but as far as Alex and the VIP party went, I was definitely on a clock. With an inaudible sigh, I switched tactics and searched for vampires instead.

Clearly, the mages had a bit of a thing about the vamps. There were far more books to do with them than there had been even for the Fae. Fascinated, I picked through all the titles. There were even a few that seemed to suggest theories on how to cure vampirism. I wondered whether they were based on scientific fact or just speculation. I'd never heard of it being possible and, I had to admit, didn't know if any bloodsuckers out there would even want to be cured, but it would be interesting to find out. Not for the first time, I wished I had more time just to spend reading the books shelved here purely for academic interest instead of for some other nefarious purpose. Still, on the bright side, I did come across *The Geography and Domestic Situation of the Vampyre*. It was a pretty old tome, having been written around the turn of the nineteenth century, but I didn't think that vampires were the sort of Otherworld creature that often modernised so it was just possible that I'd find something of use even in that old book. Noting down the details on the card, and adding it to my list of books about Evocation, I finally closed the cabinet and went in search of the texts themselves.

The Evocation books were pretty easy to get hold of, and it took me little time to track down the ones that I thought might be useful. Carrying several in my arms, I deposited them over at the same table that I'd studied at the last time, again working on the premise that if I was doing everything within open sight, then no-one would consider that I was doing anything at all suspicious. When I made it to the aisle that housed the vampire book I was looking for, there was an initiate wearing red robes signalling her status as a fifth year. She gave me a curious glance, but fortunately did nothing more than that. In fact, she didn't even appear that nervous that I'd suddenly appeared right next to her. Maybe that was because by the time the initiates reached that level, they possessed considerably more common sense than the others. I could only hope.

Trying to look as if I was doing exactly what I was supposed to be doing, I wandered down the tightly packed shelves until I found the area I was looking for. Crammed in between a treatise on the properties of garlic and a history of Vlad the Impaler that I'd actually read before, was the *Geography* book. I managed to pull it out without doing either the book or myself injury then, hugging it to my chest, took it over to the table where the Evocation titles waited.

Settling down, I turned to the index where, triumphantly, I found the London lair listed. Then I flipped over to the right chapter and began to read. I discovered quickly that the vamps' main nest was situated in an area called Kingsway in London. Back in the seventeenth century, the king at the time, William III, had been in a spot of financial bother thanks to wars with Ireland and the Continent, and had introduced a window tax to help pay for his armies. The more windows your property had, the more tax you had to pay. Although the tariff itself had been wildly unpopular with the masses, it had given rise to some clever tax dodgers who had simply bricked up their windows in order to avoid having to cough up. This naturally worked perfectly for the bloodsuckers as they could block out the potentially harmful rays of the sun without raising any eyebrows whatsoever. And, of course, in this day and age, keeping original detailing such as non-existent window frames was considered noble and thoughtful, so they could easily get away with not knocking out the bricks to install double glazing.

By all accounts, the house itself looked remarkably nondescript from the outside. Naturally this would be in keeping with the vamps' desire to keep a low profile. For some reason, those particular undead denizens of the Otherworld attracted more attention and speculation than any other, so staying out of view even more than the other species was of paramount importance. From what I scanned through, however, the interior was an entirely different situation. Apparently the opulence and grandeur within was on an epic scale. I tried not to snort with laughter at how much that must sting with the frugal mages. The author of the book itself possessed an incredibly sniffy tone when detailing the gold leaf adorning the walls, and the filigree marking out the door details.

As interesting as all this was, it didn't really offer much

insight into where the Ancile/Palladium might actually be housed, or what security measures might be in place. There was a sentence or two describing a trophy room, which sounded like it might fit – either that or it potentially contained remnants of previous victims, anyway. Although the vamps almost never killed anyone these days, there were certainly enough stories of what had transpired in days gone by to reach the ears of even the Cornish pack. I'd really been hoping for some kind of helpful map, with an X marking the spot where the so-called treasure would be kept. Instead, I'd just have to do all my scouting when I actually got there. If I got there.

Closing the vamp book, having gleaned all the information from it that I possibly could, I tried to put it all out of my mind for the time being and do some real studying. The Evocation books offered lots of helpful tips and guidance for how to develop and progress in that discipline, and I ended up making copious notes for all sorts of things. None of it really involved anything practical, however. I had the sneaking suspicion that Evocation was something you either did or you didn't, and that I would fall firmly into the latter category. By the time I was done, however, the sun was beginning to dip in the sky. That meant that I'd have to start thinking about what on earth I could do to suck up to Corrigan to get him to make me his date for the party. Completely out of ideas, I closed all the books and returned them to the shelves where I'd originally found them, then called out a loud and cheery goodbye to Slim, who'd somehow disappeared again in the intervening hours.

* * *

Managing to make it to the cafeteria for a proper sit-down meal this time, I was again gratified to be joined by Mary and her friends. They were all still excited about the lesson we'd had that morning, which I'd actually completely forgotten about since all of the revelations I'd had to deal with from Alex. They told me in hushed, thrilled tones about how they'd spent virtually all afternoon practising their attacks and their kicks, and how confident they all were that I'd be impressed with them. I found myself smiling indulgently, like some proud parent. Even Brock, the boy of few words, found it in himself to describe to me how exhilarating he'd found it when he'd managed to scissor kick, then punch, then spin and catch the side of his tree, all within a couple of heartbeats. I extracted a promise from them all that they wouldn't do anything stupid like try to attack anything real, and they all solemnly agreed. Of Alex, there was no sign. However, from across the room Thomas caught my eye and lifted up his water glass in a silent toast. I glowered at him, but then caught myself doing the same and raising up my own cup in return before taking a small sip too. Idiot.

I begged off the evening activities, even though both Deborah and Mary exhorted me to join in with their girlie mani-pedi session. Glancing down at my own ragged nails, I didn't think that it would really be my thing. Besides, if I was going to sneak out to contact Corrigan, I'd have to get in some sleep first. I pleaded old age, noting that the two girls looked slightly relieved that I'd declined their offer, then padded upstairs, still brewing over what on earth I was going to say to him.

Waking up several hours later, I got to my feet and stretched before peering outside. The moon, barely a sliver now, remained uncovered this night, and the stars twinkled and shone with a ferocity that seemed to mirror my own feelings. I wished that I'd had the chance to talk to Alex again so that I could run through what I might say to Corrigan, but I figured it was probably too late. In fact, it was more than possible that the Lord Alpha himself was all tucked up and snoozing away in his own bed by this point, and I wouldn't be able to speak to him at all. I wasn't sure if that would be a good thing or not. I'd just have to try again the following night, and delaying the inevitable would probably just make it harder rather than easier. Before I could stop myself, I started wondering what he wore to bed. The shifter girls, who I used to share a dorm with back in Cornwall, did tend to have pyjamas or nightdresses, unless it was around the time of the full moon. Somehow the idea of Corrigan wearing checked flannel pyjamas didn't quite fit, however. I couldn't imagine why.

Pushing the lurid visions out of my head, I thought more carefully about what I could wear myself for this night's little adventure. If I put on the suffocating mage robes again, I knew that I'd just end up taking them off as I got outside, safe in the knowledge that all the little mages were tucked up nice and snug in their beds. But parading around in my underwear this time, given that I'd have to leave the academy grounds entirely, might not be the smartest idea I'd ever had. I frowned, considering. My own clothes hadn't been returned to me, but they must be hanging around the laundry area somewhere. Deciding to venture out to see if I could repatriate them before I went outside, I wrapped the robes around my body like a sarong, rather than bothering to go through the rigmarole of trying to get them completely back on. Of course, if Thomas had deigned to give me some proper nightwear, I thought irritably, then this wouldn't be an issue.

It only took me a few minutes to tiptoe downstairs and past the kitchens to the area that my nose defined as the laundry room thanks to its clean scent of detergent. Once inside, I was amazed at the size of the place. I mean, I knew that there were initiates and mages abounding across the academy but this wasn't a laundry room, it was more like a factory. Rows upon rows of neatly pressed and different-coloured robes sat on shelves, just waiting to be returned to their owners. Despite the size of the room, the uniformity of the majority of its contents meant that I managed to locate my original t-shirt that I'd arrived in fairly easily. Squeezing it over my head, I gave it a happy little hello, then began searching for my jeans.

Unfortunately they were less easy to find. Annoyed at the idea that they might have been thrown out, I had no choice but to look for some kind of alternative. There were a couple of pairs of men's jeans and some dark trousers, but it seemed incredibly unlikely that any of them would fit. I knew that I'd have to get a move on if I had any chance of contacting Corrigan before he really did fall asleep, so I just ended up grabbing the very first thing that my hand landed on and pulling it over my hips. It turned out to be a very small micro-mini skirt in bright yellow. For a moment I gaped down at myself in horror, then gave in, zipped it up and quickly left the way I'd entered.

I jogged back along the corridor until I reached the cafeteria where I already knew I'd be able to gain access to the outside world. Repeating the actions of my previous 'escape', I pushed myself through the same window, finding it easier this time with practice. It also helped that the wounds on my hand were now completely scabbed over and no longer required a bandage to prevent any seepage. And then I was back outside, again taking in the fresh scent of the night.

Instead of heading off round the back of the main building, this time I jogged down the driveway. Having arrived here by portal, I had no idea how far it actually stretched, of course, but it seemed logical that it would be the fastest way to leave the compound itself. Thanks to my visit to the Ministry headquarters in London to confront the Arch-Mage, I was well aware that the mages placed a nullification spell against any shifters being able to make use of the Voice, the mental telepathy link that only pack alphas could initiate in order to contact their so-called subjects. It seemed pointless to me that they bothered using it here at the academy, where the likelihood of a real shifter presenting themselves seemed to be about zero, but I supposed that I should just be grateful that I'd also discovered in the course of my temporary life up in Scotland that I also had the power to initiate a Voice link with Corrigan. Not with anyone else – I'd tried that and abjectly failed – but for some reason, with the Lord Alpha and the Lord Alpha only, I could do it. As it was beyond logic that I could even hear the Voice as I wasn't a shifter, I didn't bother to examine too deeply the reasons why I could contact

Corrigan. I'd just have to hope that once I got off the academy grounds, I'd be able to use it without any trouble.

For once it appeared that my luck was in. I only had to jog about a mile down the driveway itself before I came to a set of imposing gates. I'd managed to sneak into the Ministry in London by short-circuiting the very human security system. Hopefully that would be a similar case here. However, once I reached the gates themselves, I realised that they were actually already ajar, and that I'd be able to squeeze myself through without needing to try anything extra. Surprised, and praying it wasn't some kind of crafty trap that the Dean had set just in case I decided to try this very thing, I slipped through.

Somehow, without really knowing how, I was aware of the moment that the nullification spell was no longer affecting me. It wasn't an obvious difference by any means, but it felt as if some part of my brain had been oddly muffled and now the dampener had been removed. Exhaling relief that at least the physical complications of using the Voice to beg Corrigan pathetically for a date had been removed, I moved away from the gates themselves and sat myself down cross-legged by the side of them.

The night air felt considerably cooler against my naked skull than it had done previously. It was certainly bloody cold against my uncovered legs with the daft yellow mini skirt on. Thinking that I might as well have not bothered with it at all, as it was short enough to ensure that even sitting cross-legged wasn't an issue, I rubbed my skin vigorously to try to keep warm. I knew that for all the chill in the air, it wasn't the temperature that was making me shiver.

"Come on, Mack," I whispered to myself. "You can do this."

I closed my eyes and scrunched up my face and tried the Voice.

Ummm…

Oh, great start, I told myself sarcastically. 'Ummm.' That will really grab the Brethren Lord's full attention.

I almost fell over from my sitting position when it did.

Mack, what's wrong?

The concern in his Voice was almost touching. Almost. *Hi Corrigan. How are things?*

You're contacting me in the middle of the night to ask how I'm doing?

I could almost see him rolling his flashing green eyes at me. *Uh, no. I felt bad, no, I FEEL bad about what happened yesterday. You know, at the shrink's place.*

There was silence for a moment before he answered. *Is this an apology? An actual apology from the big, bad, scary Mackenzie Smith?*

Yeah. I mentally shrugged. *I guess it is.*

There was another moment of silence that deepened until I wasn't even sure if he was still paying attention.

Corrigan? Are you still there?

I'm waiting.

Waiting for what?

Your apology.

My... It was a struggle not to let my irritation show through. It was much harder to mask your true feelings through Voice contact than through normal conversation. *I apologise.*

Thank you. So why are you really contacting me, kitten?

I, uh, thought that maybe I should do something. You know, to make it up to you. I behaved badly.

Ripples of unfeigned amusement carried over the telepathic waves. *Oh, I'm sure I could think of something or other that you could do to make it up to me.*

Kill me now. *Don't get any ideas, my Lord. This is purely on a platonic basis.*

I will try not to let the disappointment overcome me. So what did you have in mind?

I crossed my fingers tightly and hoped for the best. *I thought maybe we could meet. You know, in person. And then I could, you know, apologise. And, um, we could chat.*

Chat? About what? The weather perhaps? Knitting patterns?

You're right. This is a stupid idea. I'm sorry for bothering you. Alex would just have to come up with some other way of getting into the vampires' abode. This was not going to work.

Hold those horses, kitten. As you've gone to so much trouble to get in touch, then perhaps you are right. We should meet. And...chat. Why don't we have dinner? I know some good places that are quiet and intimate where we wouldn't be disturbed.

I really didn't like the direction this conversation was taking or the suggestive tone of the Lord Alpha's Voice. *Well, actually, Corrigan, I think it would be better if we went somewhere where there were a lot of people. You know, when you met me yesterday it was because I had anger-management counselling.*

You don't say.

I swallowed. *Err...I do say. And I find that it's easier for me to keep my temper and act like a normal person if I'm in a big crowd. In fact, it's actually part of my therapy to spend as much time out in the busy public as possible.*

That's an interesting choice of words, kitten.

What?

'Normal person'. Because you're definitely not normal and I'm pretty sure that you're not a person either. You still owe me an explanation, I think.

Well, I'd have thought that by now you'd have gotten all the information you need out of Betsy or Tom or Julia.

Despite what you may think of me, I don't tend to force my shifters to tell me things that they don't want to.

I snorted. Bullshit. If he was trying to pretend that he wasn't actually some kind of furry megalomaniac, then he was talking to the wrong person. *My Lord, in that case, you won't force me to tell you what I don't want to either.*

But you're not one of my shifters and I'm not your Lord.

Damn fucking right he wasn't. I ran out of patience. *Well, okay, whatever. I'm a normal person who happens to be free next Saturday night. If you aren't doing anything, then maybe I can come to London and we could meet. Otherwise, never mind. I understand that being the Dark Lord of the Brethren means that you're a busy man.* Or panther. Or whatever.

There was a moment of brooding silence. I held my breath, terrified that I'd pushed too hard. Then he finally spoke again. *Next Saturday causes a few problems. However, I believe I can overcome them. I have to attend a gathering with some Otherworld leaders. Will mixing in such company be a problem for you?*

I couldn't believe it was going to be this easy. I was careful to be cautious in my response, however. *As long as you're not talking demi-goddesses, then I can probably manage.*

Okay then. No demi-goddesses, I promise. Wear something pretty. I will come and pick you up at the Ministry.

Wear something pretty? I wasn't a fucking doll. *Of course. I will look forward to it.*

As will I, kitten, as will I.

I broke off the connection. A single trickle of sweat had formed in the hollow of my neck and was making its way uncomfortably down my skin. Bugger. Why did he have to be so nice all of a sudden? Feeling suddenly overcome with guilt, I stood up, yanking down my borrowed skirt to cover my freezing arse.

And then Brock staggered round the corner and stared at me in shock.

CHAPTER TWELVE

"Baldilocks," he slurred, "I was jusht, er, jusht out for a walk."

The strong reek of alcohol was emanating from his very pores. Understanding filled me, and I abruptly realised why the massive gates leading to the academy had been left open. Why I'd thought that teenage mages would be different from any other kids of the same age, I had no idea.

I smiled at him gently. "Of course you were, Brock. In fact, that's exactly what I was doing."

"Yesh, yesh." He nodded vigorously. "It'sh a lovely night." Then his mouth twisted and he sat down heavily onto the gravel.

I bent over and brought my face closer to his. "Brock? Are you alright?"

"Fantashtic." He fell sideways and proceeded to curl up into a small ball, hugging his knees to himself.

Okay-dokay. I reached down and prodded him. "You can't sleep here, Brock. You need to get back to your dorm."

He mumbled something incoherently. I sighed deeply and knelt down.

It seemed impossible that he'd sneaked out on his own, so I looked around for a moment and tried to strain my ears to hear if anyone else was coming. There was the rumble of a few distant cars, but little else. I shook his shoulder. "Brock? Where are your friends?"

He raised up a heavy arm and waved vaguely back in the direction that he'd come from. "Shtill there." He pulled himself back to a sitting position, although he was swaying alarmingly from side to side. A sudden mournful, puppy-dog expression filled his face. "Deborah'sh shtill there."

Ah. "She didn't want to come back with you?"

"No." He harrumphed. "All she wantsh to do ish to talk about Thomash." He put on a high-pitched squeaky voice. "Thomash ish sho handshome. He knowsh sho much and he'sh shtill sho shexy." He sagged backwards again then reverted to his normal voice. "I hate Thomash."

I thought I could understand that. I certainly didn't think that he was 'sho shexy' anyway. "Okay, Brock. Have you told Deborah that you like her?"

His unfocused eyes swivelled round towards me. "There'sh no point. She likesh Thomash. She jusht thinksh I'm her friend."

I patted his shoulder sympathetically. "Maybe you should do something about that."

"Nothing to do," he mumbled. "Who do you like?"

"Excuse me?"

"Who do you like?" Brock's eyes narrowed for a moment. "Do you like Thomash too?"

"No, I don't like Thomash, I mean Thomas. Not like that anyway." A sudden image of Corrigan glinting at me flashed before my eyes. "I don't like anyone at this moment in time. Now, let's get you to bed."

I stood up and pulled Brock to his feet, where he wavered unsteadily. Then I hooked his arm around my shoulder and began to half pull him towards the gates. It was a struggle getting him to move. We pushed through the small gap, my skirt snagging momentarily on the rusted catch. When I managed to extricate myself, Brock was staring at me with a funny expression on his face.

"That'sh Deborah'sh shkirt. Why are you wearing it?"

"Honestly, I'm not entirely sure. It's not really my normal choice of attire." I thought about the grooming session that both Deborah and Mary had invited me to earlier in the evening and hoped for Brock's sake that it hadn't been for Thomas' benefit. Then again, although I didn't know the contrary mage very well, I somehow doubted that schoolgirls were his type.

We made our way slowly up the driveway, pausing every few minutes for Brock to avoid falling flat on his face. He chattered away the entire time, mainly about how wonderful Deborah was, although I struggled to make out every word. By the time we reached the academy buildings, my shoulder was really starting to ache.

Brock turned towards me, a serious look in his eyes. "You know, Baldilocksh, you're okay."

I winced. "Please call me Mack."

He swayed momentarily and lost his footing, falling heavily onto me. I forced him back upright.

"'kay, Mackilocksh. But, I mean it. I thought you were shcary. You alwaysh look as if you're about to eat shomeone. But you're actually alright." He nodded to himself. "I like you."

I smiled at him. "Yeah, Brock. I like you too."

He frowned for a moment. "I don't like you like that. You're pretty but you're kind of old."

I snorted. "Thanks for the hit to my ego."

"Anytime." He grinned at me lopsidedly before staggering off to his left.

I'd been concerned about how on earth I was going to get him through the cafeteria window, but I should have known that he'd have a more sensible method of sneaking in and out. Round the back of the main building, close to where the Dean's office was, there was a small door set into the brickwork that I'd not noticed before. Brock pushed his way in, with me following. He succeeded in crashing over a small table with a pretty vase set on it that caused such a racket I was convinced that the entire academy must have heard it. However, after a few moments it became obvious that thankfully everyone else was still in the land of nod. Breathing a sigh of relief, the pair of us made our way slowly up the stairs and round to where the boys' dorms were.

"I can make it from here, Mackilocksh."

I stared at him doubtfully but he snapped his heels together and gave me a sloppy salute that suggested some flicker of consciousness, so I let him go, watching the drunk teenager weave his way dramatically towards his room. He bounced off a couple of walls, but eventually made it to what must have been his door and fell inside. Chuckling quietly to myself, I headed back to my own room too.

THE NEXT MORNING I awoke with more energy than by rights I should have had. I was feeling pleased with myself by now for having somehow managed to get the Lord of the almighty Brethren to bend to my almighty will, and particularly happy that I had a full day off to myself that I could devote to further translation. I tripped down to breakfast with a spring in my step, and poured myself my usual three cups of coffee before settling down. I had barely started on the first cup when Brock came stumbling in, with a distinctive shade of green under his usual pale skin. He sleep-walked over to the counter and got himself a giant glass of orange juice, then made his way over to me, slumping down into the chair just opposite.

He gulped down half of the glass in one go, then lay his head on the table top, squinting up at me with just one eye open. "Thanks for last night," he muttered.

I smiled and reached over, ruffling his hair. "Any time. Just don't call me Mackilocksh again, or suggest that I'm old, and we're even."

He grinned weakly. A heartbeat later both Mary and Deborah came bouncing in. Either they hadn't had as much to drink as Brock or they possessed the unnatural tendency of the young to remain hangover free. Regardless, they both sat themselves down and began telling me how much fun I'd missed by not attending their pampering session the night before. I raised half an eyebrow, whilst Brock at least looked a bit guilty, but neither of us said anything else.

Deborah proudly displayed her fingers, splaying them out so that I could appreciate her immaculately created manicure. "Isn't it a gorgeous shade of yellow?" she gushed. "It's to match this darling little skirt that I've got."

A wash of guilt ran over me. Her 'darling little skirt' was right now balled up into a corner underneath my bed. I made a mental note to sort it out and sneak it back down to the laundry later.

"We thought we might head down to the garden again, Baldilocks," chirruped Mary happily. "Do you want to come?"

I was shaking my head to decline when Brock interrupted moodily, "It's Mack."

Mary looked at him surprised, still lying prone as he was on half of the table.

"Not Baldilocks. Call her Mack," he repeated with a grumpy mutter.

I felt a warm rush of gratitude towards him. It was short-lived, however, as both Alex and Thomas chose that moment to stroll into the cafeteria together. They seemed to be having some kind of close conversation that I didn't like at all. Alex registered my presence and headed over, Thomas trailing in his wake. They both sat down next to us. Deborah's face flushed red and I could just make out her gripping Mary's arm in excitement. Brock just looked miserable.

"Goodness," I commented loudly, in a bid to draw attention away from the pair of them. "And what has happened to make the great mage trainers deign to honour us with their presence?"

Thomas scowled at me, although Alex winked. It was easy to

tell that he was desperate to find out what had happened the night before with Corrigan, but after putting me through that horribly embarrassing episode, despite the satisfaction I felt at it now, I wanted to let him squirm for a little time longer.

"Oh, we thought we'd come and see how you dudes were doing," drawled Alex with a hint of mischief flitting its way across his eyes. "You are all looking so fresh and well rested."

"Mmm," agreed Thomas, reaching over to grab a roll from the centre of the table. "It's great that you all take your studies so seriously and use every opportunity you can to get a good night's sleep so you can put your energies towards the day." There was just the faintest hint of sarcasm in his voice, that was so barely there that for a moment I thought I'd imagined it. All three of the initiates looked incredibly uncomfortable at his words, though. I smirked. It appeared that the great and mighty Thomas actually had a bit of a sense of humour. Well, who knew?

Despite her over-powering excitement at sitting next to Thomas, the fear of their night's activities being revealed was clearly too much for Deborah, and she stood up along with both Brock and Mary. The three of them made their apologies and quickly left the cafeteria, Brock tripping over a chair leg on his way in a manner that was incredibly reminiscent of his attempts at walking home the night before.

Thomas rolled his eyes. "They always think that they're the first to sneak out and get pissed."

Alex grinned and put his palm up as if to high five Thomas. When all he got was a stony-faced response, he shrugged amiably and brought his hand down instead and looked at me. "So what did you get up to last night, Mack Attack?" The hopeful tone in his voice was amusing.

I took a sip of coffee. "Not much. Had an early night actually. I can't keep up with these young folks."

He kicked me suddenly under the table and I hissed in surprise more than pain. Thomas stared at me hard. I quit beating around the bush and put Alex out of his misery. "Besides,

I wanted a quiet weekend now because next Saturday night I'm going to be rather busy."

He tried not to look too interested. "Oh yeah, dude? And why's that?"

Making a show of nonchalance, I waved a hand dismissively and said airily, "Oh, the Lord Alpha has invited me to some old party so I'll need to get my gladrags on."

He almost leapt out of his chair, but just managed to restrain himself in time. Thomas frowned. "I don't think the Dean will be very impressed that you are off gallivanting with the head of the Brethren."

I raised my eyebrows at Alex who nodded vigorously in understanding. "Oh, I wouldn't worry about the Dean, Mack Attack. I'm sure he'll be reasonable."

Thomas appeared particularly sceptical but let it go. I stood up, pushing my chair back. "Well, I've got some extra studying that I need to do. If you gentlemen will excuse me?"

Both the mages acknowledged my departure, Alex trying to communicate something to me with his eyes, but failing miserably. However, I was quite sure I'd catch up with him later so we could come up with a clear plan for what I'd do once I was at the party. Right now, I needed to spend a bit of time on myself. And that meant finally getting back to the Fae book.

CHAPTER THIRTEEN

I SPENT VIRTUALLY THE REST OF THE DAY HOLED UP IN MY ROOM, just me, a seemingly sentient Fae book and a dictionary. A couple of times there were knocks on the door, but I ignored them all. I was in the zone and determined to find out more about myself and my lineage.

I was getting faster and more adept with the translations. It was still painstakingly slow, of course, but I was starting to recognise some of the more common runes and their meanings and, while some sentences were pure gobbledegook, for the most part I thought I had a good understanding of what the book was telling me. I discovered that the dragon that had been changed into human form by the less-than-forward-thinking mage developed a 'most egregious temper and vicious bouts of rage' that cast fear into the hearts of anyone who came across his path. Said dragon was clearly unimpressed with his new body and ended up killing his would-be benefactress by burning her to a crisp. He then proceeded to rape and pillage his way through various towns and villages, occasionally impregnating the poor maidens who got caught up in his violence.

I smoothed my hands over my shorn head, feeling the soft prickles of the newly grown hair against my fingertips, wondering yet again whether I was reading pure fantasy or whether the story was actually rooted in some version of fact. That was the difficult thing with the otherworldian histories: you never really knew for sure what was real and what was just legend. Part of me did feel rather buoyed up by my discoveries, however. If this ancient (and rather frightening and nasty) creature was indeed my great-grandfather several hundred generations removed, then it meant that maybe it wasn't my fault that I had such a nasty temper. I sobered up slightly with the sudden idea that it might mean I'd never have any control over my temper or my bloodfire, and I still didn't really know how the dragon–man had developed into a race called the Draco Wyr, although I thought I might be starting to get the idea with all of his sexual rampages. Eventually, when my eyes were starting to smart and the words were beginning to swim in front of me, I snapped the book shut and went in search of Alex, hoping we could have another real conversation without the hovering presence of Thomas or the initiates around.

I picked my way around the grounds of the academy, trying first one direction and then the other. I must have passed hundreds of other initiates, most of whom managed to suddenly remember that they'd forgotten something and wheel around abruptly in the opposite direction when they saw me coming. A couple did at least smile tentatively at me, which made me feel a little bit better. I avoided the garden area where Mary, Brock and the others would be, not really in the mood for getting caught up in another teaching session just yet. At one point, however, I even saw Mage Slocombe, whose eyes widened as soon as he caught sight of me. He all but tripped over his daft black robes in his haste to get away from me before I decided to engage him in conversation. I rolled my eyes. Whatever.

Thirty minutes later, I'd circled the entire compound, garden aside, and had seen absolutely no sign of Alex anywhere. I could feel heated coils of annoyance curl themselves through my intestines. Not only did I want to talk to him about the impending party, I was also desperate to confide in someone about what I'd read in the Fae book. Alex could potentially have some new insights that I'd not thought of before. He might even have a more effective way to get the book translated. Fuck. For all I knew, he could read Fae. It wasn't something we'd ever spoken about before.

Coming out from behind the back of the Protection block, I pursed my lips and considered my options. I wasn't in the mood to continue to spend the last remaining hour of daylight searching for him. I tried to think logically about where he might be, but I drew a blank. The only thing I could think of was that he'd gone off to catch some waves. That, however, was patently ridiculous. I knew that he had been desperate at breakfast to find out more about what had happened with Corrigan, so there was no way that he'd have bunked off for the day. Besides anything, we were in the middle of the sodding countryside. I didn't exactly know where the academy was, but I'd lived beside the sea for long enough to know that it was definitely miles away from here. Otherwise I'd have sensed the tang of salt in the air. I equally doubted that the Dean would allow portals to be created just so that various mages could go hobnobbing off on personal sojourns around the country.

I wondered whether I could create a short cut for myself for finding him. Yes, my previous Divination lesson had ended badly, but we'd been in a small, enclosed space then. I was an outdoors kind of girl. There were no priceless paintings or nervous mages around who might inadvertently get hurt by my trying to see if I could invoke my inveniora to find Alex. A tiny, insistent thought nudged at the back of my mind, telling me that out of all the ideas I'd ever had, this was by far the most stupid, but I pushed it away. After all, aside from Protection, Divination was the only discipline that I'd so far even had the faintest flicker of success with, even if that success had somewhat ended in disaster. At some point, if I ever wanted to leave this place, I'd have to get better at the magic stuff. Otherwise poor Mrs Alcoon was doomed forever.

I chewed my lip, deciding. There wasn't a soul around me so I really didn't see what harm it could do. I sat down on the damp ground to begin. Then I stood back up again. Maybe it was better to try it standing? Damnit, I really didn't know. I tried to concentrate, reminding myself of what Higgins had done the previous week to get me started. All I had to do was reach inside myself, find the so-called energy that he'd spoken of and imagine it as a thread so I could pull it out. I reckoned that where I'd gone wrong before was trying to pull it out with too much force. If I just tried to be a teeny-weeny bit more gentle, then surely I'd have more success.

Closing my eyes, and oddly that seemed to help, I pictured a smoky ball inside of me. I thought that perhaps I could feel the energy that I'd yanked on before, so I gave it a little tug, trying to pull it through my body. I felt a slight burn as I did so, but it was different to the usual sensation of my bloodfire heating up so, emboldened, I kept tugging. I felt it snake its way up through my chest and across my shoulders, then filter out slowly down through my arm. Then I flicked my fingers and opened my eyes.

Almost immediately a bead of red smoke appeared, lazily casting itself out into the air. Yelping with delighted surprise, I watched it curve its way around my body, almost as if it had a mind of its own. I couldn't believe it! I'd actually done something right for once. Realising that I wasn't quite sure now how to make it trace after Alex so I could find him, I silently willed it to track him down. The inveniora ignored me and just lazily continued to spin round me, creating odd shapes in the still air of the early evening.

"Find Alex," I commanded sternly.

The red smoke twisted its way down to my feet and lay there heavily, like some kind of bizarre lap dog.

"Find Alex Floride," I urged it again, feeling irritated all of a sudden.

Still nothing happened. Abruptly the sound of voices floated over the top of the buildings towards me, and I felt a surge of sudden fire flicker inside me at the thought of being discovered experimenting with something with which I'd already almost killed someone. As soon as the heat hit my system, however, the inveniora took off, rushing away from me and towards the edges of the compound at a hurtling speed. Invigorated into action, I took off after it.

Unlike other manifestations of the tracking spell that I'd seen, mine didn't veer even slightly. It shot through the air like an arrow, leaving behind a trail that could have been drawn with a ruler. I didn't have time to pause to think about it, however, I just ran, trying to keep up with the front of it. Before too long it reached the edges of the grounds, zipping its way into an impenetrable bed of flowers, bushes and trees. Without thinking twice, I followed it in, ignoring the scratching branches that pulled at my skin. My own progress was now considerably slower but, if anything, the inveniora itself appeared to pick up speed. I hopped and ducked and dodged my way through the thicket, cursing Alex and wondering what in the hell he was doing hiding in the middle of a bush. The powder-blue robes that I'd been forced to wear yet again impeded me even further, continually getting caught on various branches and brambles. The hem that was trailing at my back snagged stubbornly on some kind of thorn and I had no choice but to stop to use my fingers to free it. When I stood back up, I realised that the inveniora had stopped just up ahead and was hovering in the dark, still air.

My heart was suddenly thudding deep in my chest. I couldn't help but think of the last time I'd wandered into a thick copse and come across the cloth deposited by Iabartu. Worry filled me with what might have happened to Alex and whether, once again, it would end up being my fault. Gingerly picking my way forward, I pulled up my robes to avoid catching them on anything else, but tensed all my muscles in case I suddenly needed to attack.

As I got closer, I realised that the red snaky smoke was hanging right in front of a looming bricked wall. Obviously I'd reached the outer fringes of the academy grounds, and that beyond here the mages' influence dissipated. Did that mean that Alex had left the compound? Puzzled, I leaned forward, realising that there was a crumbling gap in the stone next to where the inveniora had stopped. Without thinking, I reached out to push my fingers through and touch it. As soon as I did so, however, I felt something wet.

Rubbing my fingers together to work out what it was, I peered at them through the gloomy cover of the trees. Whatever it was, it felt thick and gloopy. Definitely not blood, I registered with a dim surge of relief, but definitely not anything entirely natural either. It hadn't rained for days, so it couldn't be a puddle of mossy rainwater that had collected, and there was far too much of it to be dew. Anyway, it was completely the wrong time of day for that. I lifted my fingers to my face and sniffed cautiously, then immediately recoiled.

Whatever it was, it smelt dark and rotten, not dissimilar to the unpleasant whiff that cockroaches somehow managed to give off. What the fuck was it? I could see now that the strange liquid was dark and shiny, with something of a purple tinge to it. I didn't like this at all.

I was about to call out to see if Alex was for some reason on the other side of the wall, when I heard my name being faintly called from behind me, albeit from some distance away. I wiped my fingers on a nearby leaf, trying to rid myself of the gloop, and then turned back. The voice called again, and I frowned, now more puzzled than ever. It sounded like the hippy mage himself.

Eventually emerging back from out of the undergrowth, I spotted him, hands on hips as he stared at me.

"Mack Attack, where the hell have you been and what the hell have you been doing? Sheesh, I've been looking all over for you!"

Pissed off, I glared at him. "Well, I've been looking for you too, Alex. I've been all over the sodding compound, and then when I couldn't find you, I conjured up some inveniora to find you and–"

"You did what?"

"You heard me," I snapped.

"Dude, that was an idiot move to make."

"Well, dude, it led me here, didn't it? What have you been doing in the bushes, eh?" I waggled my eyebrows at him to prove I was serious.

Alex just looked confused. "I have no idea what you're on about."

"You've never been in there?" I jerked my head back to where I'd just come from, somewhat deflated.

He shook his head, looking at me as if I was crazy. "No, I've not. And besides, until you reach Level Three, you can't control inveniora to run any kind of proper search. You've been running around aimlessly, with some kind of stupid death-wish on your shoulders."

"Nothing went wrong. It didn't cloud up like last time or try to smother anyone!"

"You were lucky," Alex said grimly. "This kind of stuff isn't a toy, Mack Attack. There's a reason why there are trainers making sure nothing goes wrong when the initiates practise."

"Jeez, who rattled your chain? Chill out, Alex."

"You're telling me to chill out? Seriously? The girl with the worst temper this side of the equator? Because she's not actually a girl, but instead a fucking dragon?"

"I'm not a dragon," I stated emphatically, "I'm a Draco Wyr. And if it wasn't for that fact, then you wouldn't have anyone to help you sneak into a fucking nest of vampires to steal a bloody chunk of wood!"

Alex and I both glared at each other. I realised I was letting my temper once again get the better of me and tried to calm myself using Bryant's deep breathing suggestions. At the same moment, I think Alex also recognised the idiocy of the situation and relaxed.

"Sorry Alex. I'm finding all this very stressful, I guess."

"Me too, Mack Attack, me too." He stretched his hand out. "Friends?"

I took it and shook vigorously. "Always." We smiled at each other and the tension evaporated.

"I've cleared things with the Dean, dude," Alex said. "He'll let you go out and party it up on Saturday. Did Lord Shifty cause you any problems?"

"No," I answered. "He was actually pretty easy to convince."

Alex was exultant. "See? I told you! And all those times that you thought he'd smite you down for not being a shifter. He's actually a fairly reasonable guy."

"I'm not convinced of that yet," I grumbled. "He's still on some kind of power trip." The 'wear something pretty' command continued to irk me. "I have to find something to wear for the party too."

"Don't worry, mate. I'll sort that side of things out. Come on." He held out his arm for me to take and we started walking back to the scattered buildings.

On the way back, I told him about the Fae book. Alex was astonished. "Seriously? Are you sure it's the same book?"

"I'm positive." I added in the details that I'd managed to translate so far.

"Whoa, that's far out, Mack Attack. So you really are descended from dragons, then."

"I don't know, Alex. This could all just be legend. And it might not have anything to do with me. It certainly doesn't clear up anything as to the reasons for why my mother dumped me with the shifters, or what else my blood can do."

"It's a start though. I can't read Fae so I can't help you in that department, unfortunately. Why don't you get in touch with your fairy buddy?"

"Solus? He won't come near anything to do with the mages or

the Ministry, you must know that. Anyway, he's a Fae, and they're untrustworthy by nature."

"You trusted him enough with your friend, Mrs Whatserface."

"Alcoon," I said absently. "Mrs Alcoon." I felt a tug of guilty melancholy at the thought of the older woman. "I didn't have all that much choice at the time. And he got what he wanted in return."

"Which was?"

"To find out what I really am."

"You told him? About the Draco Wyr stuff? Mack Attack, you just said you couldn't trust him!"

"I also just said I didn't have a choice. And I suppose he's not given me up so far." Although the stupid fairy had trodden pretty close to the line a couple of times, I thought ungratefully.

"Six days' time, Mack Attack. Once this party's over, then we can concentrate on getting you up the levels and out of this place as soon as possible. Then you can sort out Mrs Alcoon, and the Fae, and find out who you really are."

Amen to that, I whispered to myself.

CHAPTER FOURTEEN

THE FOLLOWING FIVE DAYS SCAMPERED BY REMARKABLY QUICKLY. Lessons started up again on Monday, and I received exactly the same terrified rabbit-caught-in-headlights reaction from both Slocombe in Kinesis and Barton in Evocation. And I had the same success in both those lessons as I'd had the previous week, which of course amounted to absolutely zip. Nada. Nyet. I was getting damn good at staring at stones, however.

I'd been hoping for a little more from Illusion, as at least this time I had a full lesson's worth of time in which to learn. But again, nothing really happened, other than me being forced to count to ten several times over whenever the trainer started up her hacking cackle at my pitiful efforts. I was learning to keep my mouth shut at least, and I managed to go the full week without maiming anyone or damaging any more property. There was no time with Alex to spend on Divination; instead we took the opportunity of having the peace and quiet to be able to discuss and plan out different scenarios for my impending heist. I was just trying hard not to focus on what could happen if I got caught by the vamps.

On the brighter side, I was also finding myself getting on better and better with Mary and her friends. I had little in common with them, but Deborah didn't have a mean bone in her body, and Mary's constant stream of chatter always helped make me feel just that little bit less stressed or worried. I spent a fair bit of time chatting to both Brock and Aqmar, and Brock in particular was opening up to me. We had a lot of deep and meaningful discussions over meals about the rights and wrongs of magic, although we entirely avoided talking about what might or might not be happening with his love life and his momentous crush on Deborah. I didn't push it.

By the time Friday rolled around, and I had Protection again with Thomas, I was starting to feel more in control of myself and my emotions. I'd spent more time in the library, and was starting to feel an odd fondness for Slim and his curses. I'd also found the time to translate a little bit more of the Fae book, although it pretty much just explained how my potential (probable?) ancestor met his own demise at the hands of the rather unfortunately named Bolox, a warrior who set a cunning trap involving a sacrificial virgin (who sadly bled to death in the course of the proceedings) and some kind of elaborate gold mesh net. Bolox nearly hadn't made it out alive himself, as the dragon-man had reverted back to his true form in his final death throes and had gouged a deep enough chunk out of the warrior's shoulder that he almost died from his injuries afterwards.

Back in the virtually derelict Protection building that Health and Safety would have had a field day with, I found myself looking forward to what Thomas had to offer. Over the past week, we'd managed to maintain a cool ambivalence towards each other whenever our paths crossed. My hair was already almost half an inch long and I was still tempted to keep it shaved if for no other reason than I'd be able to keep rubbing his face in how much of a prick he'd been. But when I met him for our second round, he was all relaxed smiles.

"So, Initiate Smith, you've been encouraging the younger ones to attack using the element of surprise and the unexpected, have you?"

I was certainly surprised that he no longer chose to make more of my teaching of his pet subject, and just nodded.

"Well then," he continued, "let's see if you can practise what you preach."

He motioned me towards the centre of the gym, and then stood in front of me, his entire body proclaiming a calmness that I found bewildering. His stance was completely open and vulnerable, and I couldn't begin to see how he could possibly be successful.

Thomas laughed at me. "You look confused, Initiate. T'ai chi ch'uan is not about tension or the centrifugal force that modern fighters so mistakenly rely on. Rather it involves looseness in order to subdue potential aggressors with the minimum amount of effort. Your task is not to fight back, but merely to avoid my own attacks." He bared his teeth at me in the semblance of a grin. "I doubt you will cope."

Bullshit. I grinned at the mage, confident that this was going to be a piece of cake.

He began to gracefully extend his arms in a move reminiscent of our previous lesson's drills. "When your body is emptied and vacant of force and tension, your muscles relax and a resolute strength takes its place. This strength, you shall discover, is superior in every way to all other forms of attack."

I watched him, waiting for the moment when I could block his movements and prove to him yet again that anything I could do would best him. He was moving so leisurely and deliberately that it required no effort on my part to track his movements, until all of a sudden he whipped out with his fist and caught me in my stomach, causing me to double over and exhale all the air I had left in my lungs. I was so stunned that he'd managed to hit me with such strength when he was moving around so slowly, that I barely managed to stand back up before he lashed out again, this time with his foot. He connected with my leg mid-thigh and, yet again, I went down.

"Keeping your body weight on one foot alone aids the

movement and attack," Thomas intoned, spinning around like a ballroom dancer in slow motion, and flicking out again to knock me on the side of my head. "Using two feet to equally distribute your weight impedes your agility." He cast around with his arms, then brought them together and bowed.

I straightened up and stared at him, aghast that he'd found it so easy to attack and connect. The rage within me that set my bloodfire roaring threatened for one moment to overcome my thoughts, but I counted to ten instead and concentrated on regaining my breath.

Thomas smiled at me, pleased. "I didn't think it would take you such a short time to manage not to reflexively return my assault."

I had to admit that I was rather taken aback myself. I figured it was because I knew that he wasn't really going to hurt me all that much.

I shrugged. "I guess I'm just a fast learner." I twisted my body to the side, trying to snap out the pain that still throbbed from my stomach muscles. "But explain to me, Mage Thomas, why these techniques didn't work before?"

He cocked his head. "What do you mean?"

"In the cafeteria. Before. When I attacked you. You didn't try any of this stuff or, at least, you didn't manage to beat me, anyway. That was an easy win for me." I wasn't trying to goad him; I was genuinely curious.

"Ah, well, you were actually fighting me that time. It's a whole different ball game when your opponent is not only using magic but is also seeing things through the veil of emotion." He inclined his head. "You are a superior fighter to me, of that there is no doubt. Hence you managed to beat me in the cafeteria. And I admit, I am still feeling the effects of it now. However, that doesn't mean that I can't still teach you more than a few things to make you an even more effective attacker. Good teachers don't seek to train their students to be as good as they are, they seek to make them better."

I was shocked by his honesty, and mulled over his words all the way to the portal for my session with Jacoby Bryant. I even half imagined that my trip through the portal was less nausea inducing than usual because I was so caught up in thinking about what he'd said and how he'd acted. I'd certainly been warming to Thomas since the previous week, but now I was wondering if I'd gotten him completely wrong. Sure, he'd been rude when I'd first arrived, but then maybe he'd had good reason to be. I tried to imagine what it would have been like down in Cornwall if some unknown mage had shown up because the Brethren had ordered us to teach them to be like shifters. Even for myself as a non-shifter, I knew I'd have been disgusted.

Entering the reception area, and seeing exactly the same girl who I'd barked at and flamed at the week before, made me also half expect to see Corrigan striding through from round the corridor again. However, this time the girl stayed behind the desk and I felt the briefest flicker of disappointment that clearly the only other person I'd be seeing this time would be the counsellor himself. I told myself that I should be grateful: the last thing I needed was to see the Lord Alpha before our so-called date. He'd probably just make some snarky comments about my attire. Nope, I didn't want or need to see him. Definitely not. No. No. No.

I discussed with Bryant what had happened during the preceding seven days, leaving out any mention of my now somewhat more doused bloodfire, of course, and we spoke about what had worked and what hadn't. He was pleased with my progress and I felt an unexpected thrill zip through me at doing so well. Perhaps there was hope for me yet. He recommended that I continue with the techniques he'd already shown me, and then I left without further incident.

However, the next morning, when I awoke, I could feel little spikes of flame flickering through my toes and fingers. I lay in bed for several moments, ignoring the discomfort it provided, purely trying to calm myself down and use all the tips I'd been given. Despite the numerous talks that Alex and I had had about how to act once I got to Kingsway, I was still feeling nervous and more than a little scared about how it would pan out. I really didn't want to let him down, but stealing from the undead right now seemed like a suicide mission. I imagined myself keeling over at Corrigan's feet in dramatic, dying-swan fashion, and him raising one sardonic eyebrow at me for bringing it all onto my own head in the first place. For one thing, I still didn't actually have anything to wear. Despite his promises to the contrary, Alex still hadn't come through with a suitable outfit. At this rate I'd have to squeeze back into Deborah's micro-mini, which remained under my bed as I'd not quite managed to guiltily sneak it back into the laundry yet.

A knock at the door startled me out of my reverie. I reached over and twisted the doorknob, swinging it open to see who it was.

"Hey! Baldi...I mean, Mack! How's it going? Ready for the big date?" It was Mary, with Deborah in tow. Naturally, they'd gotten wind of my impending evening.

I forced myself up to a sitting position. "I can't wait."

Mary shot me a look of suspicion at my unenthusiastic comment. "You know, the reason why you are feeling like this, Mack, is because you haven't yet been beautified."

Uh, say what?

Deborah grinned at me. "We've spoken to the boys and they've agreed that it's fine to put off today's training session till tomorrow. So we have all day to help you get ready for this evening." Her eyes gleamed in anticipation.

"All day?" My mouth hung half open. Really? How long did it take to have a bloody shower? It wasn't exactly as if I had any fucking hair that needed doing. "I don't think–" I began, before Mary placed her finger on my lips, shushing me.

"That's enough. You can thank us later."

I tried to think quickly. If I could hunt down and defeat the various nasties that the Otherworld had to offer, then surely I could find a way to extricate myself from two girls. "I can't get ready yet," I said triumphantly, seizing upon a reason. "I don't have anything to wear."

"Don't you worry your pretty little head," tutted Deborah. "I've spoken to Mage Floride and it's all in hand."

I might have to kill Alex for not putting a stop to this, I thought grimly, as the pair of them pulled me out of bed and down to the communal shower room.

Several hours later, I'd been plucked and waxed and prettified half to death. I was sitting grumpily in a swivel chair in the girls' dorm room, feeling none too impressed. Deborah wandered back in with a cup of coffee in one hand and a dress in the other. The aroma of the rich coffee cheered me up no end. I tried to avoid looking at the dress.

"Here we go," she trilled happily. "Coffee and party wear!"

I reached out for the steaming mug but Deborah snatched it away, out of my reach. I growled at her.

"No, no, no," she said with a saucy wink, "you get the coffee after you've put on the dress."

"But I'm naturally a very clumsy person," I pointed out reasonably. "I might spill the coffee down the dress."

"Hmm, you're right," she said thoughtfully. "I'll drink the coffee, you put the dress on."

Cursing the world under my breath, I stood up and snatched it out of her hands then stomped off to the bathroom to change. Pulling it off its hanger, I had to admit that it was an arresting colour. Pillar-box red, it screamed 'Look at me!'. That was all very well, I thought, if I wanted to attract attention. However, it didn't strike me as the sort of garment that you'd wear if you wanted to sneak around undetected. Some sort of black ninja combo would surely be more suitable. I knew that the girls were only trying to be nice, and thought that they were helping me snag Corrigan's attentions, but Alex at the very least could have gone for something a bit less obtrusive.

Squeezing into it, I performed some extraordinary

callisthenics to reach around and do up the zip, forced to breathe in deeply as I did so just so that it would go all the way up. I smoothed it down and scowled. It was too low and too short and I looked absolutely bloody ridiculous. A seventeen year old might be able to get away with this, but a woman in her mid twenties just looked as if she was trying far too hard. And how in the hell was I supposed to manage running if I needed to get away fast? It was so tight, I'd be lucky if I managed to even sodding walk.

"Coooeee!" called Deborah. "How does it look?"

I yanked open the bathroom door and stalked out. "It looks fucking–"

"Amazing," breathed Mary.

"Drop-dead gorgeous," sighed Deborah. "You're so lucky. If I had a dress like that to put on, then Mage Thomas would definitely notice me."

I bit back the comment that was already on my tongue and forced a smile onto my face, stomping over to the mirror to take a look. Then I had to admit that it did look pretty amazing. They'd shaped my eyebrows so that instead of giving the impression that I was permanently in a bad mood, I looked groomed and sophisticated. The make-up they'd trowelled on had evened out my complexion and made my eyes look wide and sultry all at the same time, while the dress fitted snugly in all the right places. I swivelled my hips around for a couple of admiring seconds. Okay, maybe it looked alright after all.

"Something's missing," stated Mary firmly from behind me.

Deborah jumped right in. "Accessories, darling, accessories!"

"Yeah! If you take off that necklace, then I'm sure I can find something else that'll match much better."

I touched my hands to my neck. I'd almost forgotten all about the thing that hung round there. In the ensuing mess of discovering that I hadn't needed to shave my hair off after all, it had completely slipped my mind to tell Thomas that he'd have to work out a way to get it off me. Now didn't seem like the right time to tell either Deborah or Mary that it was stuck there.

"No," I said emphatically. "The necklace will have to stay."

There must have been something in my facial expression that brooked no argument because for once the pair of them backed down. That was until Deborah produced a pair of shoes from behind her back.

"Well, if you won't change your jewellery, then the least you can do is change your shoes."

Absolutely no way. I would not be able to walk half a yard in those things. Unfortunately for me, the pair of them were already at my feet, forcing them on and strapping them up with some kind of complicated leather bands. I felt about half a foot taller, and already felt like they were starting to pinch. I took a couple of steps and almost tottered over. Oh great. Mack, the killer cat burglar who crawls to every destination. Brilliant. I was about to start pulling them right back off again when there was a quick knock at the door and I looked up to see Alex.

He looked mildly astonished at my appearance, but recovered quickly and tapped his watch. "We need to vamoose, Mack, er, Initiate Smith, I mean."

Sighing heavily, I wavered my way over to him, much in the same manner that Brock had walked when he'd been falling-down drunk. I could see the corners of Alex's mouth tipping up as he tried not to laugh and I had to resist the urge to punch him. I could do this, I thought defiantly. It was only a dress and a pair of shoes, for fuck's sake. Saying goodbye to Mary and Deborah, and thanking them as graciously as I could for their ministrations, we headed out the door and down to the waiting portal. Ruefully eyeing the shimmering gateway, I felt slightly sick. So much for the perfectly applied make-up.

I'd been concentrating so hard on not falling over that I hadn't even noticed that the Dean was also outside, standing there waiting. He looked me up and down, a sneer on his face. "Trying to impress someone?"

"No." I didn't even bother reacting further. He just wasn't worth it.

"I expect you to remember that you're a representative of this institution. I know most of the people you will be socialising with and, believe me, I will hear about it if you do anything that even hints at tarnishing our reputation."

I stared at the mage. One good thing about the stupidly high heels was that I was now taller than him and literally able to look down upon him. It was a nice feeling. "Oh, if you know so many of them, then it's a real shame that you weren't invited, Dean Michaels," I said sweetly.

His eyes shot daggers at me. "The responsibility of running this academy means that I cannot afford the opportunity to go out hobnobbing at will."

"Of course," I murmured, trying so very hard not to laugh. I glanced over at Alex, who was standing beside me, a ball of visible tension. "We'd better go, Mage Floride."

He nodded and took a step forward, vanishing through the portal. I followed, hoping that I wouldn't trip over after finally managing to get one over on the Dean.

CHAPTER FIFTEEN

I THREW UP AS SOON AS WE ARRIVED IN FRONT OF THE MINISTRY headquarters. Alex was good enough to look pointedly away until the contents of my stomach had been completely purged, then he helped me back up to my feet.

"You know, Mack Attack, antagonising the Dean is not going to help your cause."

"He started it," I said sullenly, all too aware that I sounded just like a petulant child.

Alex shook his head. "You're going to need to learn to bite your tongue more."

I nodded briefly, not wanting to acknowledge the truth of his words, and he handed me two slim, short daggers. They weren't silver, which was probably just as well considering who my date was, but they still looked happily lethal.

"Here," he said. "I picked these up because they'll fit perfectly with this dress."

He moved over to me, instructing me to lift my arms. Then he slid one under each armpit. "There's a specially made sheath built into the fabric," he explained. "If you need to use them, and I would urge that you do so only as a very last resort, then you can slide them out within a heartbeat." He looked terribly unsure of himself. "I know very little about weapons, but I've been assured that these are of the highest quality. I had to hock my favourite surfboard to get them, although goodness knows why a troll would want to go surfing."

Startled, I peered up at him, thinking that I had a pretty good idea about which troll he was referring to. Before I could ask him about it, however, a lazy, arrogant voice from across the other side of the street called over. "Are you ready to go yet or are you bringing the wizard with you?"

Corrigan. Dressed to the nines in a perfectly tailored tuxedo, it was still more than possible to see the effects of his lifestyle from the rippled muscular bulges under the expensive material, even from the other side of the darkened street. Realising that he'd have noted Alex's proximity to me when he slipped the knives under my dress, and probably mistaken it for something else entirely, a faint twist went through me. He always seemed to think the worst of me with men. Or maybe it was the best of me that he thought I had so many apparent admirers. Regardless, it was wrong. I shouted over that I'd just be a second then I turned back to Alex.

He was shaking where he stood and I knew it wasn't from the cold. "It'll be alright," I said softly, sounding a hell of a lot more confident than I actually was. "This will be easy."

"I'll never forgive myself if you end up getting hurt, Mack Attack."

I smiled at the mage. "Hey, this is a good plan. I'll get the Ancile, replace it with the Palladium and no-one will ever be any the wiser."

He passed me over a smallish clutch that contained Athena's little statue. "Be safe."

"I will." I leaned over and gave him a peck on the cheek, gripping tightly onto the purse. Then I turned back to face Corrigan and the music.

The Lord Alpha was leaning against a shiny black limo, arms folded, looking rather bored. I took a nervous step forward and felt myself waver ever so slightly, then I picked up confidence and managed to move a little faster. Halfway across the road, however, I felt my left heel start to wobble. I pushed out my arms to try to balance myself, but it was too late and I ended up careering onto the cold, hard tarmac with a loud ooph of exhaled air.

Corrigan began laughing. I picked myself up and glared at him.

"Yeah, lap it up, fuzzball," I hissed, annoyed with myself.

"Striking fear into the hearts of all who cross her, ladies and gentleman, I give you Mackenzie Smith," he intoned dramatically.

"Fuck off."

He shrugged. "Okay, then," and began pulling open the door to his 'look at me, I'm a rich bastard' car, as if to clamber in and leave me stranded.

I scowled at him. "Very funny."

Corrigan smirked. "Just remember that you're the one who invited me out on a date. You might want to show a little more humility and gratitude."

"This is not a date," I stated firmly. "It's merely an opportunity to smooth things over in order to avoid any future confrontations." And to steal a thousand-year-old statue to prevent a civil war in the Ministry, and death and destruction everywhere else, but I wasn't going to go into that at this particular moment in time.

He licked his lips predatorily, as if promising future 'confrontations' that I had no desire to think about right now. I swallowed hard, then shakily tottered my way across the final few feet to him. Holding open the door, he gestured me inside with a flourish. I took one quick glance back at Alex standing forlornly in front of the Ministry, and then got inside.

Once we were both ensconced within the limo's interior, it smoothly took off. It had the unmistakable smell of new car lingering about it. Despite myself, I was impressed.

"So things are going well in shifter-land, then?" I commented.

Corrigan didn't answer, and instead reached over into a small cabinet and pulled out a bottle of champagne and two chilled glasses. What the hell, I figured, I needed something to calm my nerves. He poured me a glass, which I gulped down and drained, then set aside.

He blinked at me, a streak of gold flashing its way across his jade-chipped eyes. "Thirsty?"

"A bit," I sniffed. "Maybe I just need some Dutch courage to get through this evening." Then it occurred to me that was probably a stupid thing to say, so I backtracked hastily. "Just because until very recently I thought that you were going to slaughter me and all my friends once you worked out that I wasn't a shifter, of course."

"Yes," he murmured. "We'll need to talk about that one day." He poured me another glass, but this time I ignored it. Taking the edge off was one thing, but getting drunk was most definitely not a good idea. "So, the mage. He's the one from Cornwall, right? The one who sneaked you through the portal."

And there we had it. I was just surprised that it had taken him this long. "He didn't sneak me through the portal. I asked him to help me get through it and he obliged. Because he's nice. And that's what friends do for other friends."

"Put them into life or death situations?" There was an edge to his voice.

"Help them in their time of need."

"It may have been more helpful if he'd gone through with you. But you didn't want that, did you? You were seeking glory and wanted the spotlight all to yourself."

I felt the heat rise up inside me at his baiting. "Glory? I was trying to stop Iabartu from murdering anyone else."

"We still haven't really established why she was trying to murder anyone at all." He leaned back against his seat, and eyed me.

Okay, I saw where this was going. He was still trying to glean from me what I really was, and he thought that he could manipulate me into getting annoyed and blurting it out. Not gonna happen. I concentrated on letting the bloodfire dampen back down, and then smiled calmly back. "Instead of annoying each other, why don't we see if we can get along?"

Corrigan grinned, baring his teeth. I shivered.

"Okay then," he purred. "You look nice in that dress. It was… thoughtful of you to dress up."

I could play this game. "You look well turned out yourself."

Mutual appreciation society now in full swing, I felt brave enough to pump him for a little information. "So," I said casually, "where is it we are actually going?"

Corrigan laughed humourlessly. "You know exactly where we're heading."

Oh, shit. I thought quickly, trying to remember what he'd said before, sure that he'd not specifically mentioned where we were going. Play dumb, Mack, play dumb. "Um, no. You just said that it was a gathering for the Otherworld leaders, that's all."

"And you just happened to be free to go out only this night. After almost biting my head off less than twenty-four hours before." His eyes narrowed. "Let's quit the play-acting, kitten. For some reason, you are desperate to get into this party and you're prepared to use me to do it."

My stomach dropped. Was I really that obvious? Corrigan shrugged, but there was a lack of insouciance about it, and instead the appearance of barely controlled tension that was frightening. He leaned back towards me and whispered, "So don't think that I am for one moment going to let you out of my sight to go off and do something stupidly reckless."

I hesitated for too long before squeaking, "I don't have any ulterior motives, Corrigan. You're just determined to think the worst of me."

"Hmm, we'll see about that, shall we?"

Insides churning, I stared at him, wide-eyed and nervous. Of course it had been too easy getting him to agree to bring me to this party. He was just toying with me, much in the same way a cat does with a mouse. Realising that I was that mouse pretty much terrified me.

Fortunately, before I could say anything else that would just dig my own grave deeper, the car pulled up. Corrigan got out, not waiting for the driver to open the door for him. I did the same. The street we were on was brightly lit with lampposts, but I still felt that I could imagine all manner of nasty things hiding in the shadows, ready to jump out and attack. The building itself looked exactly as it had in the old book I'd found in the mages' library, although now that I was here in person it felt considerably more imposing. The bricked-out windows in particular gave the whole place a sinister edge. Corrigan moved round to my side and held out his arm. I stared down at it for a moment, feeling pointlessly furious that he'd suggested he didn't believe that I was here just for him. I wasn't, of course, but that didn't mean that I couldn't still be annoyed that he didn't trust me. Forcing myself to remain calm, I placed my hand on his outstretched arm, noting the rock-hard steel of the muscles beneath. Then we walked up to the entrance of the vampires' lair.

The door to the house was lacquered black and so shiny that I could practically see my face reflected in it. I was half tempted to breathe onto it and write my name in the ensuing condensation, but I managed to resist. I was all too aware of Corrigan next to me, all spicy citrus hardness. His knowledge that I wasn't here to chew the fat with him was going to cause considerable complications to my plan. I'd need to hope that once I was inside, I could find some way of getting separated from him as somehow I didn't think that he'd help me retrieve the Ancile. The weight of the Palladium itself felt heavy and cumbersome in my purse as I clutched it tightly in my free hand.

Without knocking, the gleaming door swung open as we approached. Inside I could see several guests already milling around in the hallway, the chat and buzz of your average, run-of-the-mill cocktail party reaching my ears. Just beyond the threshold stood a youngish-looking man. He wasn't a vamp: his skin wasn't pale enough and he didn't possess the lingering smell of death that I'd registered before on my one and only previous encounter with a member of the undead. I'd just have to hope that he wasn't a mage who'd been recruited specially as security to sniff out anything untoward.

Corrigan stepped inside and turned, stretching out his arms so he could be frisked. He kept his eyes trained on me the entire time, a half-amused expression skittering across his face. While it seemed to me to be a pointless exercise – the shifters' weapons were their claws and teeth that could be accessed virtually whenever they decided to transform – it didn't stop my mouth from going dry. If they searched my bag and found the Palladium, or frisked me thoroughly enough to find the daggers, then I was done for. It probably wouldn't reflect very well on Corrigan either.

Once he was done, he gave the Lord Alpha a brief, respectful bow, and then motioned me forward. Alex and I had discussed this already. We'd considered having him place an illusion spell on me, in order to escape any undue attention. However, bloodsuckers were notoriously adept at sensing magic, and we figured it would no doubt simply send me flying back through the door. Instead we'd decided to focus on a few simple diversionary tactics. I smiled at the man, stepping inside and praying that the times I'd practised this through already were going to be enough. I turned round, just as Corrigan had done. The man started patting me at the hem where my dress began, moving upwards with the perfunctory attitude of a professional. As soon as he reached my waist, I dropped the clutch, spilling its contents – or at least some of them – on the floor. Alex had made sure that there was a second pocket built in to the purse so it could be opened without the little statue being displayed. A tube of lipstick, comb, compact and tampon all rolled out very deliberately onto the smooth cream carpet.

"Oh my goodness," I gasped, "I'm so sorry. How embarrassing."

I made a move as if to kneel down to collect up my scattered belongings. Of course I couldn't actually kneel down or I'd end up skewering myself on the concealed daggers that the doorman's hands had been just about to reach. Fortunately, as we'd planned, or at least rather hoped when we planned, the man knelt down himself for me, scooping everything back up, then handed me the clutch. Chivalry, as it turned out, was still alive and kicking. I'd tried to tell Alex that it wouldn't work, that any bouncer would notice the unnatural weight that would attest to the statue's presence as soon as it was lifted. Alex told me that he'd be so embarrassed by the appearance of a tampon that he wouldn't even begin to twig that anything was amiss. Score one to Alex: he was right.

I took the purse back from him and smiled as genuinely as I thought I could manage. "Thank you so much! You're terribly kind."

He smiled back at me and bobbed his head, then moved aside so both Corrigan and I could enter the house properly. My heartbeat drummed a relieved tattoo against my chest, and my bloodfire relaxed back into a more gentle sear in the pit of my stomach. Alex was clearly a bloody genius and phase one of 'breach the stronghold' was complete.

Corrigan took my hand again and placed it on his arm. "I have to admit, I'm impressed," he said in a smooth undertone. "However, you got lucky. My shifters would never have fallen for that."

I blinked up at him. "I have no idea what you're talking about."

"Of course you don't. I am going to find out what it is you're really after, you know, kitten."

"Only the pleasure of your company, oh great Lord Alpha of the awe-inspiring Brethren," I replied without a hint of irony in my voice.

Corrigan choked. I ignored him, and we moved inside to our left. A waiter approached, carefully balancing a tray of drinks, and offered them to us. I delicately picked one up at the stem and sipped from it, surveying the crowd. It was easy to tell who the vampires were. Several stood around in little huddles, discussing what appeared to be weighty matters in low voices. There were a few black-robed mages, including, I noted, His Magnificence himself, the Arch-Mage. For a moment I panicked, thinking that he must be here because he knew what Alex and I were up to, and he was going to put a stop to it. Then I told myself to breathe. Of course he'd be here. If there was going to be a gathering of the Otherworld's leaders, then naturally the head of the mages would be present. Telling myself to get a grip, I continued to sweep my gaze over the assembly, attempting to judge where any potential threats might spring from.

Catching sight of one surprisingly familiar face, I grinned. I hadn't expected my old buddy Tom to be here. He bounded over happily, bowing first to Corrigan. "My Lord Alpha," he said formally.

Corrigan nodded. "You know Miss Smith, of course."

Tom beamed at me. "I almost didn't recognise you without any hair! What the hell happened, Red?"

"It's a long story," I muttered.

"It suits you," he said, probably lying between his teeth. "And that dress is hot! I don't actually think I've seen you wear a dress before. Sexy!"

Corrigan noticeably stiffened at my side. "Where is your fiancée?"

"She's not feeling very well, my Lord. She decided to stay at home." He suddenly looked worried. "But she wanted me to thank you for inviting us along."

I could bet I knew exactly why Corrigan had bothered to do just that. He was trying to throw me off my game by reminding me of my old life. Well, I was stronger than that. Irritated by Tom's subservient attitude, even though I knew it was part and parcel of the role he'd so eagerly volunteered for, I couldn't help myself.

"So, Tom, are you enjoying serving the Brethren or do you wish that you were still back in Cornwall?"

He flicked a nervous glance at Corrigan and cleared his throat. "Well, I wouldn't call it serving the Brethren."

"Tom here has been promoted," interrupted the Lord Alpha smoothly, "because he's a very helpful and loyal wolf."

I pulled my arm away from him and spun round to look him in the eye. "And of course you demand abject loyalty from all your subjects, don't you, my Lord."

His eyes gleamed. "For someone who spent so much time living with a pack, you seem to have a remarkably weak grasp on how all this works. The hierarchy keeps the system working. It prevents discord. Not only that, but it's in our blood and in our genes. To pretend otherwise would be to deny ourselves our true nature. Without the Way Directives and the chain of command, the pack wouldn't exist."

I knew that Corrigan was right. I'd wholeheartedly believed in that hierarchy when I'd been part of it. It was the lifeblood of the shifters; it created the sense of family that I'd been missing so much since my departure from it. It helped to prevent rogue shifters from branching out and causing chaos, and it meant that weaker members were always protected. But that still didn't mean I had to like it at this particular point in time. "Well, it certainly makes your life more comfortable," I snapped.

Careful, kitten. His whispered Voice brushed my mind. *Remember that you're supposed to be my ever-so-willing date. If you continue to look as pissed off as you do right now, then you'll draw attention to yourself. And I don't imagine that will help your plans, whatever they really are.*

I gritted my teeth. Tom switched his weight from foot to foot, apprehensively watching the pair of us.

I don't have any plans, I shot firmly back, then smiled sweetly at him and turned to face Tom.

"I hope that Betsy isn't very sick."

He gave me an uneasy smile. "No, it's nothing serious. But

she's tucked up in bed with a hot water bottle. She's gutted that she didn't get the chance to come and catch up with you though."

"And Julia?"

"She's gone back down to Cornwall. Anton needed her for some things."

My eyes narrowed at the mention of my former nemesis. However, I was saved from making any further unpleasant comments by the loud clinking of a glass towards the front of the room.

"Ladies and Gentlemen of the Otherworld," boomed a deep voice. "Welcome to Kingsway. We encourage you to sample our humble offerings, partake of our wine and use this opportunity to mix and mingle with friends. This unique event offers much scope to forge new contacts and prevent unnecessary conflict, and we are honoured to welcome you."

"Trumped-up little shit," commented Corrigan drily.

I shot a surprised look at him. Then the crowds cleared and I could see the owner of the voice. It was definitely a vampire, and he reeked of power. His eyes were blood red, and his smooth, unlined face gave me the creeps. He raised his glass, eyes wandering over the room with the blaze of self-satisfaction. When his gaze fell upon me, his eyebrows raised in unabashed interest and curiosity. I felt an involuntary shiver run through me and, without thinking, moved an inch closer to Corrigan. Then, irritated with myself, I moved away again.

"Don't fret about it," the Lord Alpha drawled. "He has that effect on most people."

Wanting to snarl back a retort that I wasn't afraid of a stupid vampire, I pressed my lips together, forcing myself to stay quiet. I took another sip of my drink instead, looking around hopefully for some snacks. A tuxedoed waiter came up and whispered something in Corrigan's ear.

He leaned over to me. "I need to go and do some of my jumped-up, arrogant Lord of the Brethren stuff now," he said, his breath hot upon my cheek. "Be good." He raised his eyebrows meaningfully at Tom, and then me, making it clear that I had a babysitter who would no doubt dog my every move.

I smiled unconcernedly, wondering if I could persuade my old sparring partner to give me a break and let me sneak off. The flicker of obedience that Tom returned to his alpha, however, suggested otherwise. With silent confirmation of Tom's loyalty, Corrigan placed his empty glass on a nearby tray and lithely sauntered off.

Tom looked at me sadly. "I'm sorry, Red, he's my alpha, I have to–"

"I know, Tom, I understand." I sighed and looked around the room, noting several other shifters, each of them watching me with brazen, unabashed vigilance. Great.

Frustrated, my hand curled around the glass I was holding. How the fuck was I going to manage finding the bloody Ancile now?

CHAPTER SIXTEEN

I MULLED OVER MY OPTIONS. IT APPEARED THAT I HAD SCANT FEW at this particular point in time. I probably should just have come clean with Corrigan and told him the truth; I wasn't really doing anything wrong per se – in fact, it could be said that I was doing the right thing by returning the statue to its rightful owner. Well, sort of rightful owner anyway.

I drained my glass of champagne and wandered over to a waiter to get it replaced, Tom trotting faithfully at my heels. Picking up a fresh glass, I felt a pair of eyes watching me. I turned, half expecting it to be yet another shifter, and then realised that it was someone entirely different. Solus, or rather Lord Sol Apollinarus, Seelie Fae, was lounging languidly on the other side of the room. He lifted his glass and toasted me lazily. Ignoring Tom, I walked over to him.

"Solus."

"Dragonlette. Bald dragonlette. How are you?"

"Oh, just peachy. How is Mrs Alcoon?" I asked.

"Sleeping," he answered, twirling the stem of the glass in his hand. "I've been concerned about you, you know."

"And why's that?"

"You've been bleeding. More than once." He jerked his head towards the scabs on my hand. "I sensed it."

I raised my eyebrows at him. "Well, clearly you weren't concerned enough to come and check to see if I was alright."

"You know I can't do that. How is life with the witches and wizards treating you, anyway?"

"They really don't like being called that," I murmured.

"They're a bunch of hocus-pocus con-artists," interjected Tom with a note of bitterness.

I stared at the werewolf by my side. "Tom, that's hardly fair! They've helped shifters out lots of times. And they don't con people."

He grumbled at me. "Since when were you their freaking champion?"

I rolled my eyes in exasperation. No wonder they had this stupid party every year. Someone needed to do something to keep all these idiots from each other. "You met Alex. He's nice! In fact, he's my – our – friend! He knows as much about me as you do."

"Yeah, well, that was before I knew what they were really like."

Solus ignored my ripples of outraged indignation and gracefully extended his hand. "Tom, I don't believe we've officially met."

Tom stared at the Fae for a moment, then shook his hand. "You were at the restaurant that time."

"Indeed I was," Solus said smoothly. "It's a pleasure to make your acquaintance."

Tom muttered something uncomplimentary about Fae in general. I watched Solus' eyes harden for just a heartbeat before returning to normal.

"Tom, do you think you could give us a moment?" He began to shake his head, but I interrupted. "You can stand just over there. I only want to talk to Solus for a minute in private."

He glared at me, then stomped off, positioning himself just a few feet away.

Solus raised his eyebrows. "Don't you trust the little wolf any more?"

"Corrigan's got him on a short leash. Look," I said quickly, "I need your help."

"Again? Dragonlette," he said, shaking his head in mock disappointment, "this is becoming a bad habit."

"Please? It's important."

He sighed dramatically. "Very well. What do you need?"

"Just to get out of this room without every single shifter trailing after me. Can you glamour them or something?"

Solus glanced about. "I can manage three or four but I'm afraid you've got more than that hanging off your coat-tails."

"I know," I said grimly. "But I wouldn't ask if I didn't need to."

He frowned, considering the matter. "You won't have long. Maybe three of four minutes."

"That's okay," I said. If that was all the time I had, then that was just what I'd have to work with. I'd just have to hope that the Ancile really was being kept in the trophy room that *The Geography and Domestic Situation of the Vampyre* had described. Come to think of it, I thought, looking around for a moment, I hadn't yet seen any gold leaf on the walls.

"So what will you give me in return?"

I thought for a moment. Of course it had been stupid of me to think that the Fae would help me out of the goodness of his heart. And even I wasn't enough of an idiot to ask him what he wanted in return. A few ideas flipped over in my head, and then a bolt of inspired lightning hit me. If this worked…

I put on a serious look. "I don't want to do this, Solus. It's only because I'm desperate."

"Go on," he said, eyeing me with a disturbingly hungry expression.

"Well, I have this book, see? I'm pretty sure it's one of a kind. I found it first up in Inverness, in fact right before you showed up. Then it turned up again in the mages' library. I'm sure it's the same one and that somehow it's sentient."

"What would I want with a sentient book?" Solus waved a hand airily around. "My life is far too exciting to bother with reading."

And that, Solus, is one of the reasons why I will never entirely trust you, I thought, keeping my mental fingers crossed. "It's a Fae book. Rather beautiful, I might add. But very old. And it goes into lots and lots of detail about dragons."

He started. "Dragons? You mean..."

I nodded. "Yes, I do. So with this book, this sentient book, you can know more about the Draco Wyr than anyone else on the planet. In fact, more than anyone else on any plane." I licked my lips. "Well, apart from me, of course. Knowledge is power, Solus. While I'm reluctant to give you such knowledge so easily, I can see I have little other choice at the moment."

He held my gaze steadily. "So you would promise that this book is worth reading, would you?"

"Certainly. I give you my word on that." Especially if you can read it for me and tell me what it says, I thought.

The Fae thought about it. I held my breath.

"Okay then. Give me the book and I will sort out your little shifter problem."

I exhaled. Praise the gods. Now I'd just have to finagle my way into getting him to tell me what was actually in the book without him realising that I'd not actually read much more than the first chapter. I felt a slight twinge of guilt, then dismissed it. This was the sort of thing the Fae did all the time with their tricksy bargains. I just happened to be playing them at their own game for once.

"I can't get you the book right now, of course. It's at the academy. But I leave every Friday for a couple of hours to go to anger-management counselling." Solus started to laugh. I ignored him. "You can meet me there and then I'll give you the book."

"It's a deal." He spat on his hand and held it out. I did the same and then we shook.

Solus crooked an eyebrow at me. "If you have access to the mages' library, then why is the old woman still asleep?"

Puzzled, I just frowned at the Fae.

"Honestly, dragonlette, for an apparently smart girl, sometimes you can be incredibly dim. The spell they put on her had to come from somewhere. And it will be written down somewhere. Just find the book that it's written in and then you can find out how to free her."

I stared at him, completely nonplussed. A vision of the off-limits catalogue cabinet swam into my head, along with the fact that Slim was constantly reminding me to stay on the ground floor. I smacked my palm against my forehead. I was a fucking idiot.

"And so turns on the light bulb," drawled Solus.

The cogs in my brain geared up. "I was told that only the Ministry Council could actually remove the spell."

"Well, of course you were told that. If every mage had access to it, then it would never work, would it?"

I thought about it. Assuming that I could find a book with details about how to remove the spell, and that I was able to do it myself, not only would I be breaking my word to the Arch-Mage, but I'd be pretty much damning myself and potentially Mrs Alcoon forever. I already knew that there were few places to hide from the reach of the mages. And yet if I could free her now... I pondered carefully. It wouldn't hurt to have a back-up plan in case everything fell to shit at the academy.

Solus was watching me carefully. "You could always come and live in Tir-na-nog. You'd be safe there."

I snapped my head up at him. He sighed. "I'm not a mind-reader, dragonlette. It's just not hard to work out what you might be thinking."

"I don't want to go to Fae-land."

He shrugged. "Think about it."

I breathed out. I didn't like the lack of honour that those kind of actions would highlight. But I would have to think about it, and seriously. In the meantime, however, I had to concentrate on the matter in hand. I raised my eyebrows pointedly at the Fae.

He sighed. "Give me a minute to put things into place."

"Wait!" I stopped him and reached down to my shoes and began undoing the complicated straps.

I could feel Tom staring at me from the other side of the room. I mimed that my feet were hurting, which was actually true, and yanked the offending things off. Suddenly I felt about two feet shorter. I handed the Fae the shoes and he looked at them in disgust, as if I'd given him a pair of live snakes.

"Now you can begin," I said.

Solus closed his eyes briefly and muttered something inaudible. Then he opened them and grinned at me. "Get ready."

I stood there for a moment. Everyone around me continued as before. Irritated, I opened my mouth to speak, but before I could there was an almighty roar of rage from right outside the window. The ground shook and half the guests ducked down, covering their ears.

"It's a wendigo." The Fae was looking incredibly smug.

"Huh?" I gaped at him.

"A wendigo. A cannibalistic nightmare of a beast. I've summoned it. It's not happy."

The thing roared again. People began running for the door – whether to get away or to try to kill the thing, I had no idea.

"Is it dangerous?" Bloody hell, I certainly didn't want anyone's blood on my hands for this.

Solus shrugged. "Only if it eats you." He gave me a little nudge. "You'd better go now."

I looked around, realising that the shifters were transforming in an explosion of fur and cloth, ready to do what shifters do best and save the proverbial day. Tom was already in wolf shape and leaping out of the door. I reached up and pecked Solus on the cheek, then ran.

Floods of different people were pushing past me in a rush to get outside. Even the vamps seemed to be taking heed of Solus' wendigo creature, and were pelting out the front door, fangs elongating. It would take their combined efforts virtually no time at all to dispatch the thing. I hoped for its sake that Solus would transport it back to wherever it came from before they managed to do so.

Ducking underneath and shoving my way through, I hiked up my dress so that I could actually move freely. Satisfied that everyone's attention was on what was outside rather than in, I quickly leapt up the stairs, my bare feet hardly even touching the ground as I flew up. As soon as I reached the first floor, I curved round again and continued upwards. The trophy room was, according to my potentially defunct research, on the second floor towards the back of the house. I could still hear shouts from the different denizens of the Otherworld as they rushed to meet the wendigo outside. It roared again, and the foundations shook, but I ignored it as I completed my ascent, one sweaty palm clutching the banister and the other gripping my clutch with the Palladium inside.

I swung round, hitting the second floor. There were several doors to choose from. Fuck. Which one would it be? I launched myself towards the end of the landing and tried the very last door. It was locked. Not wanting to leaving a trace of myself if I didn't need to, I didn't try kicking it open for now. Instead, my hand twisted the knob on the second door. This one opened easily. However, all there seemed to be inside was a full-size snooker table and a dartboard. I guessed the vamps enjoyed their indoor sports.

Shutting the door again, I sprang to my right and tried again. The catch on this one was a bit stiff and I ended up having to put my shoulder to it to force it open. I felt around for a light switch on the wall, found it quickly and then flicked it on, illuminating the entire room. This was it. Heat rippled through my veins, snaking its way out from my heart and down to the tips of my extremities. I sucked it up, for once enjoying the focus the bloodfire gave me. Then I ducked inside the room and shut the door.

The entire room was covered in wall-to-wall glass shelving. I scanned each one quickly, hoping that I'd find the Ancile. There was a dizzying array of purloined gold plates, jade carvings, and stunningly opulent and heavy-looking jewellery. There was even a mummified head that made me grimace as I shot by it. Still no wooden statue, however. I moved to the other wall and began side-stepping along, skimming each section. No. No. No. No. Maybe? No. I jerked my head each time in a tiny motion of negative affirmation. Another distant roar rumbled through. Damnit, I was running out of time.

And then I saw it. It was sandwiched between two dusty-looking pieces of armour, and backlit by a green bulb. My bloodfire flared in approval. I felt along the glass, trying to get hold of the catch that would open the unit and let me swap the objects. Cursing, I realised I couldn't feel or spot anything that might open it up. From somewhere an alarm bell starting ringing. I jumped for a moment, before working out that it was from too far away to be a result of my actions, so I continued, moving my fingers along to try to find the secret. I could almost hear my bloodfire screaming at me to hurry up, to just punch through the sodding glass: come on, come on, you've done it before.

I shook my head. No, there had to be another way. If I smashed the glass then the vampires would know that someone had been here, and that could ruin everything. But it was to no avail. I just couldn't find the damn switch to give me access to the Ancile.

I took a step and inhaled deeply, sucking the air into my lungs. Then, almost without thinking, I raised up my left hand. The familiar glow of green flame twinkled at me. Using just the very edge of my pinky, I shot out a tiny stream of fire. As soon as it hit the glass, I had the horrible feeling that it was just going to bounce back, but instead it sizzled and spat for a moment before disappearing. The glass front stayed stubbornly closed. Fuck, there had to be a way to make it open without destroying the whole thing.

Staring down at my other hand, a thought hit me. I quickly reached over and began to pick at the freshest scab, pulling it away from my skin until a single drop of blood oozed from underneath. I dabbed it onto the tip of my index finger, then leaned forward to the glass, smearing the drop onto the flawless surface. Something clicked and buzzed and, my bloodfire singing as I watched, the gigantic pane slid to the side, revealing the bare shelf underneath. Without thinking further, I scrabbled in my purse and opened the second compartment, squeezing out the Palladium and gripping it hard.

I was just about to reach over to swap it with the Ancile when Corrigan interrupted, making me drop the small statue. It bounced onto the floor and underneath an embroidered and uncomfortable-looking chair.

Where the fuck are you, Mackenzie?

I noted dispassionately that he was now omitting his stupid nickname for me. So that was the key, I thought. Just defy his orders and run away from his shifters, and then he'd call me something at least vaguely sensible. It wasn't quite my preferred name, but it was close enough.

In the bathroom, I answered back. *Powdering my nose.*

He snarled in my head, his Voice reverberating around my skull. I ignored it and scrabbled round on the floor, managing to grab hold of the Palladium. Then I sprang back up, scooped up the Ancile, taking very great care not to let any of my blood touch it, and carefully stood the Palladium in its place. The wise carving of Athena stared compassionately out at me. I gave her head a little rub for luck, and then quickly ran back over to the edge of the glass and gave it a push, hoping it would close again.

Luckily for me, it did, sliding shut with another click. I wetted my fingers with saliva and rubbed away at the spot of blood. It left a tiny smear on the glass, but there was little I could do about it now. I crammed the Ancile into my purse, zipped up the compartment, and then ran back out the door, only just remembering to flip the switch to turn the lights back off again as I did so. I made it to the stairs and leapt down, clearing them in one jump. Landing at the bottom, I bent my knees just enough to spring back up again and dart around in order to be able to descend to the ground floor. People were starting to wander back again, a few looking somewhat stunned and others looking pleased with themselves. I jogged down the last few stairs, disbelief and relief mingling together with the retreating bloodfire in my system.

And then I banged straight into a vampire.

CHAPTER SEVENTEEN

I RECOILED SHARPLY, REALISING ALMOST STRAIGHTAWAY THAT IT was the bloodsucker who'd welcomed everyone in. The one that Corrigan hadn't seemed to like very much.

He stared at me expressionlessly. "What were you doing upstairs?"

My mouth dried. Every molecule of my body was screaming at me to take a step backwards, but there was no way I was going to give this guy the satisfaction.

"I...er..." I was lost for words. The vamp's red eyes were utterly mesmerising.

"Honey! There you are! Did you find the bathroom?" The dulcet tones of the Lord Alpha were, for once, music to my ears.

He wandered up and placed an arm in a laid-back manner around my shoulders. At least, to a casual observer it would have looked laid-back. Personally I could feel the coiled tension ready to burst through at any moment. It was a miracle that he'd not inadvertently shifted, in fact. I glanced down at his clothes. He was still wearing his tux, so had either taken the time to carefully undress and fold it up somewhere before joining the wendigo attack, or hadn't bothered getting involved. I voted for the latter somehow.

I injected an appropriately whiny tone into my voice. "No, it's not up there. That creature out there has almost made me wet myself."

I flicked a glance back up at the vampire who was still standing in front of me, almost preternaturally still. Uh oh. Probably too much information. He watched me unblinkingly for a moment, then looked down at the oozing scab on my hand. He sniffed delicately. And licked his lips. I was pretty sure that at that point my heart stopped beating. The faintest furrow traced across his forehead and I felt a flicker of dread. Could he sense that my blood was different even from scenting just that small amount?

"Aubrey, this is Mackenzie." Corrigan's arm tightened infinitesimally across my shoulders. "Say hello."

I flapped my eyelashes and aimed for vapid. "Hello, Aubrey. I love your eyes. They're so...red."

"You're not human," said the vampire slowly.

I smiled brightly. "No, no, I'm not."

"She's a werehamster," Corrigan casually interjected.

Aubrey's lips pursed thoughtfully. "Fascinating. I've never come across one of those before." He pronounced the word 'those' as if he were discussing a vaguely interesting species of insect.

"Aubrey, do you know where the bathroom is?"

He lifted a long, elegant white arm and pointed down the corridor. I registered with a kind of sick absorption that the colour of his fingernails perfectly matched that of his eyes. Ugh. Painting on a smile that was about as genuine as that of a Photoshopped model, I slipped out from under Corrigan's ever-tightening arm and temporarily escaped, heart pounding.

Once inside the restroom, I closed the door and twisted the lock, then leaned against the wall for a second, trying to breathe deeply and stay calm. I'd done it. Aubrey might be suspicious, but if he looked around, he would notice nothing out of the ordinary. For a moment I wished that I could use the Voice on Alex and let him know that it was mission accomplished. When I got out of the academy, I'd really have to think about investing in a mobile phone.

I pushed myself off the wall and stepped over to the sink, turning on the tap before splashing cool water on my face to calm myself down completely. Then I stared into the mirror, and realised that all I'd really managed to succeed in doing was to smudge Deborah and Mary's carefully applied make-up, so I pulled out a paper towel and began to dab carefully, trying to get the worst of it off.

Corrigan popped back into my head. *You're a fucking idiot.*

What do you mean? I was simply a bit scared of that incredibly loud roaring sound from outside, and needed to hide somewhere in case its owner came into the house. I continued wiping at my face, aware that I'd somehow managed to give myself two large black eyes. Fucking hell.

Funnily enough, I know enough about you to know that you are not the type to run away from a fight. You're far more likely to run headlong into one and get yourself killed.

I stopped my dabbing for a moment, hand frozen in mid air. *Did anyone get killed?*

No. The thing vanished into thin air before anyone could do anything.

Relieved, I continued my self-ministrations. *Well, I guess it's just lucky that all you big, strong shifters were around to keep everyone safe.*

Mackenzie, have you done something that I need to know about? Something that is going to cause problems with the vampires?

I pondered that for a moment, then decided that I was in the clear and he didn't need to know. *Nope.*

I'm not sure that Aubrey bought that story about the werehamster.

I appreciate you doing that. Sticking up for me, I mean. I know it might have potentially made things difficult between you and him. I meant it. I did appreciate what he'd done. He could easily have thrown me to the wolves. Or the vampires, at least.

Corrigan was silent for a moment. *You're welcome. Now get the fuck out of there so that we can leave.*

I'm actually a little bit busy.

Now, kitten.

His tone suggested that if I didn't do what he asked, then he might quite possibly feed me to Aubrey himself, morsel by fleshy morsel. I stared at my now entirely make-up smeared face and shrugged. It wasn't as if I'd be hanging out with this crowd again any time soon. Or ever.

Leaving the restroom, I received a couple of very odd glances. I grinned happily back, and then wandered up to Corrigan and tapped him on the shoulder. He turned round and took one look at my face and cast his gaze heavenwards as if to say 'Why me?' I smiled at him brilliantly and took his arm.

"Hello gorgeous."

You are not funny.

Suit yourself, my Lord.

You look better without that stuff anyway.

I tried to ignore the little thrill that his words sent through me. Then Corrigan jerked his head towards a couple of shifters who were leaning against the wall. They immediately sprang to attention and fell into step behind us. I rolled my eyes.

"Where are the rest of your obedient servants?"

"Strangely enough, there was a rather large, angry, bellowing creature outside that conveniently appeared out of nowhere. They felt the need to shift so they could attack it and protect the likes of you. Now they're a bit too naked for this crowd."

Ah, of course. That would include Tom as well, then. "Thanks for the reminder. Although you'd think that you lot would learn to come better prepared and bring a change of clothes."

A flash of hot, angry gold passed through his eyes. "You'd think that us lot could attend a party without being attacked by a monster suddenly materialising."

We passed Solus, who doffed an imaginary hat to me and smiled, displaying very white and very sharp teeth. Of my shoes there appeared to be no sign. Oh well. Missing nothing, Corrigan let out a low rumble of a growl.

"He's a fairy."

Yes, yes, he is.

"I've seen him before."

Yes, yes, you have.

"In my bedroom."

That's right.

"Right after I kissed you."

Oh. Yes. Okay. After that.

"Why is he here?"

I gave in. "It's a party, Corrigan. Why is anyone here?"

We emerged into the night air. I was feeling very proud of myself. I had resisted the appeal of the Lord Alpha admirably, despite the way he fitted so snugly into his tuxedo. I'd not lost my temper at all. I'd even been able to think clearly and use my bloodfire to good effect when raiding the vamps' trophies. I had the Ancile in my purse and the Palladium was safely where it should be. I wriggled my bare toes against the cool, hard tarmac. All was right with the world.

Corrigan halted in the middle of the road and turned to face me. He had clearly used his Voice to say something to our two followers, because I just caught them out of the corner of my eye melting away into the night. They wouldn't have done that unless he'd ordered them to.

"I have no idea why everyone else bothered to show up," he said darkly, "but you can bet that you're now going to tell me exactly why you did."

And then he twisted my arm, lifted my body in the air as if it was as light as a feather and flipped me down onto the cold, hard ground. He bent over me as I groaned.

"I don't like being used, kitten."

I lashed out and caught him on the jaw, forcing him to reel backwards. "Then why did you let me come along in the first place?"

I jumped to my feet and faced him, trying to remember to relax my body in the same way that Thomas had during our last t'ai chi lesson.

"I mistakenly thought that it might be entertaining," he growled. He stepped forward and grabbed my arm, spinning me round and pinning me against his body so that I could barely breathe.

I kicked backwards, connecting with his shin, then twisted away. I was tempted for a moment to pull out my concealed daggers. But that would have been against the unwritten rules, so instead I sucker-punched him. He doubled over for half a beat, then straightened, but I could see that my shot had been effective.

"Aren't you being entertained now?" I inquired.

"Having the time of my life," he grunted.

He lunged forward, catching me round my waist and flipping me again. However, this time I was ready and twisted myself in the air so that I landed square behind him. I karate-chopped the back of his neck, but he barely registered it. Damnit.

I was waiting for his next move, and grinning to myself behind his back, when his entire body tensed. I couldn't read which way he was going to go.

"Don't move, Mack."

Hmm. I tried to think. Was that a 'Don't move so I can beat you to a pulp' comment, or a 'Don't move so that then you do move and I still beat you to a pulp' double bluff comment? I was still working it out when I realised he'd called me Mack.

"Corrigan?"

He snarled. My bloodfire leapt in response. This wasn't the play-fight of a cat any longer.

"I mean it, Mack, stay behind me." His face twisted round and I realised that he was in mid shift already, black fur springing out on his cheekbones. He leapt up into the air, tuxedo bursting off and the gigantic shape of black panther taking hold.

Without thinking twice, I stuffed the clutch holding the Palladium down the back of my dress, hiked up the hem and crossed my arms to pull out the daggers from the sheaths under my arms. If something out there had Corrigan worried, then it had me worried. I moved over to the side, and then I spotted it.

Hovering in the air, and looking more like shadow than substance, was a wraith. This seemed too much like coincidence. My purse, with the Ancile stuffed inside it, felt heavy against my back. I stared at the thing in front of us. There hadn't seemed to have been a flicker of doubt in Alex's story about the Palladium that the vamps had caught Tryyl with and tortured him to death. And yet…

"Where issssss it?" the shadow rasped.

Corrigan, now in pure were-form, snarled again and launched at it, lethal, gleaming claws outstretched. He leapt through the thing's entire body, as if it were as insubstantial as air, and appeared behind it looking slightly dazed and shaken. He shook his giant panther body, muscles rippling under the sleek black fur and bright emerald-green eyes flashing, then lunged forward again, this time jaws ready to clamp onto the wraith's leg. His teeth snapped together, a hiss of black mist streaking outwards from where his mouth connected, which then clouded back in to re-form. The wraith reached out and grabbed the large cat by the scruff of the neck, flung him to the side and knocked him against the body of a parked car.

Alrighty then. Just to be doubly sure, I twisted my wrist and let one of my daggers fly through the night air on a direct collision course with the wraith's head. As suspected, it didn't even slow upon contact; it just cut through the shadow form and landed with a clatter on the pavement opposite. The wraith didn't even blink.

"Giiiiive me it," it hissed again.

I dropped the other dagger, appreciating that it would be useless now. It might have been more helpful if it had been pure silver, but it wasn't and I couldn't cry about it now. Corrigan was staggering to his paws, wavering a bit with a slight concussion.

Bloodfire heat tickled at me from the bridge of my nose and behind my eyes.

"You're going to need to tell us what it is you're after," I said calmly, although I had a pretty good idea of what it might be. "Otherwise how can I fetch it for you?"

The wraith quivered in the air. "You. You haaaave touched it. Where issssss it?"

I clenched my fists for a heartbeat then outstretched my palms, knowing without looking that the now familiar flicker of green fire was back. From behind me, I heard the door to the vamps' house that we'd only just exited opening and the sound of running feet coming out to join us. I didn't hesitate, however, and sent out a stream of flame right towards the looming shadow.

The wraith screamed and clutched its stomach where my fire had connected. Yahtzee. I shot out another and another. It fell down, half collapsing. I was about to combine both hands to create a stream of double impact, when I was abruptly shoved out of the way by something cold. Blinking, I stared and saw that a vampire was hurtling himself forward. Unfortunately, the wraith was also starting to recover and threw out a dark arm, pulled on the vampire's hair and ripped its head clean from its shoulders, then tossed it away with a sickening thump. I tried not to notice that the head bounced several times, with the now lifeless tongue of the vamp hanging out of its mouth.

Corrigan, still shaking his head slightly to rid himself of what was no doubt considerable fuzziness, returned to my side.

You know what it wants. His Voice was grim.

"Yeah," I said aloud. "But before you say anything, I don't have it. The vamps do."

Because it wasn't the more dangerous Ancile that was digging uncomfortably into my back that the wraith was after. It wanted the pointless and powerless Palladium that was now sitting snugly behind the glass of the vampires' trophy room.

A figure joined us. "So, Initiate Smith," the Arch-Mage stated calmly, "we find ourselves on the same side."

"That we do, Sir," I agreed.

The Arch-Mage jetted out a snake of blue light. It circled round the wraith, binding it into one place. I flicked my own flame forward, this time catching it on the side of its face, and sending it recoiling backwards. The wraith screamed. Not in pain but in sheer unadulterated rage. I could feel Corrigan's werepanther body tensing at my other side, preparing for another attack.

Don't. You can't win this one, my Lord.

He growled, but I ignored him and flicked out another arc of green fire that rose high into the air then curved back down, landing squarely onto the wraith's face.

"I'm starting to wonder whether it was such a good idea to host this party," came the chill tones of Aubrey from somewhere behind me. "There seem to be far too many uninvited guests."

"Hey," I snapped irritably, "this one's all on you."

As if to illustrate my point further, the wraith shrieked again. "I waaaaaaaant it!"

"It's after the Palladium."

The vampire started. "How do you–?"

He didn't manage to finish his sentence, however, because right at that point the Arch-Mage groaned. "It's too strong," he gasped.

I half turned and realised that he was drenched in sweat and shaking. Shit. We didn't have much time left. I twisted back towards the wraith again and sent out as much fire as I could potentially muster. But it was too late. The Arch-Mage's binding light was wavering and the wraith grinned emptily then pushed against it. The blue circle snapped and the Arch-Mage collapsed to his knees. The wraith snapped itself away from my approaching flame and drew itself up, towering over us. It pulled back one shadowy dark arm. I concentrated. Focus the fire, Mack, I told myself. Focus the fire. If I could just muster up enough energy…

Corrigan barrelled into me, knocking me down as the wraith's lethal swipe came whizzing over my head. Then it shot up into the air and vanished.

CHAPTER EIGHTEEN

I picked myself up off the ground, aching all over, and turned angrily to meet the werepanther head on. "What the fuck did you do that for?"

Corrigan began to shift, black fur retreating against his skin and bones cracking as he re-formed back to human. He pulled himself up and bared his teeth at me. "For the same reason you told me not to attack."

I cursed him, trying very hard to ignore the fact that he was stark naked, all tanned, steel muscles set into an aggressive stance of flat-out male perfection, and turned back to the Arch-Mage who was still on his knees.

"Are you alright?" I asked, helping him up.

"I'm good," he gasped, although the pallor of his skin suggested otherwise.

I turned to look at Aubrey, whose gaze was on my fallen dagger that was gleaming against the grey tarmac of the road. He flicked his eyes up at me and I shot him a disarming smile and shrugged, as if to say that it wasn't my fault that his bouncer hadn't noticed it.

His red eyes flashed. "I hadn't realised that werehamsters were so aggressive." He leaned forward, displaying his fangs, the corner of his tongue curling round to lick one, lapping at the sharp point. "Or that the pack was capable of using magic."

Corrigan planted himself in front of me. I scowled. I didn't need his sodding protection.

"Why don't you tell us exactly what it was that thing was after," he growled.

I couldn't see Aubrey's face any longer but I could picture the expression on it.

"Ask your girlfriend," he spat. "Somehow she seems to know." He began stalking back off to the house.

I sidestepped my way out from behind Corrigan, and called after him. "Hey!" He ignored me. "That was Tryyl, wasn't it? You didn't kill him, you just tortured him and then let him go. No wonder he's pissed."

The vampire spun round. "Idiot. You can't kill wraiths, they're already dead. And what do you know about it anyway, little girl?" His eyes fixed on the Arch-Mage. "All contracts are meant to be confidential."

I started in surprise. Oops. I hadn't known that.

The Arch-Mage coughed, still feeling the effects of the fight. "Not all mages work alone, Aubrey, you know that."

"Yes, but since when did the wizards work with the beasts?"

Both the Arch-Mage and Corrigan visibly stiffened. I rolled my eyes. These guys really had to get over themselves.

Aubrey's gaze switched back to me and he jabbed a finger in my direction. "There's more to you than meets the eye, and I'm going to find out what it is."

He twisted round again and continued for the safety of his lair.

"Yeah," I shouted back. "And what about the Palladium? Obviously there's more to that than meets the eye too!"

The door slammed shut in response. I exhaled a cloud of disgusted air and then pulled my dress back down over my thighs, feeling the sudden brush of the cold. I wondered what had happened to Solus and whether he'd run off at the first sign of action. Untrustworthy Fae. Irritated, I turned back to where the wraith had been hovering. There was something there, lingering. I took a few steps forward and realised with a sinking feeling what it actually was.

Corrigan joined me and knelt down, touching it, then raised his fingers to his nose and recoiled in disgust.

"Fucking hell!" he swore. "What is that?"

I didn't know what it was, but I knew where I'd seen it before. It was the inky dark gloop that I'd found on the wall of the academy. The wraith must have sensed the Palladium was there and had gone to find it. The wash of relief that flooded through me that we'd gotten the statue out of there before Tryyl had decided to attack was overwhelming.

I just shook my head slightly. "It doesn't matter. It's the vamps' problem now. They created this situation in the first place anyway."

Corrigan's eyes narrowed. "How?"

I looked at the Arch-Mage for permission and he nodded, so I filled Corrigan in on the details, leaving out, of course, that until about half an hour ago I'd been the one with the Palladium in my possession.

Once I'd finished, I checked with the Arch-Mage that I'd gotten the details right.

"Yes. Although Aubrey is right that all contracts are confidential. I assume that it was Mage Floride who told you about it." His eyes were hard. "I will have words with him."

I pursed my lips. If that was the worst thing that came out of all this – well, that and one dead vampire, anyway – then things were not that bad. Alex was a big boy; I was pretty sure he could deal with one telling-off.

An engine started up nearby. The Arch-Mage glanced at me. "I can give you a lift back to the Ministry so you can transport back to the academy. Don't you have shoes?"

I looked down at my bare feet. "Not any more."

The mage shrugged and turned towards the car. I glanced

over at the still disturbingly naked Lord Alpha. Didn't he even feel the bloody cold?

"Is that okay with you?" I inquired, attempting to maintain a dignified front.

He growled. "What, you're asking me for permission now?"

I shrugged. "We were on a date. It seems appropriate."

"I thought you said that it wasn't a date. And the bloodsucker is right. There is more to you than meets the eye, and somehow I can't help thinking that you had more to do with the events of this evening and that thing than you are letting on."

I blinked innocently up at him. "You always think the worst of me."

"Perhaps I'm just following your lead. You don't tend to think much of me either."

I gave him a sad half-smile and turned to go. Corrigan's hand snapped out and latched onto my arm, pulling me towards him. I let out a little squeak. His skin burned its way through the fabric of my dress as he pressed my body against his.

"You really did look lovely tonight, kitten," he breathed. "And after all you put me through this evening, I think the least I deserve is a good-night kiss."

And he inclined his head towards mine. I squeaked again, but this time the sound was muffled as Corrigan's lips hit mine. A squiggle of hot heat zipped through me all the way down to my toes. His hands cupped my face as the kiss deepened and everything else around us faded into obscurity. My arms reached up involuntarily round his neck and I leaned in to him.

A car horn sounded, blaring into the now empty street. I jerked back, coming to my senses, and pulled away. Corrigan glinted down at me with the definite expression of the cat who'd got the cream.

"Are you feeling entertained now, kitten?"

My insides fluttering with annoying little flips of happiness, I glared at him. "Why the fuck can't you just call me Mack?"

He laughed throatily, and I turned away and padded stormily

down the street to where the Arch-Mage was waiting.

Corrigan called out after me. "You will tell me what you really are and what is really going on sooner or later."

I shook my head as I walked away. No way, my Lord Furriness, no fucking way.

* * *

Once I was safe in the back seat of the car, the Arch-Mage beside me, I couldn't get the memory of Corrigan's kiss out of my head. I could still taste him on my lips. Damnit. With everything else that was going on, an entanglement with the Brethren Lord was the absolute last thing I needed. My life was complicated enough. I had a pretty good idea how it would go if things progressed any further. I'd jump into bed with him, we'd have utterly mind-blowing, earth-shattering great sex and then, with the chase over, he'd dump me and move on to the next thing. In the meantime, the mages would hate me even more, and across the entire Otherworld my name would be mud. I'd be just another pretty thing that had climbed into bed with the all-powerful leader of the shifters. Just another conquest. I'd seen enough photos on the Othernet of Corrigan and various dates hanging off his arm to know what he was really like. Not only that, but it was not beyond the realms of possibility that, put into the vulnerable position of pillow talk, I'd blurt out to him exactly what I really was – not human, not a shifter, not a mage, but instead a Draco Wyr. There were already too many people who knew the truth about me. I was just lucky that so far I'd been able to trust all of them enough not to use it against me. The memory of Iabartu's actions were still fresh in my memory. And besides, Corrigan was just intrigued by me because I kept saying no. Next time I'd just have to say no to myself as well.

I leaned back against the leather-upholstered seat and felt my purse with the Ancile within it digging into my back again. Reaching behind, I pulled it out and stared unseeingly down at it.

"So," the Arch-Mage began with a hint of steel in his voice, "tell me exactly what is going on."

Looking up, I found his gaze fixing me into place. "I don't know what you mean, Sir," I replied tiredly.

"First of all," the Arch-Mage ticked off, "you know about the contract that Floride had with the vampires to retrieve the Palladium. Despite your prior relationship, I find it difficult to believe that he would reveal it to you without some kind of reason. Secondly, you left the academy in order to go to the gathering tonight with the Lord Alpha. I had not previously been under the impression that the two of you were romantically linked, regardless of the frisson in the air between you tonight. I can only deduce, therefore, that you had some other reason for attending. And," he moved forward, "I expect you to tell me what that was."

I sighed deeply. I was getting a bit tired of the same old stuck record. "I just needed to get out of the academy. It was becoming a bit stifling and I needed a break."

I had no idea what Alex was planning to do with the Ancile now that we had it in our possession, and if he wanted to come clean with the Arch-Mage, then that seemed like a good thing to me. But I wasn't going to betray him, no matter what my personal opinion on the matter was.

The Arch-Mage's eyes narrowed. "Don't forget that you are under my jurisdiction."

Despite his occasional friendly overtures, the Arch-Mage was certainly no pushover.

"How could I forget that?" I said irritably. "You've still got Mrs Alcoon trapped in stasis."

"You know the terms," he said sternly.

"And you know that it should be becoming clear that I'm no mage. Therefore there's no need to worry about me going rogue. So there's no need to make me stay at the academy."

"And yet you managed to invoke inveniora just last week. Therefore there is indeed magic inside you."

I grimaced inwardly. I was damned if I did show signs of magic and damned if I didn't. My thoughts flicked to the potential existence of the spell book that could solve all my – and Mrs Alcoon's – current problems. Bugger. It was such a bad idea and yet so very, very tempting.

The car stopped, pulling up outside the Ministry and waiting for the large, heavy gates that I'd once sneaked through to open up. I glanced up towards the building and saw Alex emerging from the front door. He'd obviously be anxious to find out what had happened.

"Last chance," said the Arch-Mage grimly as the car drove up the short driveway.

I kept my lips firmly buttoned. He sighed, then got out, marching up to Alex. I stayed in the car for a moment, watching. Alex hung his head, whilst the Arch-Mage's lips continued to move, obviously berating him. Eventually, he lifted up his chin and said something back. I noted the Arch-Mage's shoulders pulling back in anger, and as I climbed out of the car, I hoped that I wouldn't be forced to intervene.

"You have to understand, Your Magnificence," protested Alex, "that you needed to have deniability. You know what's going on with the Council."

Ah. Did that mean that Alex had spilled the beans then? The pair of them turned to me as I walked up. I looked at Alex and he nodded back ever so slightly. Okay then. I zipped open the clutch's second compartment and pulled out the Ancile, holding it out.

Alex's breath exhaled in a whoosh. "You did it. You're the dude, Mack Attack, you really are."

The Arch-Mage stared at the thing, before asking, "May I?"

I nodded in the affirmative. I was glad to get it out of my possession. With the luck I had, I'd trip and cut myself and soak the thing with my weird-ass blood, and then all hell would break loose.

He turned it over in his hands, examining it. "The similarity with the Palladium is remarkable." He gave a short laugh. "It's ridiculous that the wraith and the vampires are desperate to have the Palladium when really this is the object with all the power."

Alex's eyes widened in alarm. "Wraith? You mean Tryyl?"

I lifted up a shoulder. "I assume it was Tryyl. You didn't think to mention before that wraiths can't be killed and that he was still after his bloody statue."

"I thought he was out of the picture," protested Alex. "And anyway, you can kill wraiths, you just need to find the bones of their original human form."

"It doesn't really matter," I said, waving a dismissive hand. "It's only the Palladium that he wants and now that's at Kingsway. He won't bother us any more." I neglected to mention that if we hadn't managed to switch the two statues when we had, then Tryyl would have been bothering us a very great deal. I felt slightly bad for the vampires, but, hey, they were undead creatures of terror, not all that dissimilar to the wraith, in fact. They'd work it out.

The Arch-Mage cleared his throat. "I'll take this and dispose of it so that there are no further problems."

Relieved, both Alex and I nodded vigorously. Yes, thank the gods, please do.

He fixed a stern look upon the pair of us. "But don't ever attempt to do anything like this again. I appreciate that your intentions were pure, however your actions could have caused irreparable damage."

I opened my mouth to retort that we'd actually saved the fucking day, but Alex nudged me hard so I snapped it shut again. The Arch-Mage turned on his heel and headed inside the front door of the Ministry headquarters. Alex put up his hand. Not really my thing, I thought, but…I jumped up and high-fived him. We grinned at each other.

"And that's the end of that," he said happily.

"Amen."

CHAPTER NINETEEN

THE NEXT DAY THE SKIES WERE GRIM AND OVERCAST, REFLECTING A dull grey sheen across everything. However, my own mood couldn't be dampened by the weather and, in total contrast to the weak, washed-out colours of the world, I felt sunny and chirpy. Alex's Palladium problem had been solved, Solus was on his way to doing my work on translating the Fae fire book for me and I now had nothing to concentrate on or worry about apart from actually starting to learn some proper magic stuff and then getting the hell out of the academy.

I was overwhelmingly tempted to see if I could indeed find the spell book that would enable me to provide Mrs Alcoon with her freedom a whole five years before it was theoretically due, however my current misgivings about the end result that such a project might entail meant that I was prepared to stick to my word and, at the very least, give the actual studying part a shot. Maybe I'd even work out how to reverse the spell on my own. It was amazing what one good night's sleep could do to provide clarity, I thought, while wandering out to the back of the academy gardens for my postponed teaching session. Similarly, I'd managed to compartmentalise the annoying niggles about Corrigan and put them away deep inside me, including his knee-weakening kiss, at least for now. In fact, I was starting to wonder whether coming to the academy might be the best thing that had ever happened to me.

Even Mary seemed to notice the difference, as she commented when she caught up with me. "You're just less prickly, Baldilocks. I don't feel like you're going to spontaneously bite the head off the nearest person any more."

Of course, she put it down to her genius action of bestowing me with a nickname. Deborah, who appeared a few minutes later, seemed to think that it was more to do with the contented feeling of 'lurve', as she described it. However, even her insinuations that I was an all-round calmer person thanks to the attentions of Corrigan rather than anything I had achieved myself, didn't put a dent in my relaxed state. The events of the night before seemed a lifetime away and, by the time that Brock and Aqmar bounded up, all eager to begin round two, I was beaming in satisfaction as Deborah and Mary hurled themselves at each other, trying to catch the other off balance.

Aqmar grinned his usual boyish hello, whilst Brock smiled shyly. I set them off on the same exercise as the girls, and then stood back and watched. After a while, it became patently clear that the four of them were purely relying on luck, rather than skill or observation, to land their hits. I interrupted them and got them to sit down in a row on the damp grass and pay attention. This had always been Tom's failing too.

"You need to keep your body from betraying you," I said seriously. "If your opponent pays enough attention, then they will know where you are going to hit next, and they'll not only get out of your way but also have the opportunity to hit you back."

"Aw, man. Baldilocks, this is just the same shit that we do in Protection already," complained Aqmar.

I frowned down at the teenager. "Well, maybe there's actually a reason why you spend so much time on that sort of stuff." I thought about Thomas and our t'ai chi ch'uan lessons. Maybe we had more in common than we realised. "But if you get this right, then I promise I'll also show you some attack moves," I said, relenting.

"Far out!" They all look pleased.

Momentarily amused at the impatience of youth, I began. "You tell me," I said, positioning myself into a typical fight stance. "Where am I going to go next?"

"Right," said Mary confidently.

"How do you know?" I inquired.

"Uh," she dissembled. "I don't, I'm just guessing."

"Is it left?" asked Deborah.

I relaxed my body for a moment and gazed at them all in exasperation. "You can't just guess. You have to know. If you don't know, then don't say anything."

I returned to my initial attack position and asked again. "So, which way?"

They stared at me, blank expressions on their faces. Then Brock put a tentative hand up into the air.

"We're not in school, Brock. You don't need to do that."

Slightly flustered, he lowered his arm again and coughed. "Backwards. You're going to go backwards."

"And how do you know that?"

"Your centre of gravity," he said, pointing at the lower part of my stomach. "It looks kind of, I dunno, off."

"Well, let's see then, shall we?" And with a sudden spring, I flipped backwards, twisting in the air until I landed on my feet in exactly the same position, only now two metres back.

The others broke out into spontaneous applause. I grinned at Brock. "Well done. Now you try it."

The teenager stood up and took my spot in front of the others. He relaxed his body completely, in a way that I recognised from the philosophy of t'ai chi. However, a tiny muscle throbbed in his right cheek, giving him away. It was a minor tell, and one that not many would notice.

The others still weren't sure, but I let them try first anyway.

When I told him he was going to leap to the left, he appeared particularly deflated.

"It's a tiny thing, Brock. Your cheek twitches on the right-hand side so I know you're going to head to the left. You just need to practise your facial expressions in the mirror as much as your body language and then you're there. Not even Thomas will be able to work out which way you're going then."

Unfortunately it was completely the wrong thing to say. Brock brightened momentarily at my words, but then so did Deborah when I mentioned Thomas, making Brock sink down back into himself. I cursed my big mouth.

The session continued for another hour and, as promised, I showed them how to do a few kicks and spins that really looked more impressive than they actually were, but that pleased the four of them no end. When we wrapped up and started to head back for dinner, I pulled Brock aside, then let the others go off ahead.

"What is it?" he asked anxiously. "Did I do something wrong?"

"No, goodness, nothing wrong," I reassured him. "But you've got to sort this thing out with Deborah."

His gaze flickered down to the ground and he looked downright miserable. "She's not interested in me, Mack. She's only got eyes for Mage Thomas." He spat out Thomas' name as if it was a curse.

"But she doesn't know that you like her in that way," I said gently. "If you tell her, then she might see you in a new light."

"Or she might never talk to me again."

"Well then, she's the idiot, not you. You can't regret not doing something, Brock. You should only regret the stuff that you actually do. At least then you're in control. Believe me, you'll feel better about yourself."

He sighed. "But what would I do? What would I say?"

"Well, what is she interested in?"

"Mage Thomas," he said huffily. When I gave him a stern look, he relented. "Fashion, make-up, that kind of thing, I guess. Which makes her sound like a bimbo, but she's not, Mack, she's really not. She's sweet and funny, and always thinks of others. She'd never hurt anyone, not intentionally. And she's really clever. When she's thinking really hard, her nose wrinkles and when she's happy, really happy, she lifts up just one corner of her mouth in a kind of half smile."

I reached out and squeezed his shoulder. Yeah, he had it bad. "So is there anything at all you could do to get her attention?"

"I don't know. I thought about getting her some flowers or something once. She's got hay fever though."

"You don't have to buy her something. Usually it's not what you buy a girl that she'll like about you, it's what you do instead. Something really thoughtful that'll make her see you for what you are."

"You're right. But it's coming up with that thoughtful thing that's the difficult part." He ran his hands through his hair in frustration.

"Yeah, I guess it is."

We walked back. My efforts at matchmaking were about as successful as my own love life currently was, I thought ruefully. Cupid certainly didn't have anything to be afraid of from me.

* * *

THROUGHOUT THE REST of the week, everything continued as if Saturday night hadn't ever taken place. I felt like I'd somehow been dropped into a world of safe mundanity. Other than the fact that I was at an academy of magic, that is.

My Kinesis lesson went as usual. I entered the room, sat myself down on the edge of Slocombe's little chalk circle and watched the same pebble again for hours whilst the mage stood as far away from me as he could possibly get without hiking up his black robes and running away. I was aware of him flicking nervy glances towards me, perhaps in case I got upset and decided to pick up the little stone and fling it at him, but I resolutely remained in place, trying to focus. I'd done a little reading in a spare hour I'd had to kill at the library about how to begin with Kinesis and be successful. It hadn't helped. No matter what I did or how I concentrated, the rock stayed determinedly in the same spot.

Evocation was much the same, although I hung back at the end feeling confident enough to brave a touchy subject with the teacher without losing my cool.

"So," I started, as he was gathering up his things.

The mage shot me a terrified look. "Yes?"

"Do you know Mary? She's a Level Four initiate."

He nodded and made to leave. However, I took a leaf out of the Dean's book and blocked the doorway. "She told me a couple of weeks ago that she was summoning a dryad."

The mage smiled proudly, despite his obvious unease that I was trying to engage him in conversation. "Yes, she's very talented." He eyed me up and down. "I don't think you're ready for that level of summoning just yet."

I almost snorted, but somehow managed to keep it inside, choking slightly instead. I couldn't summon a flea, I was hardly going to be able to manage it with something life size. Besides, that wasn't what I was after. "From what I know of dryads," I said cautiously, "they don't like it very much when they are far away from their own habitats. You know, their trees. In fact, they find it quite painful to be away from them. Or so I've heard, anyway."

From the horse's mouth, in fact. I'd had a long conversation with one that I'd come across in the woods in Cornwall on that very subject. She'd been very skittish and at first unwilling to talk, but I'd been equally determined to find out more about her and her people. It had become a bit of a personal challenge after John had given me an incredibly embarrassing dressing down in front of the entire pack when I'd been about thirteen and had mistakenly chosen a dryad's tree to use for target practice. With enough persistence, she'd given in and we'd ended up becoming friends of sorts. Well, no, that was a lie actually. She stopped running away screaming every time I approached her is what I really meant.

The mage blinked at me owlishly. "They're only summoned for a very short period, Initiate Smith. They're not in any distress."

Actually I was pretty sure they probably were. When I said this to him, he muttered some comment about the 'hippy arguments of tree-hugging humans' and pushed past me. I let him go, although I wasn't ready to drop the matter just yet. I figured that I could speak to him about it again the following week. And the week after. And the week after that. After all, that was how I'd gotten to know what dryads thought in the first place, so it was bound to work on a mage sooner or later. Even if he displayed the same kind of nervous, gazelle-like tendencies as the dryad had. Sooner or later I'd break him down and get him on side.

Perhaps the most shocking event of the week, however, was my Illusion lesson. I'd set off from the cafeteria after lunch, allowing for just enough time to get there. And then somehow, despite being sure that I could confidently find my way round the whole campus, I got lost. Again. It felt like I kept somehow missing the building. I'd walk past Divination and Evocation, and the ground-keepers' little shed. There was the gap in the wall, which the wind blew through and could virtually yank you off your feet if you weren't paying attention. And then I'd end up at the end of the buildings beside Protection without ever seeing the Illusion block at all.

Knowing what was happening, that the mage who was my teacher was just playing with me or testing me or something again, didn't particularly help matters. It was a particularly drizzly and cold day, and the raindrops kept landing on the back of my neck and dripping down uncomfortably against the skin of my back, whilst the tips of my fingers were starting to go ever-so-slightly numb. The idea of her sitting comfortably in the warm classroom sent shivers of irritated bloodfire heat through me. But, remembering my training, I counted to ten as slowly as I could, and pushed the flames back down again. Then, when I turned around to head back for another circle to see if I could find the door, I saw it. It was just a glimmer, an odd little hint along the edge of the cobbles that something wasn't quite right and didn't quite fit. I walked over and stood in front of it, then reached out with just my pinky and gently poked it. All at once, the glimmer enlarged in front of my eyes, bulging and elongating like those old magic mirrors you used to find at funfairs. After blinking a few times, I even found the door and managed to make my way upstairs without missing too much of the lesson time.

Gratifyingly, my Illusion teacher didn't cackle gratingly this time when I found my way up to her. Instead she cracked into a smile and patted me on the shoulder. Even better, when I was finishing up dinner that evening, listening to the teens chatter about their day, Thomas wandered over, black robes swishing behind him. Deborah let out a small whimper of excitement when she caught sight of him. Out of the corner of my eye, I noted Brock's shoulders slump ever so slightly. Fuck.

"So, Initiate Smith," Thomas said, drawing out the syllables, "I hear you finally had some success today."

The others turned to me, their eyes widening.

I shrugged. "Some," I acknowledged, unable quite to keep the grin off my face.

"Well done."

I could tell that Thomas meant it genuinely and my smile broadened.

"You should join me tonight for a drink, at the local pub in an hour or two. It's very close to the academy." His eyes flicked over the rest of my table. "I'm sure a few of your friends here will be able to tell you how to get there."

I swear that every single one of their faces flushed red in unison at that point. Trying to give them some measure of dignity, I avoided looking at them and stayed fixed on Thomas. "I'd love to," I said simply.

He inclined his head, and then strode off again.

"You're so lucky," breathed Deborah, quivering.

"Why?" snapped Brock. "Who wants to hang out with a teacher?"

She sent him a dark look then turned her attention back to me. "If I could just find my yellow skirt, then I'd come and join you. Rules be damned."

"Well, it's not so much 'rules'," I replied to her, "as the law. You're under age."

"Pah! Rules schmules."

"Have you still not found that piece of fabric yet, Deborah?" asked Aqmar.

Her mouth twisted. "No. And I've looked bloody everywhere."

Oops. I really had meant to have sorted that out by now and returned it to the laundry room.

Aqmar snickered. "That's probably because it's so small, you'd need a magnifying glass to find it anyway."

She punched him on the arm and the pair continued to bicker. I glanced thoughtfully over at Brock, who still looked miserable, the cloud of an idea forming in my head. I excused myself, then drifted over to the laundry room to see if this time I could find my jeans. I scouted up and down a couple of shelves, before eventually realising that they were sitting there, in plain sight, next to a pile of orange robes. Picking them up, I stroked the soft denim lightly, then jogged up to my room and stripped off the robes, changing quickly. Both my t-shirt and Deborah's skirt were still under my bed so I retrieved them together. I sniffed the t-shirt, and it didn't seem too bad, so I pulled it on over my head. The skirt, however, I took back down to the laundry room and shoved into a washing machine, and added a bit of powder before turning it on. Then I headed out.

The academy gates opened automatically for me when I reached the end of the driveway. Well this was a whole lot easier than when I was trying to sneak out without being noticed, I thought wryly.

I wandered down the quiet country road, wondering where in the hell I actually was. It didn't seem beyond the realm of possibility that an entire five years' time could pass me by and I still wouldn't be any the wiser as to which part of the country I was in. I figured it was probably a deliberate act on the mages' part. Even though it was still technically winter, the night was only just starting to edge in, with the sky turning a dark purple and the stars only just beginning to appear. There was a hedgerow lining the single-lane country road. Yep, it could be pretty much anywhere.

Before too long, the twinkling warmth of what I presumed to be the local pub began to appear up in front of me. This was a true country inn, the sort that townies would travel miles and miles for, in order to enjoy an 'authentic experience'. What the owners of it thought of their more regular clientele from the academy I could only begin to wonder.

As I neared the building, the letters on the old-fashioned hanging sign began to become more legible. 'The Ball and Chain'. Hmmm. Would that be the crystal ball and the mages' slavery chain, then? I snickered quietly to myself, before entering. Thomas was already up at the bar, hunched over a pint of something amber-coloured and frothy. He looked odd out of his robes, in that strange way that teachers always seemed to do when you caught them out of their natural environment of school. I beckoned the barman over and requested the same as Thomas was having, then settled down myself. It felt damn good to be out of the academy – and without any other tasks, problems or counselling sessions to have to worry about.

"Hey," I said, aiming for light and friendly. Clearly, I could do chatty small talk with the best of them.

"Hey," Thomas greeted me back. Well, at least he wasn't much better.

The barman set the brimming pint in front of me. I took a sip and then leaned back on the stool, eyes closing momentarily in pleasure. Yeah, Corrigan and his mates could keep their champagne and caviar lifestyle. A pint of beer and a bag of pork scratchings would more than do me. I sipped again and sighed happily.

"So, do you come here often?"

I looked up at Thomas and then realised what I'd just said, and began to snort with laughter. He grinned back at me and batted his eyelashes dramatically. I snorted harder, fighting to retain control of myself then clinked my glass against his.

"I actually try and avoid it as much as possible during the week," he said seriously, once I'd managed to calm down somewhat. "It's generally not a good thing to be here when the students are."

I eyed him carefully. "So, given the chance, you wouldn't, er, you know, liaise with a student?" Thinking of Brock, I figured that the least I could do was to be absolutely sure that Thomas was immune to the charms of Deborah.

"Liaise?" He looked remarkably offended. "Is that what you think of me?"

"No, no," I protested. "It's just…" I blew air out of the corner of my mouth. "It's just that one of the girls likes you, you know, in that way, and one of the boys likes her, and I want her to like him, but…" my voice trailed off.

He stared at me. "Fucking hell, Mack. Less than three weeks and you're already fully embedded in teen drama town. Do you not have anything better to do?"

"Hey, I need some distraction and entertainment if I'm going to make it through the next five years." That thought depressed me. "Sorry, let's change the subject."

Thomas was silent for a moment, as if considering something very deeply. Then he tightened his grip on the glass and twisted round to look me in the eye. "No, let's not. Look, Mack, I really am sorry for how I treated you when you arrived. I'm not proud of it. You're in a shitty position and, other than a few rather spectacular blow-outs, I think you're doing really well."

I smiled at him, but didn't say anything, curious about where he was heading.

"Not only that, but you're helping the kids out with those Protection lessons. The Founder knows I'd love to be able to teach them the way that you are. Of course, we're bound by the curriculum the Dean sets out."

"You sound bitter about it."

"Oh, don't get me wrong, there are things that I definitely wish were different. But the Dean's really okay."

I must have looked sceptical because he stared at me seriously. "No, really, I mean it. He is good at his job. He cares about his students and about his teachers. But he doesn't like the Arch-Mage and you're kind of His Magnificence's pet project. So it probably wouldn't matter what you did or who you are, he'd want you out of here."

"That's just not fair," I pointed out.

Thomas laughed. "Come on, Mack, surely you know by now that the last thing life is, is fair? Has it never occurred to you that maybe it suits the Arch-Mage very well having you here? He's not an idiot, he'd have known what you'd be like and how the Dean would react."

"What I'd be like?" Careful, Thomas, I thought irritably. I might kind of like him now but that didn't mean that he couldn't still piss me off.

He rubbed his forehead. "You know. All angry at the world and stuff. By keeping you here, the Arch-Mage gets to exert a little power because he knows you'll piss off Michaels. It's His Magnificence's way of putting him in his place without anyone getting hurt. It's pretty clever really."

Just the tiniest flicker of bloodfire in the deepest pit of my gut answered Thomas' words. "No-one gets hurt? Are you fucking kidding me? There's a harmless, elderly woman stuck in bloody Tir-na-nog in a coma!"

Thomas put his drink down and his hands up, palms facing towards me in a gesture of peace. "Yeah, and you're not the kind of person to sit back and wait for five years, or however long it takes to graduate, before she's released from stasis. So if you were the Dean, what would you do?"

"What do you mean, what would I do?"

He sighed. "Imagine that your first reaction to being threatened or put in your place isn't to violently attack someone. Put yourself in the shoes of the Dean – being made to look after a student who you don't want and who you know is just there to remind you that you'll never be the man at the top. What do you do?" There was a faintly desperate edge to Thomas' voice.

I thought for a moment. Killing the student would probably be the easiest, I reckoned, but seeing as how that might not be an option... "You would do something to make the student flunk out. To prove that you were right all along that they should never have been there in the first place."

"Yes," said Thomas patiently. "And how would you do that?"

"Well, I guess I'd just sit back and watch them self-destruct. Or attack another mage. Or destroy a priceless painting. Or fail every single discipline."

"And in case those things don't work?"

"Then I might do something to help them along a little bit, I suppose. Something to make them look really bad. Like..." I threw my hands up in the air. "I don't know. Help me out a bit here, will you?"

"Where does every student have to go no matter what they are studying?"

"The cafeteria?" I asked, feeling rather stupid.

Thomas stayed silent.

Dawning realisation hit me. I was having an epiphany. And not the good kind. "The library," I said slowly. "You'd plant a trap in the library. Like maybe having an area that's off limits. That'd make that student think there were some dangerous spells there. The kind of spells that would help them get little old ladies out of trouble. And then that student would go looking for a spell book to help them out with that, and when they found it, you'd appear out from behind a corner and accuse them of cheating or lying or being dishonourable or whatever."

"Bingo."

I felt slightly sick. "That fucking bastard," I whispered.

"But you've not done it though, have you? You've shown that you're a more honourable person than that."

I wondered how much of that supposed honour was down to the fact that it just hadn't occurred to my dim-witted brain that I could even find such a book until Solus had pointed it out. What if I hadn't been quite so preoccupied or quite so thick? The little flicker of bloodfire was burgeoning and growing, licking its way along my veins with an ever-increasing ferocity. Blood roared in my ears.

"Whoa, Mack, calm down." I must have looked about ready to murder someone, because Thomas stood up and reached out for my arms. "Seriously, calm down. I'm telling you about this for a reason."

"Oh yeah? And what's that?" I snarled.

"Because I like you! I didn't want to, but I do. So I don't want you to do anything stupid and I do want you to get your little old lady out of the state that she's in. So calm the fuck down," he reiterated.

I stared at him, realising that I'd pushed my bar stool back and was now standing and facing him. Thomas' hands were gripping my upper arms with surprising strength and I was dimly aware of the barman watching me steadily from behind the polished mahogany counter, wary in case I was about to kick off inside his little domain. I took a deep breath and started to count in slow, measured steps, the flames licking their way around my heart and squeezing it as I did so.

"You need to see things from the Dean's point of view," stated Thomas in a calm, even voice. "He's been in charge of the academy for virtually three decades, churning out happy mage after happy mage. And then the Arch-Mage comes along, completely usurps his authority and plants you in the middle of things. Of course he's going to do what he can to maintain his little world."

The flames retreated from around my heart and I began to push them back down into my stomach, feeling the afterburn akin to having eaten the richest, spiciest, creamiest curry within the walls of my chest. "He's a fucking power freak," I snarled, bitterness mingling with my slowly receding fury.

"Is he?" asked Thomas quietly. "Or is he just trying to protect the traditions and the students of an institution that has been around longer than even Cambridge or Oxford?"

"I'm no danger to the students," I snapped, as the fire twisted back inexorably through my veins and arteries.

Thomas' grip eased slightly. "But he doesn't know that." He sighed. "You grew up with the shifters. There's a long history of tension between our two groups. Yes, things are better now than they have been in the past and there are treaties in place to prevent any, uh, problems from occurring that might upset the delicate balance between us, but that doesn't mean that there's not still a lot of residual antagonism hanging around."

I held the mage's gaze. "We work together. I mean, the shifters and the mages work together. To stop bad things from happening."

"Yes," he said gently. "But the enemy of my enemy isn't necessarily my friend. And the new Lord Alpha has a lot of the Council worried. He's got more control than previous Brethren leaders, and more respect. That has them concerned. They don't want the shifters to become any more powerful than they already are, because that would inevitably take away some of the influence from them."

"I'm not a shifter," I pointed out, finally pulling away from him entirely and sitting myself back down.

Thomas moved backwards, and re-seated himself too, and I sensed, rather than saw, the barman also relax and begin to start wiping down the sticky remnants of previous patrons at the other end of the bar.

"You're right, you're not. And that makes you even worse and even more dangerous. We don't know what you are. You're not a shifter, and it's clear that you're not a mage. But you can fight like a deranged ninja on steroids and you do have magical powers. It's only natural that the Dean would feel nervous about having you here. You go postal, and it's him who would get the blame for not controlling you, not the Arch-Mage for dumping you with us in the first place."

The heat had settled back down inside me to a dull thrum. "So what do you suggest?"

Thomas shrugged. "You bide your time. Be good. Keep trying at your lessons, keep making friends. Smile at the Dean when you pass him. And I mean actually smile in a friendly fashion, not with that look that you have that suggests that you've sighted your next meal and you're about to start gnawing on their flesh."

"I don't look like that!" I protested.

Thomas just smiled. "Then, the Dean will realise that you're not a threat and the Arch-Mage will realise that forcing you to stay here is pointless. And you'll be let go."

I chewed on the inside of my cheek. "Do you think they'll let Mrs Alcoon go, or is that all bullshit?"

"They'll let her go," he said confidently. "It'll just be when no-one else is paying attention any more, that's all. You have to understand what a huge loss of face it is for His Magnificence that he screwed up so royally and had someone so patently unthreatening and completely lacking in power put in enforced inhibitory gnosis in the first place."

"They weren't aiming for her." I picked up my glass again and drained it, laying it back down again sadly. "It was me they were after."

"So you see why the Dean might be afraid of you then. No-one's ever done that before – avoided having such a powerful spell take root. No-one who's human, anyway."

"I'm human," I said in a small voice.

Thomas grinned at me. "Of course you are." He motioned over to the barman. "Come on, let's get as humanly drunk as we possibly can."

I raised my empty glass in agreement. Sounded like a plan.

CHAPTER TWENTY

When I awoke the next morning, bed sheet twisted round my legs and a weak winter sun filtering in through the tiny window, my mouth felt as dry as parchment. However, otherwise I felt reasonably fine and congratulated myself silently on no other appearances of a hangover. Thomas and I had continued until the wee hours, when the barman had begun noisily and pointedly washing glasses and tidying up, encouraging us without words to hurry the fuck up and go home, so I figured I'd had a lucky escape to not be feeling any worse than I was.

"Still got it, Mack," I muttered to myself, then swung my legs over to the floor, wincing at the cold touch of the floorboards whilst pulling myself upright. I walked over to the sink and twisted on the tap, letting the water run for a moment or two, then cupped my hands to scoop up some of its delicious wet frigidity into my mouth.

I bent down to pick up my (for once) neatly folded robe from the floor where I'd left it when I had changed before going out, and felt a sudden lurch of oily nausea flicker its way into being in my stomach. I straightened up somewhat dizzily, swallowing down the unpleasant feeling, and then the pain in my head kicked in, slowly at first as a dull ache, building up with unerring swiftness into a thought-shattering pain. Groaning, I ran my hands over my head, barely registering the half inch of soft, downy hair that now covered my scalp, and pressed down on my temples. Another ripple of bilious queasiness shuddered through me. This was most definitely not good.

Somehow managing to dress myself appropriately, although it seemed to take a lot longer than usual, I stuffed my feet into my shoes and stumbled down to the cafeteria. Surely some food and some shots of stiff black coffee would set me right.

The level of noise and chatter from the dorm rooms as I passed shrieked its way through my eardrums with a level of intensity I'd barely ever felt before. It was even worse inside the cafeteria itself, the collection of voices less a hum and more a bellowing throb. The feeling of sickness inside my stomach showed no signs of easing up, so I grabbed a dry bagel and began stuffing it into my mouth, hoping the heavy carbohydrates would improve the situation, then helped myself to a cup of coffee. Deborah and Mary were already sitting down in their usual places, and called over to me with annoyingly chirrupy voices. I downed the coffee, gulping it and burning my tongue, and raised my hand to them in a weak greeting, but didn't join them by sitting down. I wasn't sure I'd manage their easygoing banter at this particular point.

However, at least seeing Deborah had nudged my memory about the skirt of hers that I'd shoved into the washing machine the night before so I returned my now empty cup and wandered back out of the dining room. The escape from the hurtful sun that had been flooding its way through the large windows was particularly welcome to my sore eyes. I walked slowly down the narrow corridor, concentrating very hard on keeping the bagel inside my digestive system rather than out, as it was threatening to do. Passing a couple of people, and keeping Thomas' words about being friendly in my mind, I grunted out a couple of hellos. The recipients looked somewhat startled and nervous, scuttling away from me. I was too tired and feeling too rough to worry about whether it was because they were still scared of me or whether it was because I looked like the walking dead, and gave up trying to acknowledge anyone else, instead putting my head down and letting my eyes focus on the cracks and grooves in the stone floor.

The clean scent of the laundry room again announced itself grandly as I entered. Stumbling over to the washing machine I'd used the previous evening, I spent several moments attempting to open the round, misted door, before working out that I had to turn the stupid thing off at the switch before it would let me click it open. Grumbling at the fact that the bloody mages hadn't worked out some easier magical way to wash and dry their clothes, I pulled out the tiny ball of yellow fabric and shook it out, then hung it up on a nearby clothes horse to dry. I was hoping that Deborah wouldn't wander in at any point during the day and discover it hanging forlornly there and take it back before I'd had the chance to do so myself. I'd just have to count on the fact that she was as yet a teenager for whom the act of washing clothes was as mystifying as Evocation was to me.

I still had an hour or so before my Protection lesson with Thomas was due to start, so I padded my way back through the main building to the library, this time scowling at the little wooden dragon on the door rather than greeting it happily. Once inside, blinking away from the sunshine that yet again was making its unabashed way inside, I cast a dirty look over at the forbidden filing cabinet before heading to the shelves instead, pulling out a random book and then making my way over to a table and chair to collapse upon. There was no sign of Slim anywhere, which was probably a good thing, as I doubted I'd be able to wisely keep my tongue inside my mouth feeling the way that I currently did. I wondered how culpable the little gargoyle was, and whether he was even now hovering around somewhere and keeping a beady eye on me in case I made a move to find the spell release book that would save Mrs Alcoon. Despite Thomas' revelations of the night before, I liked the grumpy little purple librarian and I hoped that it was purely the Dean's nefarious and cunning plan to catch me out, and not Slim's too. However, my head was throbbing painfully and the bagel seemed to have done little for the state of my stomach, so instead I curled my ankles round the legs of my chair and let my head droop down till I was slumped over the table with my eyes closed. The book, whatever it was, remained unopened next to me.

After thirty long minutes of lying prone over my arms, and still not feeling any better, I lifted my heavy head up and reached over for the book.

A voice filtered in through my consciousness from behind me. "You know that this place isn't for fecking sleeping, don't you? You've got a fecking bed."

Yeah, a fecking lumpy bed that Rip Van Winkle would struggle to sleep in, I thought irritably. "Good morning to you as well, Slim," I muttered, flicking open the book to a random page.

"Why the feck are you reading about vampires anyway?"

I looked down and realised that the book I'd plucked off the shelves was indeed a tome on the undead bloodsuckers. I shrugged. "Why not?"

"Only one fecking thing you need to know about them," the librarian spat, now hovering beside my shoulder. "The only thing they fecking care about is themselves. Remember that and you're fecking sorted."

I started to nod, but that just made my head start to hurt even more, so I abruptly stopped and instead focused on trying to read instead, hoping that Slim would take the hint and just piss off. He didn't.

"Nasty things. All fecking worried about immortality and eternal life. They know they're fecking damned for being what they are."

I wondered if that was completely true. Feeling rather damned to eternity myself with the hangover I was currently experiencing, I decided I didn't really care. I craned my neck up at Slim, eyeing him and trying to work out what I could do to make him just go away.

"You're looking a bit like a fecking vampire yourself right now," he commented.

I scowled up at him. "What do you mean?"

He cackled to himself. "Red eyes and pale skin. At The Ball and Chain last night, were you?"

It pretty much stood to reason that, given his appearance, the little pub was somewhere the gargoyle tended to avoid. "Yeah," I grunted, "And?"

"And serves you fecking right, then."

I rolled my eyes. That was easy for him to say right now. Giving up on any pretence of reading or studying, I pushed my chair back and stood up, book in hand. "I have to go," I muttered. "Protection."

He cackled again, then reached out a clawed hand and took the book from me, turning to the page I'd been on. "There is no known cure for vampirism," he read slowly. "Once turned, these creatures of the dead remain frozen in time, until such point as they are destroyed through either a weapon of pure silver or a piercing of the heart." He snapped the book shut. "Sawing off their heads or setting them alight works pretty fecking effectively too."

I stared at him. "Is that the voice of experience?"

"I'm a fecking librarian, what do you think?"

Giving up, I shuffled out towards the great library doors. "See you, Slim," I said tiredly.

"Have a good fecking day!" trilled out the gargoyle, crowing in the knowledge that my day would be anything but fucking good. Unfortunately, at that point I hadn't fully appreciated just how bad things would turn out to be.

* * *

I ARRIVED at the Protection building rather early, so sank myself down against the outside wall and closed my eyes, letting the now warm sun heat my bones. I still felt ridiculously sick and the thumping in my head showed no signs of dissipating. I felt, rather than saw, someone slide down next to me. Opening one eye, I squinted over.

"Hey, Mack," said Thomas weakly.

The mage didn't look well. The pallor of his skin was deathly pale, no doubt much the same as mine. Strangely, I felt oddly comforted that we were both suffering together. It kind of made me feel that the bond between us was even stronger. If he'd been bouncy and happy, I would probably have punched him, which might not have gone down well in terms of our slowly blossoming friendship.

I leaned my head against his shoulder. "You know I'm absolutely blaming you for this," I muttered.

He let out a weak snort. "You were the one who decided that shots of tequila were in order, not me."

A sudden flashback of me pressing a small glass of colourless liquid accompanied by salt and a chunk of roughly hewn lemon on him filtered its way into my brain. My stomach rolled again in nausea. "Oh God," I moaned.

"By the Founder," agreed Thomas. He reached into a bag beside him and pulled out two cans. "Here," he said, handing one over to me. "I thought this might help."

It was a luridly bright and familiar orange and blue, and happily cold to the touch. I pulled the tab and took a gulp, then wiped the condensation from my fingers onto my robes, leaving a smear. Thomas opened his and sipped at it delicately.

"Dudes! Irn Bru? The Scottish nectar of the hungover? You must be feeling bad."

I wasn't sure I could cope with Alex's chirpy bounce. "Fuck off."

"Yeah, Floride," mumbled Thomas. "Fuck off."

Alex stood in front of us, hands on hips, blocking the light and shaking his head in mock derision. "Oh, when will you crazy kids learn?"

Hah. Alex Floride, the sudden voice of sensible adult reason. Yeah, right. I grunted at him and took another swig of the sweet, indefinable fizzy orange drink. "Where were you last night, then?"

He cocked his head down at me. "Off trying to trace the resting place of the bones of a certain wraith," he commented drily.

I sat up a bit. "Tryyl? Did you find him?"

According to what little I now knew about wraiths, from scanning through a book the other day, if you had their original remains, then you could easily rid yourself of them by burying them in consecrated ground. And, hey presto, no more annoying, hissing shadow.

Unfortunately, Alex looked grim and shook his head. "Sadly no, Mack Attack. My inveniora was picking up zilch. Wherever they are, they are well hidden. Some magic spell of concealment, no doubt."

Thomas looked confused. "What are you two on about?"

I shook my head dismissively. "Nothing. Just some wraith that has a hard-on for a chunk of wood that the vamps have. It's not really anything to do with us any more."

Alex nodded seriously. "Yeah, it's not really our problem. But as I found the thing for the undead dudes, they're claiming that I need to sort out their wraith problem for them."

"And you can't," I said. It wasn't a question.

"Nope."

"Stupid bloodsuckers," commented Thomas. "They always think that they're better than everyone else just because they live a little bit longer."

"Well, not really live," drawled Alex.

We all grinned at each other. Thomas clambered to his feet then stuck a hand out down to me. I looked at it for a moment then took it, and he helped me to my feet. "Let's cancel our lesson for today, shall we, Mack?"

Thank the skies. "Yes," I said gratefully, "let's."

I finished the can and then crumpled the aluminium in my hand. It would be nice to cancel my counselling session with Bryant as well, but I didn't think somehow that the Arch-Mage would consider having drunk too many tequilas the night before as a good enough excuse. I sighed heavily, then made my excuses and left both Thomas and Alex to it.

Back in my room, feeling slightly invigorated thanks to the healing powers of Thomas' gift, I picked up the two books that remained hidden in plain sight at the foot of my bed and looked down at them, frowning. I'd promised Solus that I would give him the Fae book, but I had to get it out of the academy without anyone noticing first. Of course, I'd managed before when I'd sneaked both of them out of the library, but that had been a relatively short distance to have to cope with and, even then, my theft had almost been discovered. I really couldn't think of any other option, however. I'd just have to stuff it under my robes again, and underneath my armpit, and try to avoid waving my hands around or anything daft like that. At least I'd only have to contend with one book this time, not two. Solus wouldn't require the dictionary to understand what the book said. Flutterings of deep, insatiable curiosity were squirming around inside me. The weight of expectation about what information the book would provide about my heritage was not inconsiderable. I hoped fervently that my plan was going to work and that I'd be able to weasel the details out of the Fae himself.

I pulled up my robes and wedged the hardback under my right arm, then tried moving around a bit to make sure that it was secure. After a few adjustments, and finally feeling satisfied, I glanced down at the dictionary. I'd have to find some way of returning it to the library. Figuring that a problem for another day, I left it where it was and headed downstairs and back to the outside for the portal. I'd managed up till now to avoid throwing up as a result of my previous night's activities. All that was now going to be undone, I thought ruefully, by forcing myself back through the portal.

It just so happened that as I emerged back outside, concentrating on keeping the book firmly in its place so that it didn't start to slip down again, the Dean himself was appearing through the gateway. I noted sourly that he didn't look any worse for wear thanks to the travel through the portal, and swallowed down my sudden nervousness that he'd somehow discover or see the Fae book that I was hiding, and instead heeded Thomas' advice by walking up to him and inclining my head.

"Good morning, Dean Michaels," I intoned formally.

The Dean looked surprised for a moment, and a flicker of suspicion crossed his lined features. However, he nodded back to me and then passed me by, walked up the few steps into the main building and vanished through the door. Relief flooded through me that I'd managed that small feat of getting past him with the stolen book, as well as actually being able to be relatively pleasant without wanting to kill the academy principal at the same time.

The same mage from my previous visit last week tilted his head briefly, acknowledging my presence, then he waved his hands. There was a virtually imperceptible shift in the ripples of green and purple light that hung in the air advertising the portal's presence. I watched them briefly in fascination, marvelling at the ability the mage had to change the position of the exit from what I presumed to be hundreds of miles away. Then he gestured me towards the gateway itself. I thought I saw a trace of a smirk on his face, no doubt because the effect that such journeys had on my physical system had been broadcast across the magic community. My head hurt too much to feel annoyed about it, however, so I just smiled sweetly at him, carefully raising my unfettered arm to him in thanks, and then walked through as if I didn't have a care in the world.

As with all my previous ventures to anger management, I emerged onto the roof of the counselling offices. And, as expected, I vomited violently upon arrival. The hangover, unfortunately, seemed to make the entire business of portal travel even worse than it normally was, and it took me several moments to regain my equilibrium. It occurred to me that every time I arrived, the traces of my previous week's regurgitations were always conspicuously absent. Whether that was down to the weather, or to some poor minion of the counsellor who was forced to clean up after weak-stomached visitors like me, I had no idea. The thought crossed my mind that maybe there were birds scavenging around who pecked away and ate the contents of my stomach, glad for a meal during the slim pickings of the last weeks of winter. That made my stomach roll even more in revulsion so I forced myself to stop worrying about it.

I moved away from the unpleasant puddle and relaxed my arm, letting the book slide down through my robes and out onto the ground. It would probably be safe to have it in plain sight now; I had no doubt that letting it suddenly appear from under my initiate's garb whilst I was in front of the receptionist would cause a raised eyebrow. Better to make it look as if I was supposed to be carrying it with me, I reasoned.

Keeping my fingers crossed tightly that Solus would be there to take possession of the book – and that Corrigan would stay well away – I opened the rooftop door and began my descent. As I passed the photos of previous well-to-do and happily recovered clients, I realised suddenly that the framed picture that had puzzled me before was of a considerably younger Thomas, staring out from behind the glass with a slightly befuddled expression, as if he was equally surprised and confused to find himself there. He looked very different to the Thomas that I now knew; he had much more hair for a start, and his face held the promise and hope of youth. Well, well, well. Wonders would never cease. So Jeremy Thomas had been to anger management, then? He'd obviously refrained from telling me about it for a reason, and I wouldn't be so cras as to raise it with him. However, some of the things that he'd said to me before were starting to make quite a bit more sense, along with the way that he recognised when the rage was taking me over and making me abandon all reason, and how he could talk me down from it too.

As soon as I entered the counselling offices, thankfully it was clear that Solus was present. He was leaning over the receptionist's desk, holding her hands in his and smiling at her with the glint of a predator. He kissed the back of her hand with a flourish.

"Sweetheart, I need to talk in private to this young lady here. I don't suppose you could...?" His voice trailed off as his eyes widened fractionally, beseeching her to leave us in private for a few moments.

"Of course, of course!" The girl almost tripped over herself in her haste to please the Fae.

I watched, eyes narrowed, as she disappeared down the carpeted corridor and into one of the closed rooms. Turning to Solus, I raised my eyebrows at him.

He tsked. "Really, dragonlette. I don't have to resort to glamouring people to make them want to please me. Most people are happy to do me favours." He reached over and rubbed my head. I recoiled from the intimate touch, but he merely smiled. "Your hair is growing back."

"Hair does that," I said drily. "And how are you, Solus?"

"Oh, just wonderful, dragonlette."

I scowled at him. "Please don't call me that."

"Oh, but it suits you so." Solus' face took on a serious expression. "Now tell me, my little fiery one, does this suit me?" He spun around on one foot then faced me again, arms outstretched.

Nonplussed, I stared at him. "What the hell are you on about?"

"The outfit, darling, the outfit! Don't you think it suits me?"

My eyes travelled up and down the length of his body. Hold on a second...

"That looks familiar."

He beamed. "I thought you'd appreciate it."

"Solus, please tell me you didn't break into the stronghold of the Brethren to steal one of the Lord Alpha's suits?"

He patted the lapel. There was a tiny gold brooch pinned to it. I leaned closer, realised it was of a panther, and then moved back again, feeling slightly sick.

"As you wish, dragonlette. I didn't break into the stronghold of the Brethren and I definitely didn't steal any of his clothes."

"You're a fucking idiot, Solus."

"Well, I think I look rather dapper."

"It doesn't fit," I muttered.

The Fae looked thoughtful for a moment. "Hmm, you're right. The Lord of the Brethren does have a rather, well, large body shape, doesn't he? Too much muscle and brawn methinks." He waved a hand dismissively. "It's no problem, however. I shall simply have my tailors adjust the size."

I shook my head. If the stupid fairy wanted to dice with death by provoking Corrigan, then I wasn't going to get in his way. Then my eyes narrowed slightly as a thought struck me. Solus would never dress this way unless he was hoping for ultimate impact.

"Solus, is the Lord Alpha coming here? Now?" Absolutely the last thing I needed right now to cap my day off was a confrontation between the two of them.

Fortunately for me, he shook his head mournfully. "Alas, no. His Lord Furriness had indeed been planning to make an appearance, but appears to have changed his mind at the last minute. Some problem with the vampires, I believe." He winked at me. "I'm sure there will be other opportunities for us to swap fashion tips, however."

Good grief, what a thought. I rolled my eyes expressively, deciding against pandering to the Fae's ego by making a big deal about his idiotic plans. Maybe if I didn't make an issue of it, then he'd abandon his suicidal actions. I changed the subject and thrust the book towards him. "Here. As promised for services rendered. One sentient Fae book about dragons."

Solus' eyes widened greedily and he took it from me, turning it over in his hands and examining the cover. "Well, well, well, this really is an interesting find, after all."

I shrugged, trying to appear nonchalant. "When you've read it, then maybe we can get together. You know, to compare notes, swap interpretations, that kind of thing."

I watched him carefully, but he barely reacted, his attention focused on the book itself. "Sure thing, dragonlette." He flicked a glance at me and grinned, baring his sharp white teeth as he did so. "Be seeing you."

Before I could utter anything else, he vanished into thin air, leaving behind nothing but a wisp of aftershave. I sniffed cautiously, then closed my eyes briefly in dismay. Solus was definitely playing with fire. I had no idea what his endgame was, other than royally pissing off the Lord of all the shifters, but I was pretty sure that he was underestimating Corrigan if he thought he could get away with this kind of frivolous and foolish behaviour. But, I shrugged mentally, he was a big boy. As long as I didn't get caught in the crossfire, then he could do whatever he wanted.

CHAPTER TWENTY-ONE

W HEN I RE-EMERGED AFTER MY COUNSELLING SESSION WITH Bryant, who professed cautious optimism at my progress in handling my temper, the receptionist was back in her place behind her desk, giving me a baleful glance that suggested vexation at the fact that my presence had forced Solus away from her side. I gave her a smile of regret, trying to stay friendly. For her part, she at least remained briskly efficient and polite, smiling back, even though it didn't quite reach her eyes, and told me that she'd see me again the following week. She had to be wondering who on earth would pitch up to meet me then. First the Lord Alpha, then a Fae. It made my life appear considerably more important and exciting than it really was.

I wandered slowly back up to the roof, in no hurry to journey back through the portal again just yet. I paused for a moment again at Thomas' photo, wondering just what secrets he really held behind that tough yet calm exterior. I scratched at my scalp, wondering whether his hazing over the shaving of my hair and his initial reaction to me had not just been a result of my intrusion into his carefully laid-out little mage world, but instead hinted at the vestiges of a more complex personality. It made me like him more, rather than less, somehow.

When I opened the door that led out onto the roof, I was assailed by a sudden cold breeze that made me shiver. I pulled the robes around me, trying to prevent the wind from catching them too much and whipping them about, and to give myself some measure of protection against the bite of the chilly weather. The portal shimmered up ahead so I squared my shoulders and headed for it. I should probably get my next vomiting session out of the way.

I was just about to step back through, however, when something touched my shoulder. Without thinking, I reacted straightaway by grabbing it and twisting hard. The unfortunate recipient of my attentions groaned slightly before slipping remarkably easily out of my reach. Blinking, I realised who it was.

"Back already, Solus?" I inquired. My heart was beating fast and I could feel tendrils of snaky bloodfire worm their way around my veins. This was it. Now I'd know the truth without having to spend the next several years painstakingly translating the Fae tome.

Solus just glared at me, and didn't speak. Thinking that he was annoyed that I'd tried to attack him, I took a step forward to explain that he shouldn't just creep up on me without warning but he beat me to it and reached out for me instead. All of a sudden, without any advance theatrics, he grabbed hold of my blue robes around the neckline and pulled hard.

My mouth dropped open and I tried to yank myself away. "Solus, what the fuck…?"

He held on, however, ripping the fabric in one swift move, until the robes dangled off my arm, baring my skin to the cold. He stared hard at my shoulder, then looked back up at me.

"I thought things were going rather well between us," he hissed. "I help you out by summoning nasty beasts from other planes, you give me information and provide amusement and entertainment. And then," he flicked a fingertip against my bare skin, "I find out you've been lying all along."

Damnit. It had been a long shot that I'd be able to fake having read the book, but I hadn't thought that he'd be this pissed off that I'd tricked him.

I held my hands up. "Okay, okay, Solus. I'm sorry. But you have to understand why I did it."

"No, actually, I don't understand. We had an agreement and you went back on your word. You seem to have forgotten that I still have your old lady with me. What do you think is going to happen to her now?"

Err...what? Alarm bells began to screech painfully in my ear. "What? What the hell are you on about? That's completely separate to this. You promised that in return for finding out what I was that you'd keep her safe. That's not changed, Solus."

"You bitch! It's all changed. Did you give me that book just because you thought I wouldn't read it? That I wouldn't be smart enough to work it out? Because you, lady, have seriously underestimated the Fae if you did. I might be Seelie, but, believe me, I can hold my own. And there are plenty of people and creatures out there who've crossed me in the past who have lived to regret it. Now you're going to join their ranks."

He lashed out with one hand, catching me across the side of my cheekbone. It hurt like hell, but I knew that if I fought back now, everything would be lost. And I knew that something wasn't right here.

"Solus, I have never lied to you." I looked up at him, pleadingly, begging him silently to calm down and start paying attention to what was really going on in front of him. Namely that there was something in the book that had made him go all psycho and that I didn't know what it was.

"What are you?" he demanded.

"What do you mean? I'm me, Mack. Draco Wyr. We met up in Scotland, remember? I have freaky blood that does strange things."

"Except," he said grimly, "you are not Draco Wyr. And that means that you are something else. Daemon, hybrid mage, whatever. So tell me what you really are, and I might be merciful."

I stared at him in shock, reading the absolute truth of what he was saying in his eyes. I wasn't Draco Wyr? I didn't have the blood of thousands of years of dragon heritage running through my veins? I sank down onto to the ground. But it had made so much sense. The bloodfire, the crazy green flames, the bad temper. If that wasn't what I was, then what the fuck was I? Why had John thought that's what I was? I rocked back and looked back up at Solus.

"How..?" I cleared my throat and found my voice. "How do you know that?"

He put his hands on his hips. I saw a dawning realisation flit across his eyes. "You don't know," he said, more calm this time.

"Know what, Solus? Tell me what this is all about." I got back to my feet and drew myself up, looking him in the eye.

"Did you read the book?" he asked suspiciously.

"No, well, yes, I mean, I read some of it."

"How much?"

"The first chapter. It's not easy translating those bloody runes, you know! Now, tell me, please, what did it say?"

He blinked slowly then looked away, giving a short, sharp laugh. "I should have realised. You thought that you could give me the book and I'd translate it for you. You pretended at the party that you'd already read it. I just assumed that you could read Fae already. Another one of the many strings to your bow, dragonlette." He shook his head sadly. "Except now I can't call you that any more because it's not true."

"Solus," I pleaded, "tell me what it said. I'm sorry I made it seem like I'd read it. I didn't actually lie outright. I didn't say that I had actually read it. You just assumed it. But, please, why am I not a Draco Wyr? I have to know."

He gestured at my shoulder. "Because you're not marked," he said softly. "All of the Draco Wyr have a mark on their shoulder.

A claw mark. Apparently it's some kind of throwback to the original dragon who was transformed into a human."

"Yes, yes," I said impatiently. "I read that part. But some warrior called Bolox fought him and eventually killed him."

"Not before he gouged out a chunk from Bolox's shoulder. And the dragon, who by all accounts had some winning ways with the ladies and had managed to impregnate at least a few of them, did something as he was dying. So that every single one of his offspring, and their offspring, and all the begetting and begatting that followed, and all those resulting offspring, had something in common."

"What?" I demanded.

"A mark. An eternal reminder on their shoulders of Bolox and the fact that he dared to kill great-great-great-great-grand-daddy. A claw mark to mirror where the dragon had managed to fight back. And," he pointed back towards me, "you don't have one."

I gazed pointlessly down at what I already knew to be my unblemished shoulder. "Are you sure? I mean, is it definite? It's not just some old story?"

"It's true. It rings true at least, and there is no cause to doubt it. You are not of the Draco Wyr."

"I'm not a dragon," I whispered. I didn't know whether to laugh or cry. I lifted my eyes back up to Solus. "But my blood and the stuff it does–"

"Means that you are something else entirely. Something powerful and something probably not very good." His voice took on a hard edge. "All deals are off. I will give you credit for not actually lying so your Mrs Alcoon shall remain untouched. I will keep that side of my bargain even if the information I received in return wasn't true. But as we don't know what you are any more, and as you might be something infinitely more dangerous than I can even possibly conceive, then I have no choice but to inform the Summer Queen about your existence. She will know what to do."

I stared at him, my tongue cleaved to the roof of my mouth. I had no words, nothing any more to fight back with. Everything over the last year suddenly felt like it had been a lie. What if he was right? What if I was something dangerous? Perhaps that was why I kept getting so angry. One day I'd suddenly explode and go on some kind of terrifying rampage, destroying everything in my path. At least I'd had some kind of answer as to my heritage when I had thought I was Draco Wyr, even if I had next to no real details. Now I had nothing.

"I'm sorry, Mackenzie." Solus bowed formally and then, once again, vanished.

* * *

WHEN I LURCHED BACK through the portal again, collapsing to the side to retch up nothing but yellow bile, my mind was so awash with Solus' revelations that I didn't immediately notice the crowd of people out at the front. All I was thinking about was what I was going to do next and what on earth I could possibly be. I knew there was no way that I was truly human. Bloodfire aside, my tricklings of magical power proved otherwise. Then I touched the necklace at my throat and began to wonder otherwise. There had been no evidence that I could do anything magical at all until Mrs Alcoon's so-called friend, Maggie May, had placed the heavy chain around my neck. What if it was only the necklace that gave me the power in the first place? I'd had no luck in taking it off myself but I pondered the very real possibility that the green fire and the weak inveniora that I'd recently been manifesting were nothing other than traces of the necklace's power, not my own personal power. I thought about what else I could do. Hear an alpha's Voice. Initiate my own Voice to Corrigan. And to nobody else, I reminded myself. What if that was some odd offshoot of growing up with shifters that had made that happen? As far as I was aware, there had been no other human in history that had spent their formative years with a pack, so I had no other evidence from which to draw.

I suddenly smiled. It could just be that after everything, then maybe I actually was human. If I could prove it, then the mages would have to release me from my oath and they'd have to remove the stasis spell from Mrs Alcoon. And I could forget the Otherworld had ever existed. Then I remembered the strange stuff my physical blood actually achieved and the smile disappeared. I'd broken through a faerie ring. I'd also used it to snap a spell around a mage's cage to free myself from them. Even more recently, it had helped me open up the vampires' stupid glass display cabinet. Fuck. No, I wasn't human. My teeth worried at my bottom lip. What if I was, as Solus suggested, some kind of daemon?

The growing ire in the voices to my left snapped me out of my reverie. Glancing over, I was stunned to see a group of mages, most of them black robed, clustered around, and virtually all of them with flickering blue flames sprouting from their hands. I scrambled to my feet; what the hell had them so pent up and ready to attack? As soon as I was standing and tall enough to see, I realised.

Standing in front of the mages were three vampires, immediately recognisable from their pale skin and lean builds, along with the fact that one of them was clearly my old pal, Aubrey. He was holding something in his hands and arguing loudly.

"You did something to it. Put some kind of spell on it because you thought you'd play a joke on us. Well, the joke's on you. Now it's yours and you can deal with the wraith yourselves." He threw the object at the feet of the crowd of mages who, almost as one, sprang backwards. With a note of pride, I saw that Alex and Thomas were virtually the only ones standing their ground.

"We did nothing to it. You brought this on your own heads by stealing it from the wraith in the first place. The Palladium is no longer our responsibility." Alex's voice was calm, but I could definitely detect an edge of stress underlying it.

The Dean pushed forward. "You can take your piece of wood, and get yourselves the hell off our land."

Aubrey licked his lips, red eyes flashing. "Oh, don't worry. I will, as you say, get the hell off your pitiful little school's grounds. But you can keep the piece of wood. We no longer want it."

I felt hot ire flicker inside me. How dare he think that just because Tryyl was causing him a few problems, he could dump the bloody Palladium back here? There was no way I was going to let this one slide by. I walked up to the group.

"Aubrey, fair's fair. You wanted the Palladium and you got it. It's up to you to deal with the consequences."

The Dean looked more than slightly irritated that I was sticking my nose in, but before he could say anything, the vampire cast me a disparaging glance and spoke. "Oh look, it's the little werehamster." He took a step towards me. "Except you're not a werehamster, are you? I don't know what you are."

Well, master of the scary undead, that makes two of us. I drew myself up proudly. "I am a student at this school and you will not leave that thing," I jerked my head at the fallen Palladium, "with us."

The Dean stepped up beside me. "For once, I agree with Initiate Smith. You will leave and take that thing with you."

Aubrey completely ignored the Dean, keeping his gaze fixed on mine. "It was you, wasn't it?"

I took a step forward until I was scant inches away from him. It was hard not to recoil in natural disgust, but I held my ground and forced myself to maintain eye contact with him. "I have no idea what you're talking about," I stated evenly.

"You broke into our trophy room. You swapped the original Palladium for," he flicked his fingers downward, "that thing. So it is your fault and your fault alone that thirteen of our number have now been massacred by that wraith. I am holding you personally responsible."

I felt the Dean move away from me and glanced over at him. He jabbed a finger in my direction. "You! I knew we couldn't trust you. What have you done?" The venom he managed to inject into his voice was rather impressive.

Oh, for fuck's sake. I struggled to keep a hold of my temper. Why couldn't the Dean let us sort out the vampires first before he came after me? That guy had no sense of priority. I returned my gaze to Aubrey.

"I have no idea what you're talking about. Yes, I was in your house. You had a party there, maybe you remember it? I think," I paused, putting my finger on my lips in mock concentration, "yes, I think I helped rid you of a wraith then."

Aubrey licked his lips. "Do you have any idea what I am?"

"Why, Mr Aubrey, Sir," I said sarcastically, "you're a vampire. An undead, bloodsucking affront to nature. Or so I believe, anyway."

"You are in some sense correct. I am indeed a vampire. And I do definitely suck blood." He shrugged. "Perhaps that's a personal failing, but there is little to be done about it now. It does mean, however, that I'm actually very sensitive to blood. More so even than other vampires. I can scent a drop of blood from a hundred metres away."

I had a horrible feeling I knew where this was going. It didn't matter, however, I had to project confidence and bravado. "Well, bully for you. As for me, I have a similar ability in that I can sense bullshit from a hundred metres away." I smiled pleasantly at the vampire. "It comes in handy sometimes."

Aubrey's face suddenly twisted with an ugly snarl. "You were in our trophy room because you left your blood there. I know you thought you cleaned it up, but it takes more than a bit of spit and polish to hide blood from me."

Alex spoke up. "That's ridiculous," he said, swallowing. "Even if she was in your trophy room, what I found for you was the Palladium. What is there on the ground right now is the

Palladium. You know it and we know it. So pick it right back up and take it home with you."

Thomas moved up from among the crowd and stood next to Alex, balls of burning blue flame in his palms. "We are not without our own power, as you well know."

"I'm not afraid of you," sneered Aubrey.

"Well, actually, there's a simple solution to all this," the Dean interrupted. He motioned towards me. "You taste Initiate Smith's blood here to see if she really was the person who broke into your trophy room and swapped your statue with another one. If she wasn't, then you take your little Palladium back to London with you and don't bother us again. If she was, then she can deal with it and the wraith. And we will deal with her."

Oh, you absolute fucking wanker. It appeared that the Dean had just worked out how he could get rid of me without requiring some complicated trap in the library. What hadn't occurred to him was what might happen if Tryyl decided to show up here to reclaim his property. I wanted to scream at him that it was the vampires who'd created this problem in the first place by taking the Palladium from Tryyl and then torturing the poor creature. I was not the problem here and most definitely did not appreciate being made the sodding scapegoat.

"Dean Michaels, I don't think that's a very good idea," said Alex nervously. "We shouldn't give in to the vampires' ridiculous demands." I knew that Alex would naturally still be worried about what tasting my blood might mean, given that he still thought I was a Draco Wyr.

"I agree," joined in Thomas. "We should not be held hostage by these bloodsuckers. They should just take their statue and leave."

I sent silent thoughts of gratitude in Thomas' direction. Unfortunately, however, it was all for nought. Without warning, the Dean flicked out a stream of blue light, catching me on my bare shoulder where the fabric was still hanging off after Solus' investigations. I yelped in pain and looked down to see a tiny trickle of blood appear and begin to drip its way down. Fuck. Aubrey sprang forward, grasping me by the shoulders and bent his head, red tongue flicking out. I sharply pulled up one leg, kneeing him as hard as I could in the groin, forcing him to bend over double in pain.

But it was too late. As soon as the vampire began to straighten, I could tell by the look in his eye that he'd lapped enough blood. Not only did he now have absolute proof that I was the one who'd been in his trophy room, but he also had a look on his face that suggested both wonder and puzzlement. Clearly, whilst he didn't recognise what my blood was, he knew there was something different about it. And by the manner with which he was licking his lips, he had definitely enjoyed it. I thought back to Anton and what had happened with him when he'd tasted my blood, and my heart sank. Now I was really in trouble.

CHAPTER TWENTY-TWO

I REMAINED WHERE I WAS, EYEING UP AUBREY NERVOUSLY, attempting to work out what his next move was going to be. There was an unerring look of satisfaction on his face, coupled with what was most definitely the gleam of a predator. I tried desperately to think of what I could do to end this stand-off. The last thing the academy needed was to have to take possession of the Palladium, especially now that Alex had confirmed that he couldn't find the wraith's physical remains. I inwardly cursed the vamps for not being courageous enough to deal with the problem on their own, and the Dean for thinking that he could.

As the pair of us stared at each other across the divide of a mere couple of feet, I became suddenly aware of some movement from behind me. Abruptly there were sounds of a scuffle taking place, and the muffled tones of the Dean shouting something.

I half turned, trying to keep Aubrey within my line of sight, but also to see what was going on. What the fuck? My mouth dropped open in shock. Thomas had somehow jumped on top of the Dean, knocked him over and was now punching him repeatedly in the ribs. The Dean was trying to put his hands up defensively, and attempting to spark his magic into life to manage a counterattack, but Thomas' knees were positioned in such a way around the academy head's torso, pinning both him and his arms to the ground, that he was unable to move. The rest of the mages were all taking nervy little shuffling steps backwards, as if afraid to get involved.

"You great lumbering idiot!" huffed Thomas as he landed one punch. "She's one of us and you let that thing taste her." He connected with the Dean's soft body again. "Not only that, but you actually encouraged him to do it." He hit the Dean square in the face and there was the distinct sound of his nose breaking. I winced.

"Er, Thomas?"

He ignored me completely and continued his barrage against the Dean.

"Jeremy!" I yelled.

He stopped for a moment and flicked a glance up at me. But I recognised that look. I'd spent half a lifetime giving that look to others. Thomas was in the throes of utter, all-consuming rage and nothing was going to sway him from his current course. Shit. I jerked my head at Alex, who nodded unhappily, then we both ran towards the pair of them. I grabbed Thomas' right arm and Alex took his left. The mage's fists continued flying, his arms flailing in the air as we dragged him off the now prone and groaning body of the Dean.

"Goddamnit, Thomas, stop it!" I twisted myself round to look him in the eye. "Look at me! I need you to calm the fuck down. Right now."

He continued struggling for another moment or two, then sagged, a flicker of conscious light crossing his eyes. Then, seemingly from nowhere, a jet of blue light appeared from behind and struck him smack bang in the middle of his forehead. Thomas fell backwards, hitting the ground with a painful thud. I spun round, only to see the Dean half sitting, arm outstretched and a look of grim satisfaction on his face.

I launched myself at him, knocking him back down. "What the fuck are you doing?" I hissed.

"Protecting myself," replied the Dean in a voice that might have sounded physically weak but that had a ring of steel to it.

"He'd calmed down! You just attacked him out of spite!"

The Dean's sharp eyes fixed on mine. "Out of spite?" His voice rose. "Until you got here, Mage Thomas was a loyal soldier. Less than four weeks in and he's all of a sudden like a rabid dog. And rabid dogs get put down, which is exactly what I'm going to do to you, Initiate Smith." He spat the final words of my name out as if they were a curse.

I stared at him, completely taken aback by the fury and hatred in his voice. Jeez. It was a strange day indeed when I seemed to be the only one not losing it. Then a set of arms locked themselves in a steel grip around my chest from behind me and I was dragged off the Dean.

I knew who it was the instant he'd touched me, and resisted the urge to kick back and free myself. "I might have known that yet again you'd be at the centre of all this," growled Corrigan in my ear.

"What exactly is going on here?" The Arch-Mage stepped into view, hands on hips, definitely not a happy bunny at all as he surveyed the carnage the in-fighting had caused. I realised that both he and Corrigan must only just have come through the portal that remained hanging iridescently in the air on the other side of the driveway.

I opened my mouth to answer, as did the Dean, but the Arch-Mage held up a finger and hushed both of us. He glanced over at the cluster of stunned-looking mages, whose frozen inaction during the fight caused me no end of irritation, and then beckoned one of them over.

"Mage Slocombe, pray tell, exactly what has transpired here?" The tone in the Arch-Mage's voice brooked absolutely nothing but dripping disapproval.

"Err...well, Your Magnificence," stuttered the terrified-looking Kinesis teacher, "the vampires arrived out of nowhere, demanding that we take back some statue. They said that it was all her fault. That she'd stolen the original and put something in its place." He didn't even dare to look at me as he explained, despite the fact that Corrigan's arms remained locked in a steel circle around me. "The Dean struck her so that she bled and the vampire leader could test her blood to prove that it had been her," Corrigan's body stiffened noticeably at this, "and Mage Thomas didn't think it was, er, appropriate for him to have done so and he attacked."

"I see," said the Arch-Mage slowly. "I had rather hoped that the Lord Alpha and I were going to be able to defuse the situation before it got to this." He looked around our little group. "So where are the vampires now?"

My stomach dropped as I twisted my neck round the wall of Corrigan's chest and realised that he was right. Somehow, whilst everyone's attention had been on the Dean and Thomas, Aubrey and his two minions had simply vanished. My eyes fell to the ground and my stomach gave a heavy lurch. The Palladium still lay where Aubrey had tossed it, its dull wood contrasting against the frost-covered tarmac of the driveway. Those sodding bloodsuckers.

The Arch-Mage exhaled heavily and looked over at Corrigan behind me. Some kind of unspoken communication passed between the two of them, then he nodded briskly. "Fine. Have the Dean escorted to his office and Mage Thomas to the infirmary. Mage Slocombe, if you would be so kind as to retrieve the statue and place it in the academy safe until we can work out what to do with it, then that would be most appreciated."

Slocombe nodded vigorously, but I could tell that the poor guy was consumed with fear at having anything to do with the harmless-looking piece of wood that had caused so much trouble.

"I must protest!" interrupted the Dean. "I have done nothing but keep order here and attempt to sort out the situation that she has created."

Stay calm, Corrigan's Voice irritatingly instructed me.

I am fucking calm, I shot back. *It's everyone else that's going nuts.*

The Arch-Mage's eyes narrowed. "Your Magnificence," he said quietly.

"Huh?" The Dean looked confused. I, however, knew exactly what he meant and grinned, simply because the Dean himself had pulled this trick on me.

"When you address me, Dean Michaels, you will show me the respect that I deserve and use my title."

Something flared and then abruptly died in the Dean's eyes. "I apologise, Your Magnificence," he muttered.

"Very well," replied the Arch-Mage evenly. "Lord Corrigan, if you would be so kind as to come with me to the Dean's office, we can reach some kind of solution for what to do with the Palladium now that the vampires have decided to dump it back with us after all. We appreciate your continued support in this matter." His eyes flicked to me for a moment. "I believe you can let Initiate Smith go."

"I will just have a few words with her first," drawled Corrigan from behind me. "Then I shall be happy to join you."

The Arch-Mage nodded in acknowledgement, then jerked his head at the rest of the mages. As one, they all hiked up their robes and scuttled off towards the main doors, quickly disappearing inside with just a few picking up the unconscious body of Thomas and a couple of others helping the Dean to his feet then walking him inside, shoulder to shoulder. Slocombe stared hard down at the Palladium, then blinked several times until it began to rise in the air and float its own way forward. Clearly he had decided that touching it with his bare skin would not be a particularly good idea. I didn't blame him. The Arch-Mage followed them all in.

When the heavy doors thudded shut behind him, Corrigan finally let me go. I turned to face him.

"What the hell are you doing here?"

He raised his eyebrows at me. "The Arch-Mage needed a bit of help. The vampires were threatening to return the statue that you'd so stupidly swapped, and he thought that I might be able to exert some influence upon them and help rid them of the wraith problem at the same time."

I spluttered. "That I'd so stupidly swapped? You should get your facts right. All I did was give them what they'd wanted in the first place. I took back a completely different statue and gave it to the sodding Arch-Mage so that he wouldn't have a mutiny on his hands within the Council."

Corrigan's green eyes held mine. "And that worked out so well, didn't it?" he murmured.

"Fuck off," I said. "I'm not responsible for other people's actions."

"And yet somehow you remain at the root of them. I swear, kitten, sometimes you are more trouble than you're worth."

That stung. I growled at him and then turned on my heel, leaving him standing alone on the driveway. Bloody shifter.

* * *

STILL CURSING him after I'd stomped theatrically inside, I made my way to the infirmary to check on Thomas. He was lying down on a small bed, moaning softly, as I craned my neck around the door. Another mage was bent over him, murmuring something calmly to him. She turned when she sensed my eyes watching her, and shot me a look of malevolence, so I hastily left her to it. At least Thomas seemed to be coming round and the Dean's cold-blooded shot of magic hadn't done him any apparent lasting damage.

I stalked down the corridor, anxious energy balled up inside me. I was sorely tempted to head straight to the Dean's office and confront the Arch-Mage, and force him to acknowledge that the extenuating circumstances of three undead vampires on the academy's grounds meant that Thomas couldn't be held responsible for his actions. Instinctively, I knew that I probably wouldn't help matters at this point. Besides, I didn't think I'd be able to face Corrigan again and keep hold of my temper if he continued to insist that all this was somehow my fault. I was at a loss to know what else I could have done given the situation with which Alex had confronted me.

Curling my fingers into my fists and gritting my teeth, I had no idea what to do next. Until some decision was made regarding the Palladium, the Dean and Thomas, I was in limbo. I needed something to keep me occupied or I'd go insane. I considered for a moment heading to the library to see if some reading could take my mind off everything that had just happened, but I knew that I wouldn't be able to concentrate enough on even the most interesting book with my thoughts as turbulent as they currently were.

I was three steps past the laundry room when I stopped abruptly in my tracks, breathing a brief sigh of relief. I could sort out the situation with Deborah's skirt. That would keep me occupied for at least a whole ten minutes. I wheeled round and entered, noting for a pleased moment that the scrap of fabric still hung from the clothes horse where I'd left it to dry earlier that morning. I strode over and picked it up, smoothing it out. Excellent.

Unsure of where Brock would be, but figuring reasonably that the vampires' sudden appearance would have had all the students placed under lockdown, I headed up for the dorm rooms, turning left instead of my usual right. The majority of the doors were closed, but from helping the alcohol-sodden teen return to his room a couple of weeks before, I had a pretty good idea which one was his. I stood outside it for a moment, then rapped loudly.

The murmur of voices floated out towards me, and I heard some shuffling as the occupants moved towards the door. It opened just a crack and half of Aqmar's face appeared, looking surprised when he caught sight of me.

"Baldilocks! Wow, good to see you! What on earth is going on? We were told to stay in our rooms until further notice but we could see out of the window that something was going down. Were those really vampires outside? Here?"

I deliberately ignored his questions. If the Dean wanted to tell the students what had gone on, then that was up to him. It wasn't my place to put the fear of God into them. "Yeah," I said as casually as I could, "you should probably stay in your rooms or around the dorms for the time being. Um, listen Aqmar, is Brock there?"

He looked slightly put out and I could see the warring emotions on his face as he was torn between wanting to find out more about what had just happened and wanting to do as I asked. Fortunately, he eventually opted for the latter and opened the door completely. "He's here," he said finally, then called behind his shoulder, "Brock! Baldilo…I mean Mack, wants to talk to you."

There was a creak and a thud as Brock heaved himself off his bed and then padded his way to the doorway, peering out. "Hey, Mack. What's up? Aren't you going to tell us about what those vamps were doing here?"

"I have something for you," I said, again ignoring the questions.

He looked puzzled. "What?"

I pulled my arm out from behind my back and held out Deborah's now neatly folded and clean-smelling mini skirt. "Here. It's Deborah's. If you want to get in her good books, then all you have to do is give it to her. Make something up about finding it in a corner of the laundry room. She'll be grateful and you'll have an opportunity to ask her out at the same time."

Brock stared down at it. "I wondered whether you were going to come clean about that or not."

I started guiltily. I'd been hoping that up till now he'd not remembered that I'd been wearing it when I'd come across him staggering his way home.

"Well," I said, pushing it at him, "now I am coming clean. And

238

the skirt's clean too. So if you give it to her, then you'll be able to show her how thoughtful and caring you are."

He took it from me, blinking rapidly. "I don't know, Mack. Maybe you should just give it to her."

I frowned at him. "No. This is your chance, Brock. Show her what a good guy you are. Go and find her now, she's probably in her dorm, and you can return it to her. Then, I don't know, you can suggest that she celebrates by putting it on and going out with you for a drink. Not now, of course," I said hastily, "later, when everything else has died down."

He licked his lips nervously. "I can try, but…"

I gave him a stern look. "There is no try." Oh my God, did I just say that? Luckily Brock was either too polite, too young or too nervous about what I was suggesting to pull me up on it.

"Okay, Mack." He stroked the fabric lightly and squared his shoulders. "Yes, I can do this."

I beamed at him. At least I was managing to get something right today. I reached out and smoothed his hair down, then straightened his robes and pulled him out from the threshold of his room. Then I gave him a gentle push down the corridor. "You'll be fine. Do it now before you lose your nerve."

He nodded to himself. "Okay. Yes. I'll just tell her that I found it."

He continued muttering away to himself as he slowly walked towards where the girls' dorms were situated. I looked over at Aqmar, who was watching me with a grin on his face, winked at him then held up my hand.

"Fingers crossed."

He mirrored my gesture, then reached out and high-fived me. "I have every faith in the boy," he stated solemnly. "He will do us proud."

I gave him a mock salute, and then left.

CHAPTER TWENTY-THREE

I was just leaving the dorm room area, when Alex bounded up to me. "Mack Attack! Dude, I was just looking for you. Where have you been?"

I chose not to answer that. I didn't think that Alex would care all that much about the love lives of my fellow students at this particular point in time.

"Um, just wandering around," I demurred. "What's up?"

"The Arch-Mage wants to see you right away. I think he and Lord Shifty have concocted up some kind of plan." He shrugged. "It might work."

"And Thomas? The Dean? What's going to happen to them?"

Alex's mouth twisted. "Thomas is being taken back to the Ministry headquarters. The Dean is still in charge for now, but I'm not sure how long that's going to last."

Heat sparked up inside me. "They can't blame Thomas for what he did. He was just standing up for me."

"Yeah, I think they get that. I reckon they'll go easy on him. But his career as a teacher is probably over."

Damnit. Something else I had to feel guilty about. "Okay. Where's the Arch-Mage?"

"In the Dean's office. You should head there straightaway."

I peered at him. "And you? What are you doing?"

"I'm leaving right now. I don't really have time to explain because I need to shoot off. The Arch-Mage will tell you." He leaned over and gave me a peck on the cheek then turned round and darted off.

I watched him go for a moment, then slowly walked over to the office. The staircase and corridors were conspicuously empty. I wondered if all the other mages were now in hiding, hoping to avoid the fallout from what had transpired outside. My thoughts tripped over one another as I tried to think of something that I could do to help Thomas' situation. I'd fall on my sword in a heartbeat if it didn't mean damning Mrs Alcoon at the same time. Fuckity fuck fuck.

When I reached the door to the Dean's little room, I paused for a second, then took a deep breath and knocked on it. Squirming tension was fluttering away inside me. A voice from inside called out for me to enter, so I twisted the doorknob and walked in.

Both Corrigan and the Arch-Mage were seated on a small striped sofa to the side of the Dean's desk. Fortunately, there was no sign of the Dean himself. The Arch-Mage gestured to me to sit down on the chair opposite them.

"So," he said finally, after I'd seated myself and was gazing expectantly over at them, "as much as we want to keep the circle of people who are involved in this as small as possible, it appears that you are inextricably linked to the fate of the Palladium. This would have been a lot easier if you and Mage Floride had come to me in the first place."

Somehow I doubted that, but I kept my thoughts to myself and stayed silent.

"Mage Floride has left already. He is going to continue to track down the whereabouts of the wraith's original body. Once that has been located, then we can easily rid ourselves of it."

I cleared my throat. Both Corrigan and the Arch-Mage stared at me.

"What?"

"We've already established that the Palladium has no powers," I said carefully. "It's the Ancile that's the worrying object. So why don't we just give the Palladium back to Tryyl and be done with it?"

Corrigan smirked. "That's the plan. You and I are going to travel to the place where your mage friend found the thing in the first place. We'll leave it there and let the wraith retrieve it."

Oh joy. More alone time with the Lord Alpha. I ignored the little trip and flutter of bloodfire inside me.

The Arch-Mage leaned forward. "Of course that doesn't necessarily mean that Tryyl won't still come after us for having had it in our possession in the first place. That's why Mage Floride is still going to try to find his bones."

"I thought he tried that already and couldn't manage it?"

The Arch-Mage lifted a shoulder in a half-shrug. "There are a few things he can try yet. He's rather talented at Divination, as you know."

"And we'd expect that the wraith's largest bone of contention is with the vampires anyway," added Corrigan. "If he's going to take revenge out on anyone, it stands to reason that he'd go there first."

I wasn't convinced that a shadowy creature of death really had that many powers of logic and reasoning, but I wisely kept my mouth shut. I shrugged and looked at them both. "Okay then. Let's do it."

Corrigan stood up and pointed towards the Dean's desk. I noticed for the first time that the Palladium was standing rather forlornly on it. I gazed at it for a moment. Why such a small thing could cause so many stupid problems, I had no idea.

"As you have already handled it, it makes sense for you to do so again. That way we can limit our physical contact with the thing." The Arch-Mage's voice was calm, but I felt the stirrings of annoyance at his words.

"Of course. That way it's only my life that's in danger, not anyone else's."

Corrigan reached over and took my hand, holding it gently but firmly in his. His emerald-green eyes fixed upon mine. It was virtually impossible for me to look away. "I won't let anything happen to you," he said softly.

Now I just felt even more irritated. "Actually, I won't let anything happen to me. I don't need your protection. As I recall, you were pretty useless against Tryyl anyway."

His eyes flashed in anger and he dropped my hand. Fine.

The Arch-Mage laughed mirthlessly. "At least it's not just me that has issues with controlling her."

I stared at him in annoyance, mulling over whether Thomas had been right about him forcing me to come to the academy just so that he could show the Dean who was really boss. "If I do this, then you need to do something for me," I stated evenly.

"I'm not going to release you from your oath," he said warningly.

I shook my head. "Not that. But you need to let Thomas – um, sorry, Mage Thomas – off. It was only because of what the Dean let the vampire do that he flipped."

"I think you'll find that the Lord Alpha here has already considerably highlighted the error of the Dean's ways in that respect."

I sneaked a quick peek at Corrigan. His jaw was clenched but otherwise the expression on his face was unfathomable.

"Still," I continued, "he shouldn't be punished for it."

The Arch-Mage gave an imperceptible nod. "He will be given an alternative position as a gatekeeper, working out of London."

"He'll be very good at that," I said softly.

The Arch-Mage agreed. "I know. Now, take the damn Palladium and get out of here."

I scooped it up. It still felt like nothing more than a chunk of roughly hewn wood. Whatever. It was time to put the thing to rest once and for all.

* * *

CORRIGAN and I walked out to the front of the academy building, neither of us saying a word to the other. Part of me wanted to thank him for standing up for me and Thomas, whilst the other part was equally bristling at the idea that he thought I needed him to do so. Regardless of anything, I was gallingly aware of his proximity. He had slowed his steps deliberately so that I could keep pace with him without having to trot beside him, and the tiny gap of air between our bodies was achingly small.

He turned right, heading for the portal, and I was about to do the same when I heard my name being called from behind. I turned round and saw Thomas, supported by a mage on either side, and jogged back over to the steps and next to him.

"Are you okay?" My eyes scanned his face, checking to see what lingering damage had been done.

He coughed slightly. "I'm fine. You'll have heard I'm being sent back to the Ministry?"

I nodded. "The Arch-Mage promises that you won't be punished. He'll find you a place as a gatekeeper."

Thomas laughed bitterly. "Fat lot of good that will do. You know what it'll be like, Mack, more than anyone. I'll always be labelled as the crazy one who might fly off the handle at any moment. It doesn't matter whether I'm here or somewhere else." He sighed. "I thought I'd put all those troubles behind me, but I suppose I was wrong."

I moved closer and leaned in to hug him tightly. Still clutched in one of my sweaty palms, the Palladium knocked against his back. He clung on to me for a moment, then released his grip. "You've been a true friend to me, Jeremy." I looked him directly in the eyes, meaning every single word. "Stepping up to the Dean like that, after what he did…" my voice trailed off. "I hope we can stay in touch?"

He smiled and chucked me under the chin. "Hey, I'm going to need all the friends I can get."

I hugged him again, then pulled away, trying to convey silently to him how much he meant to me. Then I left him standing there whilst I jogged back to Corrigan.

"Another conquest, kitten?"

"Stop fucking calling me that," I hissed at him.

A muscle tightened in his jaw and he took my arm, beginning to pull me towards the portal.

"Hey!" I protested. "I'm not a sack that you can just shove around."

"As if I'd ever think that," he muttered, his grip tightening.

"Mack! Wait up!"

"Oh for fuck's sake, what now?" scowled Corrigan petulantly.

It was Brock. He ran over to me, a huge smile on his face. "It worked! Mack, it worked! You're an absolute genius! We're going out on Friday night, just me and her. You should have been there. Deborah was so grateful, and she gave me this great huge kiss, right here." He pointed to the side of his cheek, beaming from ear to ear. "Oh," he sighed melodramatically, "I'll never wash again."

I grinned at him. "That might not endear you to Deborah."

He laughed. "I can't thank you enough. I…" He stopped in mid sentence and a strange look came over his face. He coughed and gurgled.

Alarmed, I reached out to touch his arm. "Brock? Are you okay?"

A trickle of blood seeped from his mouth, then there was a loud wheeze of triumph from behind him. He fell to his knees, eyes wide and staring. Brock hung there as if suspended for one silent moment where the world stopped and nothing moved, and then collapsed to the ground. There was a gaping hole through the back of his robes that were now soaked in blood. Behind him, swinging in the air, was Tryyl, Brock's bloody heart clasped in his dark hand.

CHAPTER TWENTY-FOUR

THE WRAITH DROPPED BROCK'S HEART AS IF IT WERE NOTHING more than a piece of rubbish and fixed its terrible gaze on the Palladium in my hand.

"Give meeeeeeee it," it hissed.

I was still staring at Brock's fallen body, my brain trying to compute what had just happened. I was dimly aware of Corrigan shifting in an explosion of ripping fabric behind me, and his feline snarl as he launched himself into the air. Up ahead, by the steps where Thomas and the other two mages were, came the sounds of shouting as they all began running towards us.

Tryyl lunged towards me in a motion that was so swift that I barely registered it. Corrigan's werepanther form was already barrelling into the wraith, however, knocking him off his course as he sprang through the centre of his body so that he narrowly avoided connecting with me. All coherent thought left my mind. The only thing that was left was the bloodfire. The roar of it as it raged with fury and vengeance tore through my body. The flames seared my insides until there was not a scrap of my flesh that wasn't burning. Without thinking, I threw the Palladium behind me as far as it could possibly go, then turned to face the wraith.

Green fire exploded from my hands with violence and intent.

I launched twin jets out towards the shadowy form, both smacking immediately into his chest. The wraith roared in pain and anger, and sprang forward again. Corrigan hit him again from the side, lethal white teeth snapping as he struggled to find purchase in Tryyl's insubstantial form. Then, from behind, both Thomas and the other two mages joined in the attack, each sending out their own waves of attacking blue flame.

A vicious spasm contorted the wraith's body, and he let out an inhuman, bloodcurdling scream. Corrigan lunged out, claws flashing, scraping into his body. Tryyl spun round, slamming out a dark hand into the werepanther's face. He snarled and slumped to the ground. Bloodfire pounded in my ears and throbbed in my heart. I shot out again with my flames, but this time the wraith leapt lithely to the side, avoiding being hit. Then he lashed out again, cuffing me against the side of my head and sending me flying painfully down to the ground. I lifted my head, tensing my muscles to spring back up and saw the wraith twist in the air to fly forward and meet Thomas and the others head on. They continued to send out streams of blue fire, but they were having little effect, virtually bouncing off Tryyl's body and vanishing into the atmosphere. I leapt up just as Tryyl roared again and flew towards them, knocking over all three.

I ran towards the small group as fast as I humanly could, small stones pelting up into the air from around my feet. I continued to blast the wraith's dark shape with green fire, Tryyl twisting this way and that each time I landed a shot. Thomas lifted his head and, for one brief moment, his gaze connected with mine and he smiled, then he reached up to grab Tryyl's leg. The wraith screamed down at him in ire and kicked, his booted foot smashing against Thomas' skull with a sickening crack. The mage fell back down, his neck skewed at an unnatural angle.

Hot tears filled my eyes as I continued to run. Tryyl turned yet again and faced me, an ugly, bitter smile curving his shadow-filled features.

"It'sssssss miiiiiine," he cried out in a voice terrible enough to wake the dead.

I ignored his calls, bent my head down and jumped, headfirst, butting him in his stomach. His hand clawed out towards me, ripping the flesh at my neck and pulling away my skin. I fell backwards, heat exploding from every sinew in my body, ignoring the physical pain of the attack.

For a moment, the wraith looked puzzled, staring down at his hand. I realised through the wall of fire that he was clutching my necklace in his hand, his long, dirty fingernails curling round it. Then he dropped it uncaringly and spat, a stream of black blood ejecting from his mouth. It landed on Thomas' body, a thick, dark gloop of blood and spittle. My bloodfire screeched, thrumming through my skin. Heat and flames pulsated, opening up my pores and blazing out. The mages on either side of Thomas moaned. Tryyl reached down, grabbing each of them by their hair, one in each terrible hand, and slammed their heads down onto the gravel.

Fire.

Heat.

Blood.

A strange sensation filled me. My limbs cracked and my flesh twisted. I roared. Not in pain, but in vengeance. I could feel myself growing, enlarging and breaking out of the very skin that I was in. My teeth felt strange in my mouth, longer and sharper, as if they didn't belong. My bones stretched and snapped and what I felt was no longer just fire and flame, but power too. I roared again, and this time the sound was deafening. There was an unfamiliar weight at my back. I twitched, realising that I had control of it, then whipped it round. My tail caught Tryyl's midsection, tearing through him and leaving a sucking hole in amongst blackness.

I twisted my neck to the side, now towering over the shadow in front of me. I examined the tiny creature of vile death and pain with detachment. Then I opened up my jaws and snapped, ripping Tryyl's head from his shoulders and tossing it to the side. Opening my mouth one final time, I let my scream of bloody thunder escape in triumph. And then I collapsed.

* * *

It was the voices around me in hushed, argumentative tones that I first registered when I came to. The metallic, sterile tang in the atmosphere advertised the fact that I was no longer outside, but instead back inside, within the academy's infirmary. Probably on the same bed that Thomas had lain in until Tryyl had snapped his neck.

"She's not a mage. That's obvious now. But her powers indicate that the Ministry is the best place for her."

I kept my eyes shut. Maybe if I never opened them again, then I wouldn't have to face the reality of what had just happened. Was Thomas maybe still alive?

"For fuck's sake! She transformed into a bloody dragon! She shifted. To all intents and purposes, she's a shifter and she belongs with the pack." Hello Corrigan. I guess you didn't die as well then.

"Oh, really? And since when has the pack ever, or even in the last thousand years, had a member who shifts into a dragon? She is not a shapeshifter. She is not a weredragon, there's no such thing!" I figured that the Arch-Mage wasn't feeling quite so cosied up with the Lord Alpha any more. Oh well.

"Don't you think that the people who are best placed to help her with this emotionally as well as physically are those who also have alternate forms?"

"And don't you think that someone who has taken an oath to the mages, and who is able to eject fire from her hands, is best served by learning and growing with those who can teach her?"

The voices were getting annoying. I wished they'd go away and leave me alone. Or at least give me some fucking information about Jeremy.

"Gentlemen, clearly Miss Smith here has kept her identity a secret for a reason. She is afraid of what might happen were others to discover her true nature. It would be best for everyone if she was kept safely away from any dangers. We can do this. In fact, she clearly trusts us because we are already doing that for a very dear friend of hers."

Huh. That voice was new. It had an odd musical tone to it that sent flutters of irritation through me. Clearly Solus had done what he'd said he was going to do and spoken to the Summer Queen after all.

"But who exactly knows what she is? We should track them down and make damn sure that they do nothing to harm a single hair on her head."

"She doesn't have much hair on her head to harm, does she?"

Pain twisted through me. Fuck this, I had to know for sure.

I opened my eyes. "Jeremy?" It came out as a croak. Three pairs of eyes swivelled towards me.

"Initiate Smith! We're so glad that you're alright. You destroyed the wraith." The Arch-Mage shook his head in disbelief. "We never even knew that was possible."

I tried again. "Thomas?" My throat felt as if I had several sharp knives embedded into it.

"Mackenzie," the stunningly beautiful woman, with very cold, hard eyes and who I took to be Solus' Queen, cooed, "you've really caused quite a sensation, you know."

"Don't worry about that though," stated the Arch-Mage, placing a hand on my arm. "We've arranged for an oath to safeguard the memories of everyone who witnessed your, uh, transformation. A lot of students and indeed the mages saw what happened from the windows. But we've ensured that they won't tell anyone. Your identity is safe. It's just the three of us who are unbound. Some," he shot an annoyed glance at the Summer Queen as he said this, "coming later to the party than others."

Oh, fuck off. Just fuck off and tell me what I want to know. I raised myself up onto my elbows and glared at the three of them.

"I'm sorry, Mack." Corrigan's voice was quiet. I looked into those familiar emerald-green eyes and saw the flash of warm, sympathetic gold in them. "He didn't make it."

I closed my eyes and bit down hard on my tongue. It didn't help. Huge, wracking sobs flooded me, shaking me down to my core. Corrigan moved closer and reached down, then lifted me half up, hugging me gently to him. The tears ran uncontrollably down my face as he rocked me back and forth, saying nothing else. I cried into him, gasping in pain and sorrow. If I'd just got there a heartbeat quicker, then I might have saved him.

"There was nothing you could have done," he said, stroking my head. "Not for him or for the student."

I thought of Brock and the promise within him that would now never materialise. The simple joy in his eyes at his success with Deborah, success that would now never lead to fruition of any kind. He was so young, and so good. I cried harder. Corrigan said nothing else, just held me whilst it all came flooding out, pain tearing through me in ripples of numbing loss and desolation.

I don't know how long we stayed in that position, just that it was for a long time, his arms remaining in place even after I'd managed to bring the sobs under control. Eventually I pulled away and looked at him.

"You're wearing mage's robes," I commented quietly, in a bizarre effort to focus on the mundane.

He glanced down at himself and his mouth twisted. "It was all they could find at short notice." Then he reached out, his thumb gently rubbing away the tracks of my tears on my cheeks. "You'll be all right, Mack. You'll get through this."

I lifted my head up and looked him in the eye. "Yes," I responded dully, "I suppose I will."

Corrigan's hand moved to my shoulder. My own robes were still hanging off from where Solus had torn them before. "That wasn't there before."

"Huh?" I flicked my eyes down. There were three perfectly

formed and perfectly healed scars curving their way across my shoulder, just ever so lightly coming to rest against my collarbone. Solus would be pleased, I figured.

I moved away from him, planting my feet on the bare floor. "Where's the Arch-Mage?" Clearly at some point both he and the Summer Queen, if that's who she really was, had decided to leave us to it.

"Mackenzie, you really should rest."

I shot him a look that brooked no argument.

"Fine," he sighed. "I think he's in the Dean's office."

I stood upright, wobbling just ever so slightly. Corrigan moved to my side to support me, but I gently pushed him away. "No," I said calmly. "I can manage."

The journey from the infirmary to the office seemed interminably long. Real pain, not just emotional pain, was shooting through me, and I felt almost completely overcome with weariness. I was determined to do it on my own, however. We passed several students milling around in little worried bunches. At one point, I caught sight of Deborah, her tear-stained face mirroring my own. Our eyes met for a second, then I looked away. I couldn't face her. She turned to Mary and buried her face in her friend's shoulder. Mary glanced over at me with a small half-smile of sad encouragement. I grimly pushed forward.

Outside the Dean's office stood both Mage Slocombe and my Illusion teacher. They bowed their heads to me in a moment of surprising deference, then moved out of the way. I acknowledged them briefly, wishing fervently and deeply that it hadn't taken an event of this magnitude to finally be accepted by the mages as one of their own. The sad irony was that I had now provided absolute proof that I most definitely wasn't one of them after all.

The door was already open, so I limped in without knocking, Corrigan close behind me. The Dean was back behind his desk, but when I entered and he looked up, he just seemed old and tired. The Palladium sat alone in the middle of the table. I looked away from it, barely able to even acknowledge its now malignant presence and focused my attention instead on the Arch-Mage on the sofa, with the Summer Queen beside him.

"Initiate Smith!" he said warmly. "You are up and about! I'm so pleased." He half rose from his sitting position but I beckoned him back down again.

"Don't call me that."

He stopped and stared up at me.

"I'm not an initiate any more. You know there's no longer any need for it because I'm not a mage."

The Dean's head jerked up sharply at my words, but he didn't say anything.

I continued. "You will release Mrs Alcoon from stasis and release me from my oath. I won't do any harm to you or your mages. I think I've proved that by now."

The Arch-Mage opened his mouth to speak, then thought better of it. He nodded glumly. I flicked a glance over at the Queen.

"You're the Summer Queen?"

She nodded, rising gracefully and holding out her hand. I ignored it. I wasn't here to make friends. "Will you help transport my friend back here? To this plane?"

"I can do that," she answered in soft yet steely tones. "But, Mackenzie, you should know that you can come and join us in Tir-na-nog. I can assure you that you'll be safe there."

"That's all right," I answered, looking away from her.

Corrigan stepped forward. "Will you come with me? I won't force you, Mack, you know that. And I won't look after you if that's what you want. You'll have however much freedom you want."

I smiled at him gently and touched his cheek. There was a part of me that so desperately wanted to say yes. To give in, and no longer be alone. But I had things going on that I needed to sort out on my own. I had to get to the bottom of what I was and I had the feeling that I had to do it myself. The bickering between the three of them whilst they'd thought I was still unconscious proved that.

"No, Corrigan. But thank you. I need to do this on my own, at least for now."

He nodded, green eyes flicking down to the floor. I looked round at the three of them. I reckoned they were all still pretty stunned by what had happened this day. I also doubted that it was very often that anyone ever came along and told them no. But for once in my life I felt like I had the power and control to do just that.

I smiled mirthlessly at them all again, and then limped back out.

EPILOGUE

Spring was just beginning to break through the harsh chill of winter. All along the park's edge, snowdrops drooped their heavy heads in pretty cheer, and here and there the shoots of daffodils were beginning to peek up through the softening ground.

In the distance, I could hear the calls and yells of a group of kids playing football, their voices too indistinct to make out beyond the odd whoop or curse, whilst in front of me the air shimmered, flickering purple and green. Before too long, Solus appeared with Mrs Alcoon on his arm, blinking confusedly around her.

"The mages kept their word," he said, barely able to look me in the eye. "As you can see, she's awake and fit as a fiddle."

I smiled at the old lady who was still looking around at her surroundings in utter confusion.

"Thank you, Solus."

"Dragonlette, for what it's worth, I'm sorry."

"There's nothing to be sorry about. You did what you thought you had to do. I'd probably have done the same."

He stared at me. "Who are you and what have you done with Mackenzie Smith?"

I smiled softly again. "Oh, I'm sure she'll make a return one of these days."

The Fae took a step forward, then changed his mind and shuffled back. "Have you…have you tried to do it again?"

I didn't bother to insult both our intelligences by asking what he was referring to. I just shook my head and reached out for Mrs Alcoon.

"Mackenzie, dear, I'm really feeling very confused. One minute we were in the book shop, and now somehow I'm here." She looked about herself yet again. "And it appears to be spring." She frowned and turned her eyes to me. "And you seem to have no hair."

Solus moved back, giving me a quick glance and mock salute, before disappearing back to wherever he'd appeared from.

I focused on my old friend. "Mrs Alcoon, it's a very long story."

"Well, if you're prepared to tell it, then let's get settled somewhere over a lovely cup of tea." Her eyes twinkled up at me.

Damn. I had a horrible feeling I knew exactly what kind of tea she wanted. Well, just this once, as it was a special occasion…

"Okay. I think there's a little tea shop just around the corner from here."

"And where is here, dear?"

"Er, London, actually."

"And are we going to stay here?"

I cast a glance over at her and thought about it for a moment before answering. There wasn't really anyone to hide from any more and there wasn't really any reason to go anywhere else. I still wanted to find out what Solus had read in the book that I'd given him, and I definitely had some unfinished business to take care of with the vampires. The heartache I felt at the deaths of Brock and Jeremy would take a long time to heal. I took a deep breath and closed my eyes for a heartbeat, then made a decision.

"We just might, Mrs Alcoon, we just might."

Thank you so very much for reading Bloodrage!

Mackenzie and Corrigan continue their adventures in Blood Politics, which is available right now.

ABOUT THE AUTHOR

After teaching English literature in the UK, Japan and Malaysia, Helen Harper left behind the world of education following the worldwide success of her Blood Destiny series of books. She is a professional member of the Alliance of Independent Authors and writes full time, thanking her lucky stars every day that's she lucky enough to do so!

Helen has always been a book lover, devouring science fiction and fantasy tales when she was a child growing up in Scotland.

She currently lives in Edinburgh in the UK with far too many cats – not to mention the dragons, fairies, demons, wizards and vampires that seem to keep appearing from nowhere.

OTHER TITLES

The complete *FireBrand* series

A werewolf killer. A paranormal murder. How many times can Emma Bellamy cheat death?

I'm one placement away from becoming a fully fledged London detective. It's bad enough that my last assignment before I qualify is with Supernatural Squad. But that's nothing compared to what happens next.

Brutally murdered by an unknown assailant, I wake up twelve hours later in the morgue – and I'm very much alive. I don't know how or why it happened. I don't know who killed me. All I know is that they might try again.

Werewolves are disappearing right, left and centre.

A mysterious vampire seems intent on following me everywhere I go.

And I have to solve my own vicious killing. Preferably before death comes for me again.

* * *

A Charade of Magic complete series

The best way to live in the Mage ruled city of Glasgow is to keep your head down and your mouth closed.

That's not usually a problem for Mairi Wallace. By day she works at a small shop selling tartan and by night she studies to become an apothecary. She knows her place and her limitations. All that changes, however, when her old childhood friend sends her a desperate message seeking her help - and the Mages themselves cross Mairi's path. Suddenly, remaining unnoticed is no longer an option.

There's more to Mairi than she realises but, if she wants to fulfil her full potential, she's going to have to fight to stay alive - and only time will tell if she can beat the Mages at their own game.

From twisted wynds and tartan shops to a dangerous daemon and the magic infused City Chambers, the future of a nation might lie with one solitary woman.

Book One – Hummingbird

Book Two – Nightingale

Book Three – Red Hawk

* * *

The complete *Blood Destiny* series

"A spectacular and addictive series."

Mackenzie Smith has always known that she was different. Growing up as the only human in a pack of rural shapeshifters will do that to you, but then couple it with some mean fighting skills and a fiery temper and you end up with a woman that few will dare to cross. However, when the only father figure in her life is brutally murdered, and the dangerous Brethren with their predatory Lord Alpha come to investigate, Mack has to not only ensure the physical safety of her adopted family by hiding her apparent humanity, she also has to seek the blood-soaked vengeance that she craves.

Book One - Bloodfire
Book Two - Bloodmagic
Book Three - Bloodrage
Book Four - Blood Politics
Book Five - Bloodlust

Also
Corrigan Fire
Corrigan Magic
Corrigan Rage
Corrigan Politics
Corrigan Lust

The complete *Bo Blackman* series

A half-dead daemon, a massacre at her London based PI firm and evidence that suggests she's the main suspect for both ... Bo Blackman is having a very bad week.

She might be naive and inexperienced but she's determined to get to the bottom of the crimes, even if it means involving herself with one of London's most powerful vampire Families and their enigmatic leader.

It's pretty much going to be impossible for Bo to ever escape unscathed.

Book One - Dire Straits
Book Two - New Order

Book Three - High Stakes

Book Four - Red Angel

Book Five - Vigilante Vampire

Book Six - Dark Tomorrow

* * *

The complete *Highland Magic* series

Integrity Taylor walked away from the Sidhe when she was a child. Orphaned and bullied, she simply had no reason to stay, especially not when the sins of her father were going to remain on her shoulders. She found a new family - a group of thieves who proved that blood was less important than loyalty and love.

But the Sidhe aren't going to let Integrity stay away forever. They need her more than anyone realises - besides, there are prophecies to be fulfilled, people to be saved and hearts to be won over. If anyone can do it, Integrity can.

Book One - Gifted Thief

Book Two - Honour Bound

Book Three - Veiled Threat

Book Four - Last Wish

* * *

The complete *Dreamweaver* series

"I have special coping mechanisms for the times I need to open the front door. They're even often successful..."

Zoe Lydon knows there's often nothing logical or rational about fear. It doesn't change the fact that she's too terrified to step outside her own house, however.

What Zoe doesn't realise is that she's also a dreamweaver - able to access other people's subconscious minds. When she finds herself in the Dreamlands and up against its sinister Mayor, she'll need to use all of her wits - and overcome all of her fears - if she's ever going to come out alive.

Book One - Night Shade

Book Two - Night Terrors

Book Three - Night Lights

* * *

Stand alone novels

Eros

William Shakespeare once wrote that, "Cupid is a knavish lad, thus to make poor females mad." The trouble is that Cupid himself would probably agree...

As probably the last person in the world who'd appreciate hearts, flowers and romance, Coop is convinced that true love doesn't exist – which is rather unfortunate considering he's also known as Cupid, the God of Love. He'd rather spend his days drinking, womanising and generally having as much fun as he possible can. As far as he's concerned, shooting people with bolts of pure love is a waste of his time...but then his path crosses with that of shy and retiring Skye Sawyer and nothing will ever be quite the same again.

Wraith

Magic. Shadows. Adventure. Romance.

Saiya Buchanan is a wraith, able to detach her shadow from her body and send it off to do her bidding. But, unlike most of her kin, Saiya doesn't deal in death. Instead, she trades secrets - and in the goblin besieged city of Stirling in Scotland, they're a highly prized commodity. It might just be, however, that the goblins have been hiding the greatest secret of them all. When Gabriel de Florinville, a Dark Elf, is sent as royal envoy into Stirling and takes her prisoner, Saiya is not only going to uncover the sinister truth. She's also going to realise that sometimes the deepest secrets are the ones locked within your own heart.

* * *

The complete *Lazy Girl's Guide To Magic* series

Hard Work Will Pay Off Later. Laziness Pays Off Now.

Let's get one thing straight - Ivy Wilde is not a heroine. In fact, she's probably the last witch in the world who you'd call if you needed a magical helping hand. If it were down to Ivy, she'd spend all day every day on her sofa where she could watch TV, munch junk food and talk to her feline familiar to her heart's content.

However, when a bureaucratic disaster ends up with Ivy as the victim of a case of mistaken identity, she's yanked very unwillingly into Arcane Branch, the investigative department of the Hallowed Order of Magical Enlightenment. Her problems are quadrupled when a valuable object is stolen right from under the Order's noses.

It doesn't exactly help that she's been magically bound to Adeptus Exemptus Raphael Winter. He might have piercing sapphire eyes and a body which a cover model would be proud of but, as far as Ivy's concerned, he's a walking advertisement for the joyless perils of too much witch-work.

And if he makes her go to the gym again, she's definitely going to turn him into a frog.

Book One - Slouch Witch
Book Two - Star Witch
Book Three - Spirit Witch

Sparkle Witch (Christmas novella)

* * *

The complete *Fractured Faery* series

One corpse. Several bizarre looking attackers. Some very strange magical powers. And a severe bout of amnesia.

It's one thing to wake up outside in the middle of the night with a decapitated man for company. It's another to have no memory of how you got there - or who you are.

She might not know her own name but she knows that several people are out to get her. It could be because she has strange magical powers seemingly at her fingertips and is some kind of fabulous hero. But then why does she appear to inspire fear in so many? And who on earth is the sexy, green-eyed barman who apparently despises her? So many questions ... and so few answers.

At least one thing is for sure - the streets of Manchester have never met someone quite as mad as Madrona…

Book One - Box of Frogs

SHORTLISTED FOR THE KINDLE STORYTELLER AWARD 2018

Book Two - Quiver of Cobras

Book Three - Skulk of Foxes

* * *

The complete *City Of Magic* series

Charley is a cleaner by day and a professional gambler by night. She might be haunted by her tragic past but she's never thought of herself as anything or anyone special. Until, that is, things start to go terribly wrong all across the city of Manchester. Between plagues of rats, firestorms and the gleaming blue eyes of a sexy Scottish werewolf, she might just have landed herself in the middle of a magical apocalypse. She might also be the only person who has the ability to bring order to an utterly chaotic new world.

Book One - Shrill Dusk

Book Two - Brittle Midnight

Book Three - Furtive Dawn

Printed in Great Britain
by Amazon

45035683R00158